"I know you [...]
in the back," [...]

"You try something stupid and you know I'll come after you," Jake responded.

She rolled her eyes. "Look, I'm not some Denver daisy who went out for a jog this morning. I've trained for six months for this. I'm in good shape."

He didn't want to think about what kind of shape she was in. He'd seen her long, toned legs and flat belly. He'd seen the muscle definition in her arms. Yeah, she was in damn good shape, all right. So good he couldn't keep his eyes off her.

She approached him. "Let me go."

"I can't do that."

"Why not?"

"Because I'm a cop, damn it."

Jake didn't want to have this conversation. It wasn't his responsibility to judge her guilt or innocence or any of those gray areas in between. All he was supposed to do was take her back.

And he planned to do that, come hell or high water.

Dear Reader,

Once again, Intimate Moments invites you to experience the thrills and excitement of six wonderful romances, starting with Justine Davis's *Just Another Day in Paradise*. This is the first in her new miniseries, REDSTONE, INCORPORATED, and you'll be hooked from the first page to the last by this suspenseful tale of two meant-to-be lovers who have a few issues to work out on the way to a happy ending—like being taken hostage on what ought to be an island paradise.

ROMANCING THE CROWN continues with *Secret-Agent Sheik*, by Linda Winstead Jones. Hassan Kamal is one of those heroes no woman can resist—except for spirited Elena Rahman, and even she can't hold out for long. Our introduction to the LONE STAR COUNTRY CLUB winds up with Maggie Price's *Moment of Truth*. Lovers are reunited and mysteries are solved—but not all of them, so be sure to look for our upcoming anthology, *Lone Star Country Club: The Debutantes*, next month. RaeAnne Thayne completes her OUTLAW HARTES trilogy with *Cassidy Harte and the Comeback Kid*, featuring the return of the prodigal groom. Linda Castillo is back with *Just a Little Bit Dangerous*, about a romantic Rocky Mountain rescue. Finally, welcome new author Jenna Mills, whose *Smoke and Mirrors* will have you eagerly looking forward to her next book.

And, as always, be sure to come back next month for more of the best romantic reading around, right here in Intimate Moments.

Enjoy!

[signature]

Leslie J. Wainger
Executive Senior Editor

Please address questions and book requests to:
Silhouette Reader Service
U.S.: 3010 Walden Ave., P.O. Box 1325, Buffalo, NY 14269
Canadian: P.O. Box 609, Fort Erie, Ont. L2A 5X3

Just a Little Bit Dangerous
LINDA CASTILLO

Silhouette®

INTIMATE MOMENTS™

Published by Silhouette Books

America's Publisher of Contemporary Romance

SILHOUETTE BOOKS

ISBN 0-373-27215-4

JUST A LITTLE BIT DANGEROUS

Copyright © 2002 by Linda Castillo

Visit Silhouette at www.eHarlequin.com

Printed in U.S.A.

Books by Linda Castillo

Silhouette Intimate Moments

Remember the Night #1008
Cops and...Lovers? #1085
A Hero To Hold #1102
Just a Little Bit Dangerous #1145

LINDA CASTILLO

grew up in a small farming community in western Ohio. She knew from a very early age that she wanted to be a writer—and penned her first novel at the age of thirteen, during one of those long Ohio winters. Her dream of becoming a published author came true the day Silhouette called and wanted to buy one of her books!

Romance is at the heart of all her stories. She loves the idea of two fallible people falling in love amid danger and against their better judgment—or so they think. She enjoys watching them struggle through their problems, realize their weaknesses and strengths along the way and, ultimately, fall head over heels in love.

She is the winner of numerous writing awards, including the prestigious Maggie Award for Excellence. In 1999, she was a triple Romance Writers of America Golden Heart finalist and took first place in the romantic suspense division. In 2001, she was a RITA® finalist with her first Silhouette release, *Remember the Night*.

Linda spins her tales of love and intrigue from her home in Dallas, Texas, where she lives with her husband and three lovable dogs. Check out her Web site at www.lindacastillo.com. Or you can contact her at P.O. Box 670501, Dallas, Texas 75367-0501.

To Papi,
Because you couldn't put it down.

Chapter 1

He smelled adrenaline the instant he walked into Rocky Mountain Search and Rescue headquarters. It hung in the air like spent powder after a gunshot. Rich and electric and as contagious as an airborne disease to a man who lived for the high.

Jake Madigan lived for the high.

His own adrenaline had ebbed and flowed since the 4:00 a.m. call that had rolled him out of bed. As head of the RMSAR equine unit, he normally didn't attend the briefings. For most call-outs—a lost hiker or injured rock climber—Jake hauled his horse directly to the site, disembarked and took to the high country. This time, however, team leader Buzz Malone had made it a point to ask him to be at the mass briefing. Jake wondered what had drawn six men from their beds at four o'clock on a Sunday morning. He wondered if it had anything to do with the Colorado Department of Corrections van parked outside.

Shaking off the cold, he hung his duster on the coat tree,

set his Stetson on top, and started down the hall where he could hear his fellow team members settling in. In most cases, he'd been told the briefings were informal and held in the galley. This morning, however, the galley stood empty, and light blazed from the war room. A room usually reserved for the press or high-profile operations run by government agency bigwigs.

Jake didn't much care for government agency bigwigs.

He entered the war room and scanned its occupants, his eyes grinding to a halt on the two men at the front wearing wrinkled suits and grim expressions. He knew immediately the suits belonged to the D.O.C. van outside. He wondered if they'd lost one of their clientele; if they were more interested in getting their convict back—or covering their bureaucratic butts.

At the coffee station set up at the rear, medic John Maitland dumped caffeine into a disposable cup. Snagging his own cup from the table, Jake held it out. "You look like you've been up all night, Maitland."

He filled Jake's cup. "I drew baby-feeding duty last night."

Jake wasn't too keen on the domestic scene these days, but the thought of his teammate getting up in the middle of the night to feed a screaming baby made him grin nonetheless. Nine months ago John Maitland had been a confirmed bachelor. All that had changed the day he'd rescued a pretty redhead up on Elk Ridge. He was now married, with a three-month-old baby girl. Even sleep-deprived he looked happy as hell.

"Baby-feeding duty, huh?" Jake said.

"Beth is breastfeeding, but we're supplementing with bottles at night so we can take turns with the night shifts. It was my turn last night."

The word "breastfeeding" rang uncomfortably in Jake's

ears. Trying not to wince, he waited a beat then changed the subject. "What's up with the D.O.C. van outside?"

"Inmate sneaked out a gymnasium window last night down at Buena Vista."

"We on alert?"

"That's right." John looked over his shoulder to where Buzz Malone huddled with the two suits. "Escapee is a lifer, went in for second-degree murder."

The worst kind, Jake thought, glancing in Buzz's direction. A killer on the run with nothing to lose.

"Looks like that pretty wife of yours is keeping you up nights, Maitland."

Both men turned their heads to see Tony "Flyboy" Colorosa, RMSAR's Bell 412 helicopter pilot—and resident Romeo—splash coffee into a cup.

"You look like you had a late one yourself, Flyboy," Jake said.

"What can I say, Jake? Some of us actually have social lives." Tony whistled a tune as he spooned sugar into his coffee. "You should try it sometime. Might improve that surly attitude of yours."

"Yeah, and it might stop snowing in Colorado one of these days." Grinning, Maitland slapped Jake on the back.

Trying not to grimace, Jake blew on his coffee.

"Gentlemen, take a seat." Buzz moved to the head of the table. "We're on a tight clock this morning, so I'll keep this brief."

Jake took the chair next to junior medic Pete Scully.

Buzz continued. "The State of Colorado Department of Corrections has asked for our help in locating an escapee from prison. Robert Singletary and Jim Neels are with D.O.C., which is our designated agency-in-charge. Jim is going to brief you on our mission objectives." Buzz gave the floor to the man standing beside him.

Jim Neels was a middle-aged man with hound-dog features and the build of a retired linebacker. His hopelessly wrinkled suit coupled with the half moons beneath his eyes revealed he'd already had a long night. His dour expression suggested he knew the day ahead would be even longer.

"Sometime between ten last night and three-thirty this morning, an inmate escaped from the Buena Vista Corrections Center for Women," he began. "Abigail Nichols, twenty-seven years old, is a convicted murderer serving a life sentence at our facility. We're in the process of setting up a perimeter, but there's a lot of country to cover and we need your help." Neels scanned the men. "This is a search-only operation, gentlemen. If you come in contact with Nichols, you are advised to use extreme caution." His gaze fell to Jake. "Mr. Madigan, you're the only law enforcement officer on the team?"

"I'm a deputy sheriff with Chaffee County."

Nodding, Neels continued. "Aside from Deputy Madigan, if you come in contact with the subject, do not attempt to detain her or to take her into custody. Call D.O.C. for backup. RMSAR dispatch has been informed to patch you straight through. Is that understood?"

Tony Colorosa yawned. John Maitland drained the last of his coffee from his cup. Even Pete Scully looked bored. Trying not to smile, Jake leaned back in his chair, crossed his legs at his ankles and studied his boots. The men of RMSAR didn't like some suit from D.O.C. coming in and telling them how to do their jobs. They were the best of the best and had yet to encounter a search-and-rescue mission they couldn't pull off.

"This woman has a history of mental illness," Neels added. "She may have an accomplice, but we don't know who that person is at this time. Be advised that she may be armed and should be considered dangerous."

"Do you have a location?" Jake asked. "Any sightings?"

Buzz walked to an easel where a topography map illustrated the five-county area surrounding the prison. Suit Number Two came to life and pointed out the corrections facility. "This is our facility at Buena Vista. We've got a five-hour window. The average person travels at about 3.2 miles per hour on foot. We think she went west." He indicated a highlighted area. "That should put her somewhere in this yellow area here."

"Does she have a vehicle?" Jake asked.

"Not that we know of, but it's possible her accomplice left one at a predesignated point."

Jake snorted. "If she's on foot and went west, she's not going to make very good time. It's rugged country up there."

Suit Number Two grimaced. "Nichols is very...determined."

Jake wasn't sure exactly what the other man meant, but he let it go. No matter how determined, a human being on foot could only cover so much ground. "What about gear?"

"State-issue jumpsuit—gray. Blue jacket. White sneakers. That's all she's got unless someone left clothing for her at a predesignated drop-off point."

"Anyone bringing in dogs?" Buzz asked.

"Chaffee County is covering that. Forest service has notified all the area ranger stations."

"What about a physical description?" John asked.

The suit flipped the easel page, and the room fell abruptly silent. The mug shot of a young woman with a mane of curly brown hair streaked generously with platinum blond arrested the attention of every man. Jake saw wide eyes the color of a mountain lake reflecting a violet sky. Thin, dark brows. A full mouth with just enough pout to keep a man on his toes. A graceful neck that called every man in the room to crane forward to see the rest of the package.

Jake broke a sweat beneath his flannel shirt and long

johns. He stared, more than a little surprised and a hell of a lot more intrigued than he wanted to be. The lovely creature staring back at him didn't look like an escaped con. Maybe a shampoo commercial model with all that wild, sun-bleached hair.

"She's five feet five inches," Suit Number Two said. "One hundred fifteen pounds. Violet eyes. Blond hair."

The voice faded as Jake's attention zeroed in on the mug shot. Her skin was flawless and pale as sweet cream. Her expression reflected defiance and an attitude that took a hard left just short of good. Her eyes spoke of a woman's secrets and beckoned the unwary to trust her.

Jake definitely didn't fall into the unwary category. Two years ago he'd played the fool for a woman with a pretty face and a tale of woe. Her betrayal still cut him on occasion, when he let himself think about it. He knew better than most that looks could be deceiving. And he knew first-hand what it was like to be on the receiving end of deceit. He felt the knife in his back to this day, and he'd sworn a hundred times he'd never be taken in again.

"Any questions?"

Jake cleared the cobwebs from his throat. "Any idea where she's heading?"

"We found a map in her cell with a penciled-in route that indicated east. But we think it was a ploy to throw us off. We're setting up patrols to the east, but as I already mentioned we suspect she's heading west, into the higher elevations." Checking his watch, the suit turned the floor over to Buzz.

Buzz looked at Tony Colorosa. "Flyboy, what's the situation on the weather?"

Tony came to attention. He might be the resident Romeo, but he took his job as chopper pilot serious to the extreme. "Weather Service put out an advisory about an hour ago. There's a low-pressure system to the northwest, building up steam and heading this way. It's packing two feet of snow and high winds that'll hit fifty knots by this afternoon. Gusts are at thirty-five right now. I'd say we have about two hours of fly time, four max before I'll have to recall to base.''

Buzz didn't look happy about sending his pilot out in iffy weather. ''That gives us four hours with the chopper, gentlemen. The rest of the search will be conducted on the ground. Tell your mommies and girlfriends you're not going to be home for breakfast, lunch or dinner.'' Buzz made eye contact with Jake. ''Where do you want to start?''

Jake looked at the map, took a few seconds to put himself in the subject's head. ''I'll drop the trailer west of Buena Vista, see if I can pick up some tracks.''

Buzz's attention shot back to his pilot. ''Flyboy, you and Scully take the chopper northwest and do a sweep. Once we hit forty knots, I want you in. Got it?''

Tony gave him a mock salute.

Buzz's gaze slid to John Maitland. ''You and I will take the ATV southwest. We'll be working in conjunction with the Chaffee County Sheriff's Office and dog team.'' He scanned the team. ''Let me reiterate. This operation is a Code Yellow. Search only. Use extreme caution. Subject is to be considered armed and dangerous. Gear up, gentlemen, let's rock and roll.''

Abby Nichols figured she'd outdone herself this time. It wasn't enough that she was freezing cold, that her fingers were numb, her feet aching with every step. Or that she was hungry, exhausted and scared out of her wits. To top it all off, she was finally going to have to admit she was lost. As if she needed that on top of the reality that her life had become one big disaster in the past year.

Then, just when she figured things couldn't get worse, she spotted the man on horseback. A quarter mile away, she didn't need to see his face to know he was a cop. She'd been around enough law enforcement types in the last year to spot one blindfolded. They had that look about them. Rigid. Uncompromising. Cold-hearted. Downright mean for the most part. The realization that he was tracking her shouldn't have surprised her, but it did, and she felt the sharp stab of fear all the way to her very numb toes.

He was a sheriff's deputy, more than likely—or maybe a bounty hunter. The thought of the latter made her shiver. That would be just her luck for some trigger-happy macho jerk to make it his personal mission to bring in the infamous Abby Nichols, the most dangerous female criminal since Bonnie Parker. The only problem with that analogy, Abby realized, was that she was innocent, Bonnie Parker hadn't been. The Buena Vista Corrections Center for Women didn't seem to care one way or the other.

She'd been tromping over clumps of buffalo grass and rocks the size of basketballs for nearly six hours. The cold, thin air burned her lungs. Her muscles quivered with exhaustion. But she didn't slow down. She'd spent the past four months getting in shape for this little excursion. Physical conditioning went a long way when you were running for your life over terrain not fit for a rock climber.

Of course, no matter how good her physical conditioning, if Abby wasn't heading in the right direction, she could end up in Omaha instead of Chama, New Mexico, where Grams was waiting with a hug and a smile and a place for her to spend the night before she began the lofty task of clearing her name.

She should have come across a road by now. Closer to the truth, she should have come across a road four hours ago. A narrow dirt road where Grams had stashed a pickup truck under an old, wooden bridge. A truck with a change of clothes, a cache of cash beneath the seat, and the ignition key in a magnet box under the hood.

Abby just couldn't understand how she'd missed that

road. She'd spent hours studying the map Grams had smuggled into the prison. All she'd had to do was follow the sun west from Buena Vista. Of course, come daybreak the sky had materialized as a smooth gray bowl and Mr. Sun had refused to show his face. That had been hours ago, and things weren't looking any better. In fact, if the clouds roiling on the horizon were any indication, Abby figured she'd be trudging through snow in another hour—or, at the least, be pounded by freezing rain. She wasn't sure which would be worse, but knew she was in for a miserable dose of Colorado weather one way or another.

Stopping to catch her breath, she leaned against a jut of granite and gazed out across the valley ahead. Pike National Forest spread out below like a page out of one of those fancy coffee-table picture books Grams was so fond of. One million acres of sparsely populated mountain terrain, white water streams and pine forests that stretched as far as the eye could see. Under different circumstances, she might have enjoyed the breathtaking scenery and mountain air. But considering she was on the run for her life, lost, and would soon find herself face-to-face with an armed man whose goal was to ruin her one and only shot at freedom, she figured her energies would be best spent putting as much distance between them as possible.

Sighing, she squinted at the figure on horseback as it wended up a trail she'd taken less than half an hour earlier. There was no doubt about it; he was gaining on her. If she didn't think of something utterly brilliant in the next ten minutes, he was going to be right on top of her.

Forcing back the rise of panic, acutely feeling the quickly shrinking distance between her and the horseman, Abby looked around. Grams had always told her desperate times called for desperate measures. Abby had never put much weight in that old cliché. But as the seconds ticked by and the window of opportunity shrank, she figured now was as good a time as any to put it to the test.

Jake loosened the reins and let his mount pick its way up the rocky terrain. He'd been tracking his subject for the past hour. As soon as he sighted her, he'd radio RMSAR headquarters so D.O.C. and Chaffee County could pull in the perimeter they'd set up to the east. If all went well—and he fully expected it to—he would have her in custody and be on his way down the mountain before dark. If he was lucky, he'd be home in time to watch the Avalanche trounce the Red Wings this evening. He'd bet ten bucks on that one, and didn't intend to lose the bet or to miss the game.

Jake was at home in the high country. He loved the hostile beauty, respected the unpredictable personality of the mountains. In the twelve years he'd been with RMSAR, he'd searched this rugged landscape for everything from lost Boy Scouts to Alzheimer's patients. He knew enough about this vast wilderness to admire the tenacity of a person who could travel for six hours and not tire or panic. For a woman without hiking gear or backcountry know-how, she'd covered some rough terrain and made damn good time doing so. He wondered if she had a destination in mind; wondered what she'd expected to accomplish out here in the middle of nowhere.

The ground leveled at the top of the rise, and he urged the mare into an extended trot. Brandywine was a seasoned trail horse and as surefooted as a mountain goat. She was raw-boned and well muscled, possessing more sense than most of his friends and a heart that rivaled the size of Pikes Peak. He'd ridden her under some brutal conditions, both terrain and weather-wise, and the mare had always kept her head and come through for him. He trusted her with his life—and a good bit more than most people.

The leather saddle beneath him creaked softly as he took

the horse down yet another steep incline. Behind him his mule Rebel Yell followed, his steel shoes clanking against the rocky ground.

The wind had picked up and was now coming from the west at a brisk clip. Jake figured he had another hour before heavy weather set in. November in the Colorado Rockies was unpredictable at best, particularly in the higher elevations. He'd gone on many a call-out, looking for weekend warriors who'd left eighty-degree temperatures in Denver wearing T-shirts and sneakers, hiked into the backcountry, and got caught in a snow storm without winter gear. Damn tourists. A little common sense went a long way in the mountains.

He traveled another fifty yards before realizing he'd lost the trail. Puzzled, he pulled up on the reins and backtracked. It wasn't like him to miss something like that. Jake had been tracking since he was old enough to ride a horse—which was shortly after he'd learned to walk. From a long generation of horse and cattle ranchers, he was as comfortable on horseback as most folks were in their cars.

Fifty yards back, he picked up the tracks again. A sneaker imprint in moist soil. A trampled tuft of buffalo grass. A broken twig where the subject had brushed against it. Then suddenly nothing.

What the hell?

Remembering the corrections official's warning that the subject could be armed, Jake scanned the immediate area, listening. It was so quiet he could hear the wind whisper through the pines. Beneath him, Brandywine grew restless, her bridle jangling as she tossed her head. The hairs on his nape prickled. It was *too* quiet. Why weren't the birds chattering?

"Whoa, girl." Wondering if his subject had doubled back, he realized he'd just made a rookie's mistake. *Damn.*

Tugging on the reins, he nudged the mare's sides with

his heels, sending her quickly backward. Simultaneously he slid the Heckler & Koch .45 from his holster and swung it upward. Adrenaline cut through his gut when he saw a pair of dirty sneakers dangling from the branch of a lodgepole pine ten feet up.

"I'm a police officer." He backed Brandywine to a safer distance. "Show me your hands."

Two hands emerged, dirt-streaked but empty nonetheless.

"Come on down out of that tree, ma'am."

Barely visible from the ground, she was perched precariously on a branch. Jake craned his neck to get a better look at her, hoping to gauge her frame of mind. The instant he made eye contact, the blood stalled in his veins. He'd never seen eyes that color. An intriguing mix of violet and midnight spun into velvet as soft as the mountain sky. Her hair was a jumble of brown streaked with blond. It fell in disarray over her shoulders, each strand curling as tight as a spring, too wild and unusual to be anything but natural.

Jake upheld his earlier opinion that she didn't look like an escaped convict. The photograph the D.O.C. official had shown them that morning didn't begin to do this lovely creature justice. From all appearances, neither did the psychological profile. She looked more rational than some people he'd run into in these parts. She even seemed a tad embarrassed at having been caught up in that tree. But, of course, she was the only blonde in prison grays around. Sitting ten feet above the ground on the branch of a lodgepole pine, she fit the bill.

"Ma'am, I'm a deputy sheriff with the Chaffee County Sheriff's Department. I'd like for you to climb down before you get hurt," he said. "Right now."

"How do I know you're really a cop?"

Her voice drifted down to him like smoke. Her accent held a hint of Appalachia. Jake wondered how in the world this lovely young woman had gotten herself into such terrible trouble with the law.

Unclipping his badge from his belt, he held it up for her to see. "Jake Madigan, Chaffee County Sheriff's Office. Come on down. Now."

He heard her sigh, then watched as she slid her feet along the branch, and moved toward the main trunk. "Okay. I'm coming. Just…wait a second. And put that gun away, will you? They make me nervous, especially when they're pointed at me."

Jake held the gun steady. "Be careful," he said.

"Like you care."

He arched a brow. "Well, I'd hate to have to haul you all the way back to Buena Vista with you screaming your head off because you broke your ankle jumping out of a gosh-darned tree."

"Believe me, mister, at this point in my life a broken ankle would be the least of my problems."

He wasn't going to argue with that; she was definitely in serious trouble. Jake dismounted and ground-tied Brandywine. He looked up to see the woman set both feet on a lower branch. The branch would have been strong enough to support her weight—if it hadn't been pecked full of holes by a persistent woodpecker. "Ma'am, you don't want to put your weight on that branch."

"Don't tell me how to climb, cowboy. I've been climbing trees since I was three years old."

"That may be true, ma'am, but—"

"I know what I'm do—"

The branch snapped with an audible *crack!* The woman yelped once, then crashed through a dozen smaller branches on her way down. Jake barely had time to holster his sidearm when a blur of blond hair and prison grays tumbled down and hit the ground with a thud hard enough to make his own spine ache.

"Easy," he said, approaching her. "Just be still a moment."

Lying sprawled on her side, she made an inaudible sound that sounded suspiciously like a curse, but she didn't move.

Oh, hell. Just what he needed—an *injured,* obstinate and pretty-as-sin prisoner to haul down the mountain. What the hell was he doing volunteering for this stuff when he could be at home shoveling horse manure?

Jake knelt, set his hands firmly against her shoulder, trying not to notice when a mass of curly blond hair swept over his hand. "You all right?"

A grunt emanated from beneath that mass of hair. "Just let me…catch my…breath."

"Can you move your toes for me?"

He looked down a stretch of leg that seemed to go on forever, saw her toes move beneath the canvas of her sneaker. "Yeah," she said.

"What about your fingers?"

She wiggled her fingers. "Wow, that really hurt."

Jake didn't think she was seriously hurt. But his EMT training—and the ever-present threat of lawsuits against police departments by disgruntled suspects—told him it was always wise to rule out the serious stuff first. "Roll over for me, okay?"

Grunting with the effort, she rolled slowly onto her back. "Ow. Oh, Jeez."

Jake's heart rate spiked when he found himself looking down into violet eyes framed by thick, black lashes and a whole lot of attitude he had absolutely no desire to deal with. He'd had his fill of women with attitude and didn't much like the idea of another helping—especially the con and liar variety.

"Anything hurt?" he asked.

"My hip hurts. And my elbow. Jeez, it feels like I landed on a rock."

"You just got the wind knocked out of you," he said.

"Yeah, well, I don't know about you, but I just happen to be partial to keeping oxygen in my lungs. Makes breathing a hell of a lot easier."

"You should have thought of that before you climbed that tree. That was a damn fool stunt."

"For the record, I'm an expert on the damn fool bit, so you may as well get used to it." Pulling a stick from her hair, she tossed it at him, then sat up.

The prison-issue jumpsuit didn't do much for her figure, but Jake couldn't help but notice the body beneath it. She was long and athletic and the material fell over curves he was a fool for noticing at a moment like this.

"What the hell were you doing up in that tree, anyway?" he asked.

She gave him a that's-a-really-stupid-question glare that was hot enough to melt snow. "Well, I wasn't building a tree house."

"Running from the law isn't very smart. You always get caught sooner or later."

"Yeah, that's exactly what I was thinking when you rode by the first time."

Jake shoved down a rise of annoyance. He could do without the smart mouth. He could damn well do without the way he was responding to those eyes of hers. Eight years in the Marine Corps had taught him discipline, and he'd lived by that code ever since. Twelve years of law enforcement had taught him control, and he'd adopted that code into his personal life, as well. The ethics came from inside the man. Jake prided himself on all those things, characteristics that defined who he was. He wasn't about to let a siren such as this lure him into the shallows so he could crash on the rocks and die a watery death.

"Are you alone?" Jake stood and stepped back.

She rolled her eyes. "You don't think there's anyone else

stupid enough to go tromping through this godforsaken countryside for six hours with me, do you?''

"Stand up," he said.

Grumbling, she struggled to her feet and began brushing the dust and dry grass from her jumpsuit.

Unable to help himself, Jake's gaze swept the length of her. The instinctive need to do so surprised him—and disturbed him more than he wanted to admit. He wasn't a gawker when it came to women, no matter how good they were to look at. He'd never had a problem with keeping his male tendencies in check. He wasn't even sure why he was reacting to this woman now—but he was—and it was starting to tick him off.

"Lace your hands behind your head and turn around," he said.

Sighing in annoyance, she reluctantly obeyed.

Only when her back was to him did Jake notice the tear in her jumpsuit. It started at her backside and stretched halfway down her thigh. The sight of velvety flesh and the white cotton panties beneath shouldn't have made his mouth go dry, but it did, and for several long seconds he couldn't take his eyes off that small, dangerous stretch of flesh.

She must have felt the draft because an instant later she craned her head around and spotted it. "Oh, great." She lowered her hands. "My pants are ripped."

"Put your hands up," Jake said.

"Damn cheap—"

"Put 'em up, ma'am. Now."

"But my pants are ripped and my—"

Jake cursed.

Compromising, she put one hand on her head, clutched the torn fabric together with her other.

He sighed. Well, wasn't this a hell of a mess?

Easing his eyes away from the flesh in question, he looked her in the eye. If he'd thought her gaze would be any less mesmerizing than her thigh, he was mistaken. He felt its impact with the force of a hammer striking the head of a spike and driving it deep.

"Probably caught your pants on a branch on the way down," he offered.

"No thanks to you." Awkwardly she kept one hand behind her head, the other clutching the tear. "I need a safety pin."

"Ma'am, I don't have anything like that."

"Yeah, you don't look much like a safety pin kind of guy. I'm sure it would be totally stupid of me to ask if you have a needle and thread in that saddlebag of yours, wouldn't it?"

Jake watched the color rise into her cheeks, felt his own discomfort grow. He wasn't sure why her request bothered him, but it did. Probably because he couldn't fault her for being modest, even if she was a criminal. "I've got some sutures we might could use. I'll have a look in my pack as soon as I get you settled. Maybe we can rig something to get you by."

Her eyes narrowed. "What do you mean by 'settled'?"

Jake didn't like the way the situation was shaping up. Procedure dictated he search her next. By no means did he want to get his hands anywhere near that body. Male officers normally didn't search female prisoners, but during the briefing the team had been warned that this woman should be considered armed and dangerous. If he'd been in town, he could have radioed for a female officer to assist to do a quick preliminary search for weapons or drugs. But he wasn't anywhere near a town, and there wasn't a female officer within fifty miles, so he was going to have to do the deed himself.

Oh, boy.

The thought shouldn't have rattled him; he'd searched plenty of prisoners before transporting them. Quick. Impersonal. Half the time he found something illegal. But for the first time in the course of his career, Jake felt as if he were out of his element. Man, he needed this like he needed a kick in the head by his mule.

"I'd like for you to step over to the tree and put your hands on the trunk for me," he said.

She rolled her eyes. "Don't tell me you're going to—"

"Ma'am, just do as I say."

"I know the drill." Clutching the material of her torn jumpsuit, she stalked over to the tree—and put her one free hand against it. Jake swore softly, but didn't ask her to let go of the tear. He figured he'd be better off if he just didn't think about that tear at all. He might be a cop, but he'd been cursed with the scourge of being a gentleman, as well. To this day he wasn't sure if that was his saving grace or his fatal flaw.

"Do you have any weapons or drugs or anything I should know about before I search you?" he asked.

"I don't have anything on me, except a truckload of really bad luck." She slapped her other hand against the tree.

Jake tried not to notice when the material parted, exposing a glimpse of her rear end and those white panties. Walking up behind her, he put his hand on her shoulder. "Spread your legs apart for me."

She did, but it wasn't far enough, and he nudged the insides of her sneakers with his booted foot. Making a small sound of annoyance, she spread her feet wider. He would search her just enough to make sure she didn't have a gun or knife. Anything smaller than that, he would just have to deal with when and if the situation arose.

Starting at the top of her head, he ran his hands over her hair. It was so thick and curly, he had to squeeze it between his fingers to make sure she didn't have anything hidden within that wild mass of curls. As impersonally as possible, Jake swept his hands down the front of her, beneath her arms, careful to check her pockets and out-of-the-way places for weapons sewn into the lining of the jumpsuit. He checked her waistband, hips, the outsides of her thighs, down her legs, even her ankles.

He tried not to notice the way she was shaking as his hands moved swiftly over her. Up until now she'd been holding her own. But there was always something demoralizing about the search that undid people. By the time he was finished, he'd broken a sweat and his own hands weren't quite steady. He could tell they were both relieved when he stepped back.

"Okay," he said. "You can turn around."

She faced him then, but Jake didn't miss that, for the first time since he'd discovered her hiding in the tree, she didn't meet his gaze.

He pulled the cuffs from his belt. "Give me your hands."

Surprising him, she offered her wrists. "Let's just get this over with. I'm cold and starving and I just want to get warm."

Jake wasn't buying the sudden cooperation. Not from this woman who'd risked her life to escape, then covered an amazing amount of terrain that would have exhausted most men.

He looked down at her hands. They were small and soft-looking. A woman's hands, he thought, only these hands were scratched and bruised. Her fingertips were red from the cold. He reminded himself that *she* was the one who'd gotten herself into this mess, not him. Still, he'd never been able to let someone suffer if it was within his power to stop it.

Cursing silently, he shoved the cuffs into his belt. "Hold on a minute. I've got an extra duster you can wear to keep the wind off you."

"T-thanks." Her teeth were chattering. "It's getting colder."

Pulling the radio from his belt to call for a chopper, Jake started toward Brandywine to get the duster. "RMSAR Homer Two, this is Coyote One. Do you read me? Over."

Jake wasn't so sure about the chopper. The winds had kicked up considerably in the past half hour. Once sustained winds reached forty knots, the Bell 412 would be grounded.

"This is Coyote One. RMSAR Homer Two, do you read me?"

"RMSAR Homer Two here, Coyote. You getting snowed on yet?"

"I'm about to. Homer, I've got a Ten-Twenty-Six. Expedite. Over."

"Roger that. Eagle went back to her nest. What's your Twenty?"

On reaching the horse, Jake glanced over his shoulder to check on his prisoner, but she was gone.

Chapter 2

Abby covered the ground at a reckless speed. She stumbled over rocks and brush, zigzagging around gully washers deep enough for a person to fall into and never climb out of. She had to hand it to Cowboy Cop. He'd been decent to her—which was a lot more than she could say for some of the law enforcement types she'd encountered in the past year—but she didn't have any regrets about taking off. No matter how decent he'd been to her, she knew what the end result would be. There was no way in hell she going to spend the rest of her life in prison for a crime she hadn't committed.

She'd only put twenty yards between them when she heard a shout behind her. Some cop cliché about stopping or he was going to shoot her. Abby didn't stop. The curse that followed wasn't cliché, but the temper behind it made her run even harder. She may have been duped a few times in her life, but she'd garnered some instincts over the years. She was savvy enough about human nature to know the man with the gunmetal eyes and slow drawl wasn't going to shoot an unarmed woman in the back.

She was willing to bet her life on that.

Fifty yards out and the terrain leveled off. She found her rhythm and picked up speed, just as she had at the track back at the prison where lifer Mary Beth Jenkins had timed her two-mile run six days a week for the past four months. Between weightlifting and running, Abby was in top physical form. Now, as her feet pounded the earth and she pushed her body to the limit, she prayed all that hard work was going to pay off.

She could hear the horse breaking through brush behind her. Cowboy Cop yelled again, but she couldn't make out the words and she didn't slow down. Burning lungs and sore muscles were nothing compared to the agony she faced if he caught her. Abby was running for her life. She'd decided the first time she'd heard her cell door close that she'd rather die than spend the rest of her life behind bars.

Of course, Fate had different ideas. One minute she was running like an Olympian, the next she was perched on the edge of a gulch, fighting to keep herself from falling into a stream where the water ran white and swift ten feet below.

Cutting to the left, Abby resumed her sprint. She knew better than to waste precious seconds looking over her shoulder, but the urge was too strong to resist. The sight of Cowboy Cop astride that big, spotted horse and gaining on her at an astounding rate made her heart jump high in her throat. Good Lord, he was going to catch her!

Spurred by panic, she ran at a dangerous speed, hurtling over fallen trees, ducking the occasional branch. Her breaths came hard and fast, the thin, cold air setting her lungs on fire.

The cop was so close she could hear the squeak of leather, the horse's hooves pounding the hard-packed earth. Sensing he was about to leap—knowing how a gazelle must feel when a lion's claws closed around its throat—she pushed harder.

An instant later he came down on top of her like a ton of bricks. Strong arms closed around her shoulders, his sheer weight dragging her down. She stumbled. Her legs tangled. Then the ground rushed up and smacked the air from her lungs.

Abby landed hard on her stomach. She tried to crawl away, but his hand snaked out and clamped over her ankle. Yelping, she lashed out with her foot. Her heel connected with something solid. His curse burned through the air.

"Stop fighting me and calm down," he growled.

Only then did Abby see her chance. Somehow she'd managed to land a kick just below his right eye. While she hadn't intended to hurt him, his instant of pain gave her the opportunity she needed to save her life. Leaning close to him, she jerked the radio from his belt and heaved it as hard as she could toward the stream.

Above her, Cowboy Cop went perfectly still.

Abby held her breath.

An instant later the sound of a splash rose over the din of rushing water. And for the first time in a year the thrill of victory gushed through her veins.

But her sense of victory was short-lived. The next thing she knew she was rolled onto her stomach, her hands jerked behind her back and a pair of handcuffs snapped firmly around her wrists. Evidently, Cowboy Cop didn't appreciate her tossing his radio.

Abby lay still for a moment, catching her breath, gathering her senses, trying to decide on her next course of action.

"Son of a gun." Rising, he stalked to the steep bank.

She watched as he chucked his boots, yanked off his full-length duster and hurled it onto the grass behind him. Not bothering to roll up his Wrangler jeans, he skidded down the bank and entered the icy water and began the hopeless task of searching for the radio. She could tell by his posture he was angry. She had to hand it to him, the man had exercised restraint so far. Guilt nudged her that she'd put that bruise under his eye. Truly, she wasn't a violent person. She downright detested violence under most circumstances. But this afternoon definitely qualified as one of Grams's "desperate" times.

She watched him wade into water that nearly reached his hips. Just the thought of venturing into that icy water made her shiver. "Lady, you are a menace not only to me but to yourself," he snarled.

"I'm sorry," she offered.

He shot her a withering look and continued his search.

His eyes were the color of flint, all rigid control and that cool distance cops seemed to specialize in. The man might know how to fill out a pair of jeans, he might even have pretty eyes, but Abby knew better than to let herself be charmed by a cop. She hated the way they looked at her. With suspicion and disdain and that nasty little hint of superiority that set her teeth on edge. Despite his finer attributes, he was a cop where it counted. And she'd be wise to remember that in the coming hours.

"Well, Einstein, it looks like you and I are going to have to ride back tonight without the benefit of the chopper." He waded through knee-deep water and stepped up onto the muddy bank.

She shouldn't have noticed the way that wet denim hugged his lean hips and muscular thighs, not to mention another part of his male anatomy she did *not* want to think about. She shouldn't be noticing a lot of things about this man, including the fact that he was undoubtedly the most handsome cop she'd ever laid eyes on.

He'd lost his hat at some point, revealing dark hair that was cropped short. His features were angular and lean with cheekbones befitting a Comanche chief. His hollowed cheeks and straight nose lent him a hardened appearance.

But his mouth was oddly soft—and sensual enough to tempt a saint.

Abby winced when he reached up and fingered the bruise under his right eye.

"I'm sorry about the bruise," she said quietly.

"The *bruise?*" A humorless laugh broke from his throat as he reached for his boots and stepped into them. "You just chucked our only means of communication and you're worried about a freaking *bruise?*"

"You should put something cold—"

"If we run into heavy weather or one of us gets hurt—"

"I'm sorry you're so upset about the radio."

"You're damn straight I'm upset! I can't believe someone would do something so incredibly stupid. Even a convict!"

"I hate to point this out, but I think you're angry because I got the jump on you."

He shot her an incredulous look. *"What?"*

"I nearly got away. That chaps your ego. That's why you're so angry."

"I appreciate you pointing that out to me, but I'm *particularly* angry because we've got over five hours of riding ahead of us and heavy weather moving in."

"Look, I'm sorry I put you in a tough spot. But I'm sure you'll get out of this just fine. This isn't personal. It's just that…I can't go back."

He choked out another humorless laugh. "I hate to be the one to break this earth-shattering news to you, Blondie, but you don't have a choice."

"I can't go back. I won't."

He glared at her. "If you've got any other quick-escape schemes up your sleeve, I strongly suggest you put them out of your mind because it's not going to happen. Got it?"

"You don't understand."

"I understand perfectly. You escaped from prison. It's my job to take you back. End of story."

"It's not that simple."

"Look, we can do this the easy way, or I can use force. It's up to you. But I can tell you, if you choose option number two, it's only going to make it harder for you."

"Cowboy—"

"Don't argue. Let's go."

"Please, don't do this." Despite her best efforts, her voice quivered with the last word. "I can't go back."

He regarded her with those cool, gray eyes. "You should have thought of the consequences before you murdered someone."

Even after nearly a year of being called a murderer, the word still made her shake inside. "I didn't kill anyone."

"Lady, do you have any idea how many times I've heard that?"

"I don't care how many times you've heard it. I'm innocent."

"A jury says you did it. The warden wants you back. That's all I need to know."

Abby knew her claim of innocence fell on deaf ears. She knew what it sounded like—a murderer's desperate ploy to buy time. She would never convince this man that she was innocent. The only person who could do that was Dr. Jonathan Reed at Mercy General Hospital in Denver. A man who'd held her heart in his palm—and crushed it right before her eyes.

"I'd rather die than go back to prison," she said after a moment.

He frowned at her. "You keep pulling stupid stunts like the one with the radio and that can be arranged." His boots sloshed with water as he stalked over to her. "Get up. We've got some ground to cover."

By the time they reached the mule a few minutes later, it was snowing. Abby had always loved snow. It made the world look fresh and new and untainted by life's problems. It reminded her of home and those endlessly long winters she and Grams had spent on the farm back in Calloway County, Kentucky, before Paps passed away.

She wondered if life would ever be that simple again.

A few feet away, looking miserable and cold in those wet jeans, Cowboy Cop shrugged into his duster. Scooping his hat off the ground, he brushed at the dried grass and set it on his head. "Come here."

Warily, she stepped over to him and stuck out her chin. "If you're thinking of brutalizing me because I tossed your stupid radio, I should warn you I have a really good lawyer. Jackson Scott Sargent specializes in police brutality and he's won every case—"

"Shut up and turn around." Frowning, he extracted the handcuff key from a small compartment in his belt.

Realizing with some surprise that he was going to remove the cuffs, she turned her back to him and offered her wrists. "Oh, well…thank you."

He removed the cuff from one wrist. "Don't thank me because I'm just letting you wear them in front because you're going to get up on that mule—"

"Wait just a—"

"And you're going to need to hold on to the horn with both hands because she's got a gait like a truck with four flat tires."

"I don't know how to ride."

"I don't care."

"If I fall off—"

"I'll leave you where you fall."

"If I get injured in any way, my lawyer, Jackson Scott Sar—"

"Shut up about the lawyer, lady, will you?"

"I'm merely forewarning you what could happen if I

don't get back to Buena Vista in the same healthy condition in which I left.''

"I'll remember that next time you do something stupid like fall out of a tree or trash our only means of communication."

She started to back away, but he tugged on the cuff. "Give me your other hand."

"Please—"

"Not after the stunt you pulled. Give me your hand. Now."

Resigning herself to being cuffed and forced to ride that obstinate-looking mule, she stuck out her hand. Far too efficiently, he snapped the cuffs into place. "Feel better?" she asked nastily.

"Sure do." He walked over to the mule. When she didn't follow, he raised his hand and beckoned her with his index finger. "We've got snow moving in, Blondie. Let's move."

Abby wasn't sure how she was going to get out of this. Evidently, Cowboy Cop was a by-the-book guy and took his job way too seriously. Well, she'd just have to keep her eyes open and hope for an opportunity. If one didn't arise, she'd just have to make her own. She didn't relish the idea of spending a cold, wet night out in the snow, but knew the weather might turn out to be an advantage.

She followed him over to the mule.

"On the count of three, I want you to put your left foot in the stirrup, your hands on the horn and hoist yourself into the saddle."

"I know how to get on." She lifted her hands and set them on the leather-covered horn. She'd only ridden a couple of times in her life. Back on Grams's farm, Mr. Smith had owned several Shetland ponies. Abby had liked them just fine with their long manes and pink noses, but she'd never gotten the hang of how to stay on their backs. She'd spent a lot of time that summer dusting off her behind.

"One-two-*three*."

Abby hoisted herself up, lifting her right leg over the mule's back.

"You're a natural," Cowboy Cop said.

"Careful, my head's going to swell." She stuck her tongue out at him when he turned his back.

Taking the lead attached to the mule's halter, he lashed it to his saddle. "You'd be wise to stay alert and pay attention to me and your mount."

"Like that's going to make any difference to me as you lead me to my death."

He shot her a frown over his shoulder.

"And we're going to get wet," she said.

"Welcome to Colorado in November." Gathering the reins, he vaulted onto the big, spotted horse with the ease of a man who rode often and well. "We would have been on board a nice warm chopper by now if you hadn't chucked the radio."

"I'll take my chances with the weather."

His eyes narrowed. "You aren't from around here, are you?"

"Not by choice."

"You've got a twang."

"I do *not* have a twang."

"You've definitely got a twang. I'd say you're from Tennessee."

"It's not a twang, and I'm not from Tennessee." When he only continued to stare at her, she added, "I'm from Kentucky."

Twisting in his saddle, Cowboy Cop reached into a large leather bag slung across the back of the saddle and retrieved a rolled-up bundle. He removed the tie and shook it. Abby was surprised to see a long, all-weather duster materialize. She wasn't sure why, but the fact that he was thoughtful enough to think of her physical comfort—especially when she'd given him the mother of all shiners *and* trashed his beloved radio—touched her.

Turning his horse, he pulled up beside her mule, so close their legs brushed. "It'll keep you from getting wet, and keep the wind off you." He reached around her and fastened the button at her throat.

It had been a long time since Abby had been close to a man—especially a man who looked as good as this one. Her heart did a weird little dip, then tapped against her ribs like a brass knocker. He smelled of leather, the out-of-doors, and healthy man. He was so close she could see the crow's-feet at the corners of his eyes, smell the tang of mint on his breath.

Her mule chose that moment to shift. Cowboy's knee bumped against hers. The touch jolted her. She hadn't intended to make eye contact with him. But one moment she was trying to avoid looking at him, the next she was staring into steel-gray eyes that were a tad too cool and a million times too discerning. His face was less than a foot away from hers and for a moment, they were eye-to-eye. His gaze never faltered as he secured the duster at her throat. She thought she saw a flash of heat in the cold depths of his gaze, but it happened too quickly for her to be sure.

And at that moment Abby clearly saw this man's only vulnerability—and suddenly realized what she was going to have to do to escape him.

If Jake hadn't experienced it firsthand, he never would have believed what had just happened had *really* happened. Not to by-the-book Jake Madigan. The level-headed lawman who always looked twice and never took anything at face value. Jake simply didn't go goo-goo eyed over women no matter how good they were to look at. And he never, ever, trusted them.

So what the hell was he thinking letting those big violet eyes of hers get to him like that?

The woman was a menace. Not only to society, but to his own rock-solid discipline. She was serving a life sentence for murder, for God's sake. If that little side note wasn't enough to persuade his libido to take an extended vacation, the corrections official's briefing that morning should have been, especially the part about Abigail Nichols's history of mental instability. Jake had seen firsthand that she was self-destructive; he'd watched her toss his radio into the stream, putting them out of communication with RMSAR headquarters and the Chaffee County Sheriff's Office dispatch. Such an act was not only foolhardy, but dangerous.

Now, on top of those man-killing eyes of hers and feminine charms he had no right to be thinking about, he also had the blasted weather to contend with.

Damn crazy woman.

The snow was coming down sideways now. Not only was Jake wet and freezing from the waist down, but he was starting to get worried. The weather had deteriorated at an alarming rate. Visibility had dwindled to less than a quarter mile. They wouldn't be able to travel much longer. The snow was already a foot deep and getting deeper by the minute. The wind had kicked up to a brutal speed and howled through the trees like a keening ghost. The drifts forming now would be large enough to swallow a man in a few hours. As much as he didn't want to admit it, they were going to have to find shelter and camp for the night.

Jake definitely wasn't going to be home in time to watch the hockey game.

Cursing the weather—and his crafty prisoner—he huddled deeper into his duster and brooded.

"Hey, Cowboy, I'm not sure if you've noticed yet, but it's snowing like the dickens."

Turning in his saddle, he looked at her, felt a quiver of an emotion he refused to name kick through him at the sight of her. Her cheeks and nose were pink from the cold. That wild mass of blond curls was damp and blowing in her face and glittered with a frosting of snow.

"Put your hood up," he said.

Raising her cuffed hands, she tugged the hood over her head. "My hands are cold."

"I was wondering when you were going to get around to complaining," he rumbled, hoping to keep her mind off the cold. Even from four feet away he could see that she was shivering. Her hands were bright red. Serves her right, he thought. But deep down inside, he didn't like seeing her shake with cold. Damn it, he didn't like the way things were shaping up at all.

"I'm not complaining," she said. "Just pointing out a fact."

"You wouldn't know a fact if you stepped on one and it stuck to the bottom of your shoe." He stopped his horse. Rebel Yell took a couple more steps, then pulled up next to Brandywine. Jake frowned at the woman. "And if you hadn't done away with the radio, we would be warm and dry by now."

"Correction. *You* would be warm and dry. I'd be sitting in a cold jail cell, contemplating spending the rest of my life behind bars for a crime I didn't commit. That's not my idea of a good time."

Jake wanted to believe it was that body of hers that had his hormones chomping at the bit for the chance to sell him out. But the truth of the matter was he'd seen something honest and true in the depths of her gaze. Something that belied her cavalier attitude and smart mouth and let him see the uneasy vulnerability beneath.

He knew better than to expect honesty from a woman like Abby Nichols; Jake hadn't been born yesterday. This woman was about as innocent as Lucifer. He knew firsthand how easily lies and deceit came to some people. Still, it didn't make it any easier to look into her eyes and wonder how she'd made such a mess of her life.

Taking off his gloves, he pulled his horse up next to her mule. "Give me your hands," he said.

She looked at him warily, but held out her hands.

Without looking at her, Jake worked her hands into his gloves. "This will keep you from getting frostbite."

"What about you?" Her gaze met his.

Jake stared back a moment too long before clucking to his horse and moving ahead of her.

"Where are we going anyway?" she asked after a moment.

"There's a hunting cabin a couple of miles from here. If it's still standing, we'll stop for the night."

"That sounds promising."

"It'll keep us dry, keep the wind off us. If we're lucky the weather will clear by morning."

"Yeah, I was looking forward to getting back to my nice, cozy cell. Tomorrow's my lucky day, huh?"

He shot her a sour look over his shoulder.

"The warden and I are tight, you know." She crossed her index and middle finger. "Like this."

Jake didn't want to get in to the dynamics of her plight. He wasn't buying her claim of innocence. Not even close. He'd heard too many lies over the years not to recognize a con when he heard one. He'd heard so many lies—from inmates and criminals and suspects—he could spot one in a dark room with his eyes closed. He'd heard lies from people he'd thought were decent. People he'd trusted. Worse, he'd been lied to by a woman he'd trusted with his heart.

That had cost him something he hadn't been able to get back. Something that made him a little less human. Elaine's lies had sucked the trust from his soul. The worst part about it was that Jake wasn't even sure he wanted it back.

Chapter 3

Jake couldn't help but worry that he'd overlooked the cabin. That he'd passed right by it and hadn't seen it because of the poor visibility. Or because he was cold to his bones and shivering uncontrollably. He couldn't help but think he was leading this woman directly to nowhere—or to a slow and excruciating death.

He couldn't get the thoughts out of his head as they rode into the driving snow. They'd been traveling at an agonizingly slow speed for two hours. He was wet and tired and growing increasingly uneasy about the situation. He could only imagine how his prisoner must be feeling. She wasn't dressed for heavy weather. She hadn't eaten or rested. Her hands were cuffed, to boot. Yet she hadn't complained. Either she was one tough cookie—or more stubborn than anyone he'd ever met.

If his memory served him, they should have passed the old hunting cabin an hour ago. His compass told him they were headed in the right direction. If so, then where the hell was it? Alarm quivered in the pit of his stomach. He wasn't one to panic—he'd been in worse predicaments in these mountains and survived. Only this time he wasn't alone. His unwilling traveling companion might be an escaped convict, but her safety was his responsibility. Jake took that responsibility to heart. With weather conditions worsening by the minute—and nightfall closing in fast—he knew it had become imperative for them to find shelter very soon or else find themselves facing a life-or-death situation.

Wind stung his eyes as Brandywine took him through snow deep enough to scrape the underside of her belly, deeper where the wind had whipped it into drifts. His face was wet and ached with cold. His hands were beyond numb.

"You okay?" he shouted over the roar of wind.

"You mean aside from the fact that I'm wet and cold and hungry beyond belief and my life is wrecked? Hey, Cowboy, I'm just peachy over here. Don't worry about me. I mean, who needs their fingers and toes when they're going to be spending the rest of their life in prison?"

Even though she was less than three feet away, he could barely make out her silhouette through the driving snow. "We'll be there in a few minutes. Hang tight, okay?"

"I've been hanging on for a year, now. A few more minutes aren't going to make much difference."

An instant later Brandywine stumbled. Jake looked down, squinting through the snow, realized she'd stumbled over the lowest rail of a broken-down fence. Pulling up on the reins, he looked ahead. Relief trickled through him when the weathered exterior of the cabin loomed into view.

Sliding off the horse, he led her to the east side of the cabin where a shallow lean-to blocked the wind and snow. Jake walked over to Rebel Yell and looked up at his charge. She gazed back at him, shivering, her cheeks bright pink within the pale oval of her face. Wisps of wet hair curled wildly around the hood of the duster.

"Nice p-place," she said. "C-come here often?"

He would have bought the tough-guy act if her teeth hadn't been chattering. An Emergency Medical Technician, Jake knew it wouldn't take long for hypothermia to set in under these kinds of conditions. He probably wasn't too far from that point himself. "Sit tight," he said. Taking Rebel Yell's lead, he tied the mule to the manger, then turned to the woman. "Lift your right leg over her neck and slide down," he said.

Holding her cuffed hands in front of her, she did as she was told. It would have worked if her legs hadn't given out the instant they touched the ground. If Jake hadn't been there to catch her, she would have fallen. But he was there, holding her close—way too close—and far too aware of how good she felt in his arms.

Startled violet eyes met his, a kaleidoscope of emotions scrolling in their depths. Jake saw awareness and caution coupled with something else he couldn't quite put his finger on. He breathed in, got a lungful of her scent, felt it knock him upside the head like a fence post. She smelled earthy and elemental, a heady mix of sweet mountain rain and woman that stirred him despite the cold. He felt the hard thump of a pulse, but he wasn't sure if it was his or hers. Just that it was racing like the wind, and he was far too wise to ask himself why.

"Careful, I've got you," he said.

"I'm c-cold." She winced. "M-my feet are numb."

"Why didn't you say something?"

"I figured it didn't take a rocket scientist to figure out it's seriously cold out here." Grimacing, she shoved a handful of hair from her eyes. "Like you care, anyway."

"It's my responsibility to get you back to Buena Vista safe and sound."

Her humorless laugh shouldn't have irked him, but it did. "More like dead or alive."

"Don't overdramatize. It's annoying."

"I'm not overdramatizing. I'm simply being realistic."

Jake knew he should step away. He should have stepped away the instant he'd felt the brush of her body against his. But she was curvy and soft against him, and her scent was doing a number on his judgment. Not to mention another part of his anatomy that seemed determined to betray him.

"Don't sweat it, Cowboy Cop. I know you're just doing your job. I'm not taking any of this personally."

When he looked into her eyes, he could tell she really meant what she was saying. "I don't want to see you hurt," he said.

"Yeah, you just want to get me back to Buena Vista in one piece so I can spend the rest of my life in prison for a crime I didn't commit. That's real compassionate. But I guess a girl in my position has got to appreciate compassion when she can, you know?"

Jake sighed. "I'm not going to get into this with you now." Releasing her, he stepped back. "I've got to get these animals fed and bedded down for the night."

He turned toward Brandywine, opened the saddlebag and pulled out a halter, lead and a bag of grain. Slipping the bridle off the horse's head, he replaced it with the halter and tied her to the manger. Scooping snow from the manger, he divided the bag of grain between the two animals. As they fed, he turned to his charge. "Give me your hands."

"Don't tell me you trust me enough to take off these cuffs."

"Trust doesn't enter into the picture here, Blondie. This is a dangerous storm, and I could use your help."

"Imagine that. A lawman needing my help."

Frowning, Jake fished the key from his belt, unlocked the cuffs, then stuffed them into the compartment. Without speaking, he turned back to the animals, unfastened the two bedrolls from the saddles and offered them to his prisoner. "Would you hold these for a minute while I untack?"

She nodded. "Maybe you should deputize me or something."

"I don't think so." He set the bedrolls in her arms, then went about untacking the animals. A few minutes later, a saddle horn in each hand, he turned toward the cabin. "Let's see if this place has a roof," he said.

"Cowboy, I'm going to be really disappointed if it doesn't."

"You're not the only one."

"I guess it would be unreasonable for me to hope for hot water."

"Best case scenario is a fire—if there's dry wood."

"Room service?"

"I've got some instant meals, jerky and a few cookies."

"Chocolate chip?"

"Peanut butter."

"Jeez, you really know how to crush a girl's dreams."

Jake moved past her and reached for the knob. The door squeaked when he pushed it open. The pungent odors of old wood and dust greeted him. "No snow on the floor," he said. "That's a good sign."

He stepped into the dimly lit interior, his boots thudding dully against the plank floor. It had been a year since he'd been inside the one-room cabin, and it was every bit as dilapidated as he remembered. He'd gone camping with Tony Colorosa and Pete Scully, and they'd run into rain. Jake had remembered the cabin from a search and rescue operation years before, and they'd ended up spending the night.

"It's not exactly the Ritz, but it'll do," he said.

"We'll have to call housekeeping. There's a pane missing from the window and it's snowing in the kitchen."

Jake looked up to see his charge stroll into the kitchen

area. She'd lowered the hood of the duster he'd given her and handfuls of brown-and-blond-streaked hair curled around her shoulders. He tried not to notice that her teeth were chattering, or the occasional shiver that racked her body. Most of all he tried not to notice that she looked more like somebody's camping partner than she did a convict on the run.

Tearing his gaze from her—and thoughts that were anything but appropriate at a time like this—he looked toward the window where snow blasted in through a broken pane. Two inches of the stuff covered the rough-hewn countertop. "I'll patch that."

"Is there a bathroom?"

Jake stared at her, suspicion flaring hot in his gut. "There's an outhouse just off the back porch."

When she started toward the back door, he reached out and took her arm. "I'll go with you."

"What? You think I'm going to run out into a blizzard?"

"After the stunt with the radio, I wouldn't put it past you."

"I may be desperate, but I'm not stupid."

"They're one and the same up here, Blondie. You do something desperate in this weather and it might just kill you."

"That would just set the world on its ear, wouldn't it?"

Jake cut her a look. He didn't like the sound of that. She didn't appear unbalanced or unduly agitated, but he remembered clearly the D.O.C. officer mentioning that she had a history of mental illness. If she decided to get crazy on him and take off, they could both freeze to death and not be found until spring. "I'll be right behind you."

"Suit yourself." Rolling her eyes in exasperation, she stalked over to the rear door and yanked it open. A blast of frigid air sent her back a step.

The outhouse was a doorless, open-air facility that left

her gaping for a full thirty seconds before Jake leaned down and told her he would turn his back while she took care of business. She wouldn't even look at him as she stepped through the door and brushed the snow off the seat. Then at her nod, he turned away and tried not to think about how long this storm might last. While she used the facility, Jake spotted the remains of what had once been a woodpile. The wood underneath was dry, but there wasn't much. Maybe enough for two days. Leaving his post, he walked over to the pile and gathered up an armload of wood.

When he straightened, he found her a few feet away, gathering kindling. Surprise and a grudging admiration rippled through him. Okay, so Miss Convict was a trooper. That shouldn't have appealed to him, but it did. He knew what people were like when they were scared. He'd seen his share of panic, even more of tears. This woman could have been the poster girl for calm.

As much as he wanted to deny it, Jake realized he was going to have to be very, very careful in the coming hours. She was getting to him despite his resolve to keep her at a safe distance. And for the first time since Elaine had walked out on him more than two years earlier, he wasn't sure he trusted his own good judgment to keep him on the straight and narrow.

Rather than shout over the wind, he made eye contact with her and pointed toward the door. She nodded, and he followed her. Once inside, he set the wood in front of the fireplace. "I'll build a fire, then I've got to get out of these wet pants. Why don't you see if you can find something suitable to cover that broken pane with?"

"I was just going to suggest that." She started toward the kitchen area where a few pieces of weathered plywood leaned against the sink.

Jake watched her out of the corner of his eye as he stacked the wood and kindling in the hearth. She was still shivering, but he knew a blazing fire would take the damp chill out of the room. It wouldn't be warm by any means, but at least they wouldn't die of hypothermia. For tonight, he figured that was the best they could hope for.

She searched the counter, tossing aside a couple of scrap pieces of wood that were either too large or too small to fit over the broken pane. Next, she looked under the sink.

He jumped a foot in the air when she screamed and scrambled back.

"What the hell?" Certain she'd uncovered a nest of rattlesnakes, he sprinted over to her, grabbed her arm and tugged her away from the threat. Her laugh stopped him cold. He glanced past her in time to see a chipmunk scurry into a fist-size hole leading to the crawl space beneath the cabin.

Another laugh erupted. "Didn't mean to scare you, Cowboy, but I'm not the camping type."

"I've noticed." His annoyance died a quick death the instant he realized how close she was. Awareness zinged between them like a stray bullet. In the span of a heartbeat, the situation went from bad to worse. A situation where he was no longer the cool-headed cop in control, but a man with a man's needs—and a man's weaknesses. She was no longer merely his charge, but a woman with violet eyes and soft flesh and secrets that beckoned a man to peel away the layers of her mystery one by one. He saw the realization in her eyes, heard it in the shuddering breath she let out, felt it in the leap of her pulse as it hammered beneath his fingers where he'd grasped her wrist.

He'd been around the block enough times to know this was a very bad idea. But he didn't step away. "You okay?" he asked.

"It was only a chipmunk," she said after a moment.

"I saw that."

"I didn't mean to scare you."

"It was only a mild heart attack. I'll survive."

She choked out a laugh. "You made a joke."

"I guess I did."

"It didn't hurt too bad, did it?" Amusement sparked in her eyes, but he clearly saw that she was shaken. He wondered if it was from the scare that chipmunk had given her, or because he was close enough to see the melted snow clinging to her eyelashes. The only question that remained was just how far he was going to let this go before he put a stop to it.

Her face was only a few short inches from his. So close he could feel the heat coming off her. See the endless violet of her eyes, searching his, seeking something elusive, asking a question he had absolutely no desire to answer. Not when the blood was a dull roar in his head and the feel of her was making his heart pound. Not when the scent of her was so keen he could practically taste her flesh.

Jake knew he should pull away, knew he should heed the alarm blaring in the back of his mind, but he didn't.

"Your pupils are dilated," she whispered.

"So are yours." His voice creaked like rusty barbed wire.

"You know what that means...."

"Why don't you tell me?"

"It means you're aroused."

"Really?" He didn't need her to tell him that. Jake felt it loud and clear, like a bomb going off right on top of him. But he also heard the warning bell clanging and the voice of reason screaming for him to stop what he knew would happen next.

She inched closer. "If I didn't know better, I might think you wanted to kiss me."

"Yeah, but you know better, don't you?"

"Do I?" She stood on her tiptoes, leaned toward him until her mouth was less than an inch from his. "I'll bet you're good at it."

The control cost him, but Jake didn't move. Sweat broke out on his back. He heard the echo of his pulse in his ears, the rush of blood through his veins. She closed her eyes, leaned closer.

An instant before contact, Jake stepped back. He wasn't sure who he was angrier with, himself for getting into the situation, or her for compromising herself. But the anger stopped the insanity with an audible snap.

Her eyes widened when he grasped her biceps, whirled her around and shoved her into a rickety chair. "Let's get something straight right now, Blondie."

She stared at him, her breaths coming short and fast. "I thought—"

"You thought wrong," he snapped. "What's the matter with you? Don't you have any self-respect? Don't you have any pride?"

"Don't you dare lecture me about self-respect."

"You need it, sweetheart."

The sudden rush of tears to her eyes took his anger down a notch, filled the space left in its wake with another emotion he didn't want to deal with. Not when he could still smell her sweet essence, feel the pang of heat in his groin.

"You don't know me," she said. "You don't know what I've been through in the last year—"

"I know what I see. I see a young woman about to give her body away because she thinks she might get something in return."

She managed to look appalled. "I wasn't going to—"

"The hell you weren't. I was reading your signals loud and clear, sister." Gritting his teeth against another jolt of anger—this time aimed at himself—Jake turned away and paced to the other side of the room. Damn, that had been close.

"I wouldn't have done...*that*," she said after a moment. Pinching the bridge of his nose, Jake laughed humorlessly. "Look, if we're going to be stuck together, I've got one rule."

She leaned back in the chair, blinking back what he hoped to God weren't tears. "I'm not very good at rules."

"All I want is for you to be straight with me," he said. "That means no games. No lying. No tricks. If you can't tell the truth, then don't say anything. Do you think you can abide by that?"

She pressed her lips together. "I wasn't going to...you know, sleep with you."

"If you weren't going to sleep with me, just what the hell did you have in mind?"

"Well...I thought maybe...I thought maybe I could distract you."

"*Distract* me?" Jake gritted his teeth. "Some other bozo in my position might have taken you up on your offer. Some unscrupulous cop might have wanted more than you were willing to give. Then where would you be?"

"I'd still be in the same predicament I'm in now."

"Yeah? And what's that? Paying your debt to society?"

"Going back to prison for a crime I didn't commit."

"You're going to have to come up with something a little more original than that because I've been in this business a long time, and I've heard every lie in the book."

"You want original?" She stood abruptly, trembling and pale, tears shimmering on ashen skin. "The night before I escaped, somebody tried to kill me. I had two choices. Leave or die. So I left. Is that original enough for you?"

Chapter 4

Abby told herself the shaking was from the cold, but she knew it wasn't. She wanted to believe the tremors racking her body were because she was scared and desperate and furious that her plan to escape had been foiled. But she knew the knot in her gut and racing pulse had more to do with the way the tall cowboy with the unfriendly eyes and dangerously sensual mouth had looked at her when she'd had her body pressed against his.

Holy cow, she'd almost kissed him! A cop, for God's sake. A man who was going to do his utmost to ruin any chances she had of saving her life. A man who was apparently hardened and cynical—and not nearly as vulnerable as she'd thought.

The most lethal kind of man there was—at least to a woman in her position.

Abby wasn't above using her feminine charms to get what she wanted. She'd seen the way he looked at her; she'd seen the heat in his eyes, discerned the weakness that made men predictable. Of course, she wouldn't have let things go too far; she had her limits. But she definitely would have gone far enough to get the job done. She wasn't sure what that made her. Desperate perhaps. She could live with that. She'd learned to live with a lot of things in the past year.

Of course, she wouldn't have to compromise herself now that Mr. By-the-Book had thwarted her plans. Damn him. Maybe she was in a lot more trouble than she'd ever imagined.

Abby realized then that she was going to have to be careful with this man. She'd nearly crossed a line. She'd nearly done something irrevocable. Something that would have made her hate herself. She'd nearly made a mistake that would have cost her another piece of her soul. Worse was the realization that for a crazy instant, she wondered if she might even enjoy it.

Oh, dear God, maybe she *was* crazy.

The cowboy stared at her, his thick brows riding low over eyes filled with a cop's skepticism. "Good try, Blondie. You get a gold star for originality, but I'm still not buying it."

She met his gaze levelly. "It's true."

"And I'm the Easter bunny."

"I don't care if you believe me or not."

"Why are you trying so hard to convince me, then?"

"Because you're my last hope."

He took another step back, a predator who'd just been swiped by the nasty claws of a much smaller, but infinitely dangerous prey. "I meant what I said about playing games," he said. "That includes making up stories. You got that?"

"That isn't a story, and I sure as hell don't consider my life a game."

"Neither do I."

"Maybe you just don't give a damn."

"I give a damn—about the law. I've got a job to do. A

job that's not always pleasant. You're not making it any easier for either of us.''

A gust of wind rattled the door in its frame. Dragging her gaze away from him, Abby looked out the grimy window to the swirl of white beyond. Despair pressed down on her. She felt trapped, like a rabbit caught in a snare with a pack of dogs waiting to tear it to shreds.

"That storm's not going to let up any time soon." His voice caught her gaze. He was watching her, his expression as hard and steely as his eyes. "Let's try to get through this without any more problems, all right?"

"I'm innocent," she said. "I didn't kill anyone. I was framed, and I'm going to prove it. I just need—"

"I don't want to hear it." He raised a hand to silence her. "I'm taking you back and that's the end of it."

Tears burned behind her eyes, but she blinked them back with fierce determination. She would not cry in front of this man. She hadn't cried in front of anyone for a long, long time. She refused to start now. If Abby Nichols had anything at all left, it was pride. Crying never helped much anyway.

Still, she was thankful when he turned away. Some of the tension drained out of her when she didn't have to meet that cold-steel gaze of his. She wasn't going to waste her time trying to convince him of her innocence. Not this hard-headed lawman who saw the world in stark black and white. Her only hope was to gain his trust one inch at a time, then slip away when he wasn't expecting it. If she didn't get a chance—if he didn't give her the chance—she would just have to make one.

"There are a some instant meals in my saddlebag," he said after a moment. "Why don't you pull out a couple, and we'll eat?"

Abby's stomach growled at the mention of food. She hadn't eaten since the previous night, and after a physically grueling day she was starved. Without looking at him, she started toward the saddlebag he'd dropped near the door. Kneeling next to the bag, she opened the leather flap. Four individually packaged meals were stacked neatly, along with a collapsible container of water. She removed two of the meals.

"All you have to do is open the meal," he said from across the room. "There's a chemical inside that heats the food."

She turned to ask him how that worked, but the sight of him standing with his back to her—his butt as bare as a baby's—made her gasp in shock. She knew better than to stare, but before she could stop herself, her eyes did a slow, dangerous sweep, covering every well-muscled inch of a body that gave new meaning to the word perfect.

All the blood in her brain did a quick downward spiral. "W-what do you think you're doing?" she cried.

He looked at her over his shoulder as he stepped into a pair of jeans and jerked them up quickly over his hips. "Getting into some dry clothes. Thanks to you, I've spent the past two hours in wet pants."

"I know *that,* but why are you...why did you..."

"You didn't think I was going to change my pants outside in the blizzard, did you?"

"I didn't think you were going to strip right in front of me!"

"Your back was turned." He faced her, and Abby's mouth went dry. "I didn't think you'd peek."

"I...didn't."

"I guess that's why you're blushing."

"I'm *not* blushing." The heat in her cheeks didn't even come close to a blush; it was more like a forest fire.

"Whatever you say."

His jeans were well-worn and hugged his lean hips like a pair of snakeskin gloves. His heavy flannel shirt hung open, revealing a muscled chest covered with a sprinkling of black hair that arrowed down to his waistband and disappeared. Abby swallowed hard and tried not to notice that he hadn't bothered with the top button of those jeans.

Oh, my.

Scooping his wet jeans and long johns off the floor, he started toward her. "What's your name, anyway?" he asked.

"M-my name?"

"Or do you prefer Blondie? That's fine by me. A lot of convicts go by aliases."

"Don't call me a convict," she snapped.

He shrugged. "Just making conversation."

"My name is Abby. Abby Nichols."

"I'm Jake."

Jake. The name fit him, she realized. Almost as well as those jeans.

"It looks like we might be stuck here together for a while, Abby. I figured we ought to be on a first-name basis."

She stepped back and watched him hang the jeans and long johns he'd been wearing neatly above the stone hearth.

"How are those meals coming?" he asked.

She looked down at the two unopened containers in her hand. At some point in the last five minutes her appetite had vanished. Maybe about the time when she'd looked over and seen... Mercy, she didn't want to think about what she'd seen. "I wasn't sure how to...activate the heat."

Coming up beside her, he took one of the meals and proceeded to tear off the foil label. "Like this. See?"

He moved with the self-assurance of a man who was comfortable with himself and didn't necessarily give a damn what the rest of the world thought. Abby watched, fascinated by his hands as the steaming food came into view.

"I hope you like chicken and broccoli." He handed one of the containers to her. "I'm partial to beef myself."

"I'd eat nails if they were cooked and warm." Abby took her food to the hearth.

He walked over to the saddlebag, removed two plastic forks and two containers of water, then met her at the hearth. "The floor's cold. You can sit on the bedroll if you want." He handed her water in a collapsible cup.

Abby accepted it and drank deeply. Slipping off the duster, she unrolled the bedroll—an insulated sleeping bag—then settled onto it with her legs crossed. Jake did the same and soon they were forking chicken chunks and broccoli from their instant meals.

They ate in silence, the only sound coming from the raging wind outside, the patter of driving snow against the windows and the occasional crackling of wood as the fire consumed it.

The chicken was surprisingly good, and Abby savored every bite with the fervor of a woman who didn't know when or where she'd get her next meal. She was going to need her strength in the coming days. As long as she stayed calm and kept her head, she could still get out of this. Jake Madigan might be an armed lawman, but he wasn't the kind of man who could shoot a woman in the back if she took off on him. All she needed was the opportunity and a little luck.

The warmth from the fire was relaxing her. Abby snuggled deeper into the sleeping bag and drifted. Her tummy was full. She could feel her cold-stiffened muscles beginning to unwind. Her hands no longer ached. She could feel her feet again. Sleepiness was starting to descend like a lavender mist clouding her brain one micro-droplet at a time.

She was aware of Jake moving around the cabin. She heard the door open. Felt the draft of cold air against her face. The clanging of metal against metal.

She opened her eyes to find him kneeling at the hearth, setting a large, scarred kettle over the embers. He looked at her intently, then turned back to the kettle. "I'm melting snow so we can wash up," he said.

Sitting up, she looked around. The windows were dark now, the interior of the cabin illuminated only by the fire. Outside, the wind howled like an angry banshee. Abby could still hear the snow blasting against the glass on the north side. Jake had taken their empty food containers into the kitchen. She must have fallen asleep.

"What time is it?" she asked.

"You got somewhere to go?"

"No, I'm just wondering."

"A little after seven."

Early evening. It felt like the middle of the night. With the storm waging all-out war on the cabin, it seemed as if they were the only two people on earth. The thought should have disturbed her, but it didn't. In fact, as she sat on the bedroll and looked around the cabin, a strange and comforting warmth encompassed her. The storm might be an inconvenience, but it would buy her some time. Besides, she'd much rather be stuck in this cabin than in a prison cell. At least here there was the hope of escape.

The water in the kettle was steaming. Abby watched Jake use one of his leather gloves to take it from the fire and carry it to the kitchen where he dumped the hot water into a larger pail of snow. She swallowed hard when he turned his back to her and proceeded to strip off his shirt.

Broad shoulders rounded with muscle came into view as he draped the shirt neatly over the back of a chair. The faded jeans he wore rode low on his narrow hips. Jeans that left no doubt about Jake Madigan's masculinity. Abby tried not to stare, but she couldn't tear her eyes away from him. The man was built like Adonis. The fire cast yellow light over the room, turning his skin to bronze, his muscled shoulders and back to a sculpted work of art. His biceps flexed as he leaned forward and splashed water onto his face. His wet skin glistened when he dipped a small rag into the water and brought it to his neck and chest, then lower.

Abby turned abruptly away and stared into the hearth, watching the flames leap over the dry wood. Her face felt hot. But she knew it had nothing to do with the fire, and everything to do with the man. She could hear the water splashing on the other side of the room, but for the effect he was having on her body, he may as well have been right next to her.

"I can warm you some water if you want it."

She jumped at the sound of his voice. He'd come up behind her. Still sitting on the floor in front of the fire, Abby had to crane her neck straight up to look at him. She tried not to look at his chest or that thatch of dark hair covering it. Oh, Lord, she wished he'd put his shirt back on.

"Um, well…yes. I'd…like that."

What was wrong with her voice?

Without speaking, he went back to the kitchen area and jerked on his shirt, then slipped into his duster. Taking both the kettle and the pail, he went out the door.

Abby's heart rate quickened. While the thought of washing up with warm water sounded heavenly, she had no idea how she would manage it with Jake around. He might be comfortable strutting around half naked, but she wasn't.

He came back through the door with a gust of wind and a swirl of snow. She watched as he set the kettle over the fire, then set the larger pail half full of snow back on the rickety table in the kitchen area.

"The water ought to be boiling in a few minutes," he said. "I found a couple of clean towels you can use."

"Thank you." Rising, she looked frantically around the cabin. It was small and sparse and offered absolutely no privacy.

The water in the kettle began to steam. Abby stared at it, then risked a look at Jake. "I can't bathe with you in here," she said in her most reasonable voice.

He cut her a look that was half annoyed, half incredulous. "I'll turn my back."

"I'm afraid that won't do. I just…can't…with you in here."

"Oh, for crying out loud."

"Would you mind terribly waiting outside for a couple of minutes? I mean, it's not like I'm going to take off in this weather."

"Lady, it's snowing like crazy with subzero wind chills. I don't feel like getting hypothermic just so you take a damn bath."

She looked longingly at the water. "Please, just give me five minutes of privacy." Her gaze traveled to the fire. "We're low on firewood. Maybe you could take a few minutes and find some more."

Heaving a sigh of annoyance, Jake walked to the hearth and removed the kettle from the fire. In the kitchen area, he dumped it over the melting snow. Steam rose into the chill air. He looked at Abby through the cloud.

"I'm going to check on the stock," he growled. "You've got five minutes." He looked at his watch. "Make it quick," he said, and walked out, slamming the door in his wake.

Abby stripped in two seconds flat, draping the jumpsuit over the table. She dipped the rag into the water and brought it to her face. The warmth felt wonderful against her skin after being out in the cold all day. She soaped up the rag and scrubbed her face and hands. She closed her eyes and the water sluiced over her, rejuvenating her, making her feel clean and warm and almost human again. She wasn't sure how much time had passed—she didn't have a watch—but after a short while, she used the threadbare towel Jake had given her and quickly dried herself. She hated to put the prison-issue jumpsuit back on, but knew she didn't have a choice. She'd stepped into the jumpsuit and had it pulled up to her waist when the door swung open.

The sight of her bare back stopped Jake cold, like a ship that had run headlong into an iceberg. He felt the impact echo through his body, a paralyzing shock that went from his head all the way down to his very cold toes.

Only he definitely wasn't cold anymore.

The woman had one hell of a nice back.

Water glistened on silky flesh that was golden in the flickering light of the fire. Her shoulders were slender and fragile. Her narrow rib cage tapered to a waist so small he could almost span it with his hands....

He felt as if he'd been hit right between the eyes with a two-by-four. For a full thirty seconds he stood perfectly still, knocked senseless, knowing he should be doing anything but admiring that pretty back. But for the life of him he couldn't bring himself to tear his eyes away.

Vaguely he was aware of the wind at his back, the sting of cold on his cheeks, the dampness of snow in his hair. He knew he should shut the door to conserve heat from the fire, but some inner warning told him he didn't want to be shut up in the cabin with this lovely creature. He knew enough about women to realize this one was a truckload of trouble. He knew enough about himself to know he was standing right in the path of that truck, that it was barreling toward him at a death-defying speed, and he was about to be plowed over.

What a way to go.

"If it's not too much trouble, do you think you could close that door?" she snapped. "It's getting a little drafty in here." Glaring at him over her shoulder, clearly annoyed and discomfited, Abby fought her arms into the sleeves of her jumpsuit. "Sometime today, if you don't mind."

Even though her back was to him, Jake averted his eyes. But not before the image of her bare back had been branded onto his brain. Soft, glistening skin that curved in all the right places. Wet curls clinging to the graceful arch of her neck. The smell of woman and soap and her own unique scent filling the air like some exotic perfume.

Oh, boy.

Giving himself a hard mental shake, Jake turned away from her and slammed the door. Gripping the knob, he took a deep breath, tried to get a handle on the quick slice of heat low in his belly. He knew better than to let the heat get to him. Not over a female inmate, for God's sake. He was a professional and took his job very seriously. He was courting serious problems by letting the sight of her turn him into a stuttering schoolboy with a bad case of hormones.

Refusing to acknowledge the power of his reaction, he stomped ice from his boots, brushed the snow from his duster onto the floor and tried to find something to look at that didn't make his mouth go dry, his pulse pound.

"Lady, I suggest you get yourself decent pronto, because I'm not going back outside." He'd tried to make his voice firm, but a peculiar hoarseness undermined his efforts.

"You agreed to five minutes."

"I gave you ten."

"I suppose cops aren't known for their ability to count."

That should have ticked him off, but it didn't. He was too busy recovering from an overwhelming bout of lust to care if she'd just insulted him.

"At least we know how to stay out of jail," he grumbled. A pang of disappointment rippled through him when she yanked the jumpsuit over her shoulders.

"You look like the Abominable Snowman," she said after a moment.

"In case you hadn't noticed, it's snowing outside."

"Ha, ha. Very funny." Zipping the jumpsuit up to her chin, she turned to face him. "Are the horses all right?"

"One horse. One mule."

"Whatever."

"I tossed them some compressed alfalfa and moved them to a more protected area out of the wind. But it's damn cold out there."

"The storm's a bad one, isn't it?"

Jake nodded, glanced out the window. He'd seen white-out conditions before. But he'd never seen anything this bad. The snow was coming down at a furious pace, the wind sending it sideways and whipping it into drifts high enough to swallow a sixteen-hand horse. It had taken him a full ten minutes to move Brandywine and Rebel Yell just five feet. Visibility was down to zero, and he'd had to *feel* his way back to the door. He hadn't expected to walk in to find himself face-to-face with the most beautiful bare back he'd ever laid eyes on.

He wasn't going to think about her back. Damn it, he *wasn't*. But his mind refused to cooperate by conjuring up images of wet, fragrant skin....

A trickle of sweat dampened the back of his neck. It might be cold outside, but things were definitely heating up in the cabin.

Jake didn't like the idea of keeping close quarters with this woman. He sure as hell didn't like the idea of things getting too cozy between them. He was a professional, not some amateurish rookie. He understood boundaries. He respected them, abided by them. This woman had a way of muddling those boundaries. He knew he was skating awful close to the edge. He'd be wise to remember she was his prisoner. An escaped convict, for God's sake. A murderer who'd already tried to use her body to undermine his discipline....

Jake didn't want to think about her body. Not now. Not ever.

Thanks to another blonde with big baby blues and a tale that had made his heart bleed, he'd become immune to lying beauties.

Elaine had shown him what could happen to a man who listened to his heart, to a man who let himself get blinded by lust. Jake hated thinking of himself as vulnerable. He was an officer of the law. A man who made decisions based on logic and experience. A man who came to those decisions through slow and cautious deliberation.

Three years ago Jake had been neither cautious nor deliberate when he'd invited a woman he barely knew into his home. He'd acted like some love-sick teenager crazed with hormones and short on common sense. As a cop, that he'd been so gullible shamed him. As a man, the experience had scarred him for life. Right now, those scars were aching with remembrance and warning him not to make the same mistake twice.

Shaking thoughts of the past from his mind, angry that he would think of Elaine now, he slapped the rest of the snow from his duster and started toward the fire to warm himself. His hands were half frozen. His face was numb. He was almost to the hearth when his left boot came down on something mushy and slick. Before he could look down, both feet slipped out from under him as though someone had pulled out the rug.

What the—

He landed on his back hard enough to drive every last bit of oxygen from his lungs.

"Oh my gosh! Jake! Are you all right?"

Vaguely, he was aware of Abby kneeling next to him. He would have cursed if he'd had the breath. But he didn't. He barely had enough wind to groan, but he managed. Barely.

"Are you hurt?" she asked.

He opened his eyes, found himself staring into a bottom-less violet gaze that would have taken his breath if he'd had any to spare. "Get...away," he growled.

"Are you okay?" she asked.

"What the *hell* did you put on that floor?"

"N-nothing."

"Or maybe you're trying to kill me."

"That's ridiculous."

Struggling to sit up, he glanced over at the floor where he'd slipped. A skimpy bar of soap glistened against the rough-hewn planks a few feet away. Jake looked from the soap back to Abby, felt his temper wind up. "Oh, that's real good, Blondie. No wonder the cops love you."

"Now wait just a moment, I didn't—"

"You just happened to leave the bar of soap on the floor, hoping you might get lucky."

"It slipped out of my hand. I—I was in a hurry to finish my bath and planned to pick it up when—"

"Or maybe you set the soap by the door and then took your shirt off hoping to distract me, so I'd break my neck."

"If I wanted to distract you, you'd know it."

Jake didn't want to go there, didn't want to think about just how hard it would be to resist this woman should she decide to test his willpower, so he let the comment pass.

She looked over at the soap and bit her lip. "I know it might seem like I did that on purpose, but I didn't."

"Well, maybe you just got lucky."

"Maybe you weren't watching where you were walking."

Gritting his teeth, Jake struggled to his feet. Damn, he was getting too old for this crap. "You're a menace, lady, you know that?"

"So, I've been told." She sighed. "Look, I didn't mean for you to fall. And I wouldn't...I didn't..."

He cut her a hard look, decided it was best if he didn't

know how she was going to end the sentence. "Never mind."

"Are you…okay?"

"Fine." His butt hurt, but he wasn't going to tell *her* that.

Tossing his duster onto the table, he stalked to the hearth and stuck his hands over the fire to warm them. Behind him, he heard a noise that sounded suspiciously like a snicker. Turning, he glared at her over his shoulder. "What's so damn funny?"

She tried to sober, but she wasn't doing a very good job of it. "Nothing."

"Yeah, that's why you're biting your cheeks to keep from laughing."

She pursed her lips, but Jake could tell she was losing the battle with her sense of humor. Damn it, she thought this was *funny*. "Go ahead. Laugh," he said peevishly.

The laugh that broke from her throat was a musical sound in the silence of the cabin, rising over the howl of the wind like the cry of a songbird lost in a storm. Jake should have been annoyed that she was laughing at him, but he wasn't. He was too enthralled by the sound of her voice to be annoyed.

"I'm sorry…but…but…" Laughter overtook her before she could finish the sentence.

"But what?"

She put her hand over her mouth, but she couldn't hold back the laughter. Her shoulders shook with it. Tears formed in her eyes. "You looked so…*funny*."

The situation *wasn't* funny. This woman, who couldn't weigh much more than a hundred pounds, had wrecked his radio, given him the mother of all shiners, then knocked him flat on his back. Him. Jake Madigan. Ex-Marine Corps officer. Chaffee County sheriff's deputy. Lawman of the Year two years running.

It should have rankled, but it didn't.

It was too damn funny to rankle.

A reluctant smile tugged at his mouth. He looked over at her. She was doubled over with laughter, and he felt a reluctant chuckle emerge. He told himself it was the stress of the situation—a combination of keeping close quarters with a way-too-attractive convict and being without radio communication during a dangerous storm—that had him wanting to laugh. But the image he must have made when he'd hit the deck was too much. A full-fledged belly laugh broke free.

"I don't see what's so funny about any of this," she said.

"Me neither," he said between chortles. "It's not a bit funny."

She pressed her hand to her stomach. "You could have been seriously hurt."

"I was."

"You should have seen your face."

"You should have seen *yours*."

She doubled over again, her hair tumbling wildly down.

Jake watched her, and felt something shift in his chest. He'd known plenty of women in his time, but he couldn't remember a single woman ever making him laugh like this. Laughter was the one thing he'd never shared with a woman. It felt good, he realized. Laughing with her felt…real. Made him feel human. Connected.

Their laughter echoed in the cabin. He watched her covertly. The fire shot blond sparks through her hair. Tons of hair that was wild and flowed like corkscrews around her shoulders. It was a crazy thought, but suddenly Jake wanted to reach out and touch her hair, just to see if it was as soft as it looked. He wanted to run his fingers through those wild curls, bring them to his face to see if they smelled like her.

His gaze swept over her. The state-issue jumpsuit was buck ugly. The material was dirt-smudged and unflattering.

But Jake instinctively knew the body beneath would be breathtaking. Even through the thick canvas material he discerned curves and softness and a woman's secret places. Secret places he wanted her to share with him.

The image of her bare back flashed in his mind's eye. He'd seen wet flesh. Feminine lines and soft curves. Fragrant skin lit by firelight and dimpled with gooseflesh. Jake's body tightened with unexpected force. Heat surged low in his groin. The power of his response stunned him, left him incredulous and more than a little disturbed.

What the hell was he thinking? He was a cop, for God's sake. This woman was his prisoner.

The realization of what he'd allowed to happen hit him like a slap. The laugh in his throat turned cold and sour. The weight of his responsibility, not only to the law, but to himself—to his own personal code of honor—sobered him as effectively as a glass of ice water thrown in his face.

He stopped laughing.

As if realizing what had happened, Abby straightened, used the back of her hand to shove a curly lock of hair off her forehead. Her gaze met his, her smile withering. Jake felt the pull of her gaze, and took a cautious step back.

The moment ended as abruptly as it had started. Breathing a sigh of relief, he cleared his throat. "We've got a long night ahead of us. We'd best get some rest."

Chapter 5

Abby snuggled into the sleeping bag and listened to the wind claw at the cabin. The floor was hard and cold beneath her and shuddered with each gust. Despite the fire raging in the stone hearth just a few feet away, she was cold to her bones.

She lay on her side, staring into the flames, thinking about fate and wishing things could have turned out differently. She couldn't count the number of times she'd felt this way, locked away in her cell, lying on her cot, alone and forgotten. The entire time she'd been in prison anger and frustration and a terrible sense of helplessness had tormented her like a painful disease. She'd been demoralized and humiliated by a system that was far from perfect—and downright cruel to those sorry few who were still human enough to feel the fangs of injustice.

A year and a half ago, she never would have dreamed her life would take such a terrible turn. Or that Fate could be so vicious. Sometimes she still couldn't believe it. Couldn't believe she was a convicted killer on the run from the law. If the situation hadn't been so dire, she might have laughed at the absurdity.

The man determined to return her to the hands of justice sat on the floor a few feet away, brooding into the fire, a steaming cup in his hands. Abby wondered what he was thinking about. Wondered if it had anything to do with that crazy moment when they'd both been laughing like a couple of kids. She told herself it was exhaustion and fear that had had her emotions ebbing and flowing like a crazy tide. But in that instant when the laughter had poured out and she had heard Jake's answering laugh in her ears, she'd felt human again. She'd felt alive, as if she hadn't a care in the world. And she hadn't felt so terribly alone.

As she stared into the fire the weight of the world pressed down on her with the force of a car crusher.

"You want some coffee?"

She started at the sound of Jake's voice and risked a look at him. "I'm fine. Thanks."

Rising, he walked over to his saddlebag. "You're shivering. Something hot will help."

She hadn't even realized she was shivering. Physical discomfort in the face of the monumental disaster her life had become just didn't seem very important in the scope of things. Her only hope of clearing her name was quickly vanishing with every hour that passed.

Jake removed a cup from the saddlebag and tapped a small amount of instant coffee into it. At the fire, he filled the cup with steaming water, then handed it to her. "It's instant, but it'll keep you warm."

"Thanks." The warm cup felt heavenly against her hands.

He didn't walk away, but stood there looking down at her. "We need to get some sleep. If the storm lets up, we've got some hard riding to do tomorrow."

Her heart sank when she saw him reach for the cuffs attached to his belt. "Oh, I get it. *You* need to sleep. Can't do it when you have to worry about me slipping out the door and riding into the sunset, huh, partner?"

"Give me your wrist."

She rolled her eyes. "You don't think I'm stupid enough to run out into this storm, do you?"

"I don't think you want me to answer that."

"Give me a break, Cowboy, will you? I've had a tough day, and I'm not up to doing anything crazy, all right?" She tried to assume an annoyed countenance, but it wasn't working. In reality she *had* been thinking about trying to slink away during the night. If he cuffed her, she could forget it. And she'd rather face the elements anyday than a knife in the shower room back at Buena Vista.

"I'm not going to run away," she said, stalling.

His jaw flexed. "Your wrist. Now."

Shaking her head in disgust, Abby set the coffee on the floor next to her and proffered her right wrist. His hands were warm and encompassed hers completely when he took it. Without speaking, he closed the cuff around her wrist, then snapped the other end around the lowest rung of a straight-backed chair.

"I'm sorry if that's going to be uncomfortable for you, but it's for both our safety," he said.

"I appreciate you thinking of my safety," she said sarcastically. "How selfless of you."

He went back to his sleeping bag and sat.

Abby sat up and tested the cuff. It was secure, damn it. Her arm was going to fall asleep. Her hand was going to be very cold by morning. It was going to be a very long and uncomfortable night.

"You going to tell me how you ended up in prison?"

She slanted him a look, trying to gauge his sincerity. "You mean, how did a nice girl like me end up in Buena

Vista serving a life sentence for second degree murder?"
Abby had stopped trying to keep the bitterness out of her
voice a long time ago. She'd never given up hope that the
truth would prevail, that she would clear her name. But the
more months that passed, the more impossible the task
seemed. "It's a long story, Cowboy. You wouldn't be interested."

"I wouldn't be asking if I wasn't interested."

It had been a while since Abby had talked to anyone
about what had happened. Her lawyer had abandoned her
shortly after the trial. She hadn't had the money for another
one and most of the public defenders assigned to her put
little energy into the appeal phase. They'd asked her all the
topical questions, made all the expected legal maneuverings.
But Abby had known by the looks in their eyes that they
hadn't cared that her life was on the line, or that she was
slowly dying with each and every day she had to spend
locked up like an animal. The sense of hopelessness had
been almost too much to bear some days. She didn't want
to reawaken those feelings now by talking to Jake. Not when
they were already pressing in on her with the same force as
the storm outside.

"Do you mind if I ask why you want to know?" she
asked.

"I've seen a lot of murderers in my time." He shrugged.
"You don't fit the profile."

The comment shouldn't have meant anything to her. But
it brought hot, stinging tears to her eyes nonetheless. Abby
couldn't remember the last time someone had said something nice to her. Or truly meant it.

"Don't say things unless you mean them," she whispered.

"I don't ever say anything I don't mean."

She gazed into the fire, taking a moment to compose herself, and the memories swept over her. Before her arrest,

she'd been young and carefree and full of hope for a future that was bright and promising. She wondered if she would ever feel that way again.

"I was a nurse at Mercy General in Denver," she began. "I worked in the emergency room. Third shift."

"What happened?"

"A year and a half ago, a patient...died during my shift. A patient I was responsible for."

He contemplated her with those smoke-gray eyes, his face grim. "How did he die?"

"It never made sense to me. I mean, he was brought in for stitches. He'd fallen and received a nasty cut." She paused, remembering, and took a deep, fortifying breath. "The next thing I knew he was in a coma. I didn't find out until later that he'd been injected with a fatal dose of Valium."

"You gave him the—"

"No." She looked down at her hands. "I didn't. I gave him a tetanus injection. That's standard procedure with a serious cut or puncture wound."

"But the police believe you did it?"

She nodded.

"Could you have made a mistake?"

"There's no way I could have gotten the two confused. The Valium and tetanus are stored in different areas of the supply pharmacy."

"If that's the case, why were you arrested and convicted?"

She paused, knowing how it sounded, frustrated that she didn't have any solid proof to back her up. "Someone falsified the chart to make it look like I gave him that injection."

"Why would they do that?"

The logical side of her brain knew she was wasting her breath. This cynical lawman wasn't going to believe her.

Her theory was wild at best—downright crazy if she wanted to be truthful about it. The information she'd pieced together from the prison library was just as far-fetched. No one would ever believe her. Some days, she didn't believe it herself.

"Someone framed me," she said after a moment.

"Why?"

"Why was I framed?" She choked out a humorless laugh. "Because the real murderer needed a fall guy, that's why."

For the first time, he looked puzzled. Abby fought down a rise of desperation. She told herself it didn't matter if he believed her. This man's opinion didn't count in the scope of things. It didn't matter what he thought of her. And there was still time for her to get away if the opportunity arose....

"I didn't think you would believe me," she said.

"I'm looking for logic. You know, motive, means and opportunity." He sipped some of his coffee. "Who would have something to gain by killing a patient?" he asked.

When she didn't answer right away, he gave her a hard look. "You don't have anything to lose by talking to me."

The knowledge that he was right made her shiver. Scooting closer to the fire, she felt the memories drifting through her like clouds in the sky, gossamer and surreal and so intangible she wanted to cry out with the need to change what had happened. Lord, she'd been so naive.

"Tell me about the patient that died," he said.

"A homeless man was brought in at about two in the morning one night," she began. "He'd been drinking, fell down in the rail yard and cut himself on some sheet metal. He was in good physical condition and just needed a few stitches. Nothing major. It was a weeknight, so things were relatively quiet. His name was Jim."

Her voice sounded like a stranger's voice, recalling scenes from the latest medical thriller. She was keenly aware of Jake watching her, her heart pitching in her chest like a small boat in a turbulent sea. She looked down, saw that her hands were clenched into fists. "Jim was a little down on his luck, but he was a nice man. He was funny and…" The old guilt twisted in her stomach. "I put him on a gurney, and wheeled him into a treatment room. He kept cutting jokes while I took his vitals and put eight sutures in his right hand. He seemed fine when I left him."

She closed her eyes, the memory pounding her. "About twenty minutes later I heard one of the other nurses call Code Ninety-nine—"

"Code Ninety-nine?"

"That's the code we use when a patient's heart stops."

Jake nodded, his expression grim. "Jim?"

"By the time I finished with my other patient, he'd already been intubated and put on life support. But the doctor believed he'd suffered serious brain damage. He died a few hours later."

To this day, no matter how hard she tried, Abby couldn't get the sight of that man's face out of her mind. The sound of his voice, his jokes, his laughter. She didn't think she ever would, knew they would haunt her for the rest of her life.

"How did that turn into murder, Abby?"

"When Jim signed in to the emergency room, he wrote on the form that he was indigent and temporarily homeless and without family. Well, that wasn't true. He had a family. They were estranged, but they evidently cared about him because a few hours after his death, two of his grown children showed up at the hospital, asking questions, demanding answers. It was a terrible, terrible scene.…" Her voice broke, but she trudged on. "At first, his death was ruled the result of natural causes. But the man's family had the body shipped home to Dallas and autopsied. The autopsy revealed he'd been injected with a lethal dose of Valium."

Jake's brows pulled together. "Why would someone inject him with Valium?"

Abby looked over at Jake. He looked interested. She wondered if he would believe her if she told him the truth. If she told him that it was, indeed, her own mistake that had cost her so dearly. Only it didn't have anything to do with a dose of medication, and everything to do with trusting the wrong person.

Hope coiled in her chest. She closed her eyes against it, felt a wrench of despair nudge it aside. Right. Like Mr. By-the-Book was going to believe *her*. Crazy Abby. She wondered how he would react when he found out she'd lied to the police. When he found out about all the other things she couldn't bring herself to tell him.

There was no way he was going to believe her. He was too strait-laced. Hell, after she'd told the last public defender the truth, he'd recommended a psychological evaluation and a mental health facility instead of prison.

The memory sent a chill through her.

"I don't know," she whispered. "All I know is that I didn't kill him."

"Who did?"

"Someone who was there that night. Someone who wanted me to take the fall. Someone who knew I would be easy to frame."

"Why would they think you would be an easy frame?"

She swallowed a bubble of panic, looked over where her cuffed hand trembled against the chair back and concentrated on stilling it.

"Why would someone think you were an easy frame?" he repeated.

With some difficulty, she met his gaze. "Because of my past."

"What past?"

When she didn't answer, he scrubbed a hand over his

face, glanced over at the fire. "Are you talking about your emotional problems?"

The words speared her like a saber. Because she was a convicted felon, her health records were no longer confidential, but fair game to just about any official who needed access. "So, you know about that."

"The corrections officials put out a profile on you to local law enforcement. That was part of it."

Shame and pain mingled and became a single, profound ache that spread into the deepest reaches of her heart. Abby knew most people equated emotional problems with insanity. She'd heard it a hundred times over the years. They'd called her Crazy Abby. First in high school. The name had surfaced again after her arrest. *Crazy Abby.* The high school senior who wigged out after her mama pulled the plug on her old man. The troubled teenager who didn't speak for six months. The young woman who spent her seventeenth birthday locked in a mental institution.

Abby closed her eyes tightly, blocking out the pain.

"What past?" he pressed.

She wanted to answer, longed to get the truth out in the open. The anguish and betrayals lay like sour food in the pit of her stomach. But with the truth lay the revelations. Revelations she wasn't ready to share.

Especially with such an honorable man as Jake Madigan.

Jake wasn't sure what was going on with this woman. For a man who prided himself on his ability to read people, he was having one hell of a time figuring her out. One thing he did know for sure was that it was hard to sit there and watch her hurt.

He shouldn't have let it bother him. He'd seen plenty of suffering in his time. Hell, he'd been on the receiving end a few too many times himself to let it get to him now. But the pain shimmering in her eyes was raw and soul-deep and touched him in places he'd just as soon keep off limits.

He did *not* want to deal with this. Abby Nichols was turning out to be bad luck piled on top of bad luck. He knew better than to let himself get sucked into the maelstrom that was her life. Damn it, he *knew* better.

But as the firelight reflected in her eyes, he felt himself drawn to her in the most fundamental ways. Ways that went against everything he'd ever believed possible about himself. Jake trusted his instincts. As a lawman, he relied heavily on those instincts to guide him through a complex world full of good and bad and a vast gray area in between. And while those very same instincts were telling him to beware, something deeper and not quite so black and white was telling him she wasn't a cold-blooded killer.

Jeez, this was a mess.

"All I can tell you is that I didn't kill that patient," she said after a moment.

"The police thought differently. So did a jury."

"That's because they were presented with false evidence."

"What false evidence?"

"A syringe with my fingerprints on it."

"Why didn't your lawyer get to the bottom of it?"

"Because she was fresh out of law school and didn't have the experience for a case like mine."

Jake thought about the syringe and frowned. "That syringe with your fingerprints on it is physical evidence. Physical evidence doesn't lie, Abby."

"When's the last time you gave an injection without using latex treatment gloves?"

He knew where she was going with this. Virtually all medical professionals used latex treatment gloves these days. For a variety of reasons that protected not only the medical professional but the patient, hospital regulations notwithstanding. Her argument was sound. Unless, of course, she'd been too rushed to deal with gloves because she hadn't wanted to get caught....

The scenario gave him a queasy feeling in the pit of his stomach.

But Jake wasn't going to play the what-if game with a convict. It didn't matter that her story was plausible. That she was hurting. That she didn't seem like a murderer. Jake might trust his instincts when it came to his job, but he didn't when it came to women. Especially *this* woman.

Jake's job was to take Abby Nichols back. He was an officer of the law, for God's sake. A man who saw clearly the dividing line between right and wrong, as well as that dangerous area in between. He didn't cross lines. Just because she didn't *look* like a murderer didn't mean she wasn't one. He knew all too well that looks could be deceiving. He refused to be taken in by another pretty woman with an unlikely story and the kind of body that could make a man believe in crazy possibilities.

"I'm going to turn in," he said after a moment.

"Had enough truth for one night?"

"Let's just say I've heard enough." Rising, he walked over to the fire and set another log atop the embers. He didn't want to identify the uncomfortable tug in his chest as conscience. Damn it, this woman's guilt or innocence was *not* his concern. It didn't matter than his instincts were telling him to listen to her. His instincts had been wrong before when it came to women, and he'd paid a terrible price.

"You should put some ice on that black eye."

He'd forgotten about the shiner. Prodding it with his index finger, he winced. Oh, yeah, he had a shiner, all right— a big one judging from the level of tenderness. In another day or two the color was going to bloom like a spring flower. Man, when the rest of the team saw it, they weren't ever going to let him live it down.

He looked over at her, felt a ripple of compassion go through him at the sight of the cuffs. The chair back was too high. When she lay down it would cut off the circulation to her hand. As cold as it was in the cabin, he didn't want that to happen. He fingered the key compartment on his belt. His conscience nagged. The only other option was to cuff the other end to his own wrist, but he didn't want to spend the night that close to her.

Hell.

"Snow would probably work," she said. "Put some in a towel and use it as an ice compress. It might stop some of the bruising."

"It'll be fine."

"Up to you."

He hadn't intended to approach her, but his legs seemed to move of their own volition. He knew better than to trust her. He didn't, in fact. But that didn't mean he could stand to see her cuffed to that damn chair all freaking night.

"I can't take off the cuffs," he said.

She looked up at him, wariness and uncertainty etched on her features. "I won't run."

"Yeah, and my name is Frosty the Snowman." Pulling the key from the cuff pouch on his belt, he unlocked the cuff from the chair and snapped it over his own wrist.

Her eyes widened. "You're not going to—"

"I just did."

"But, you can't—"

"Shut up and get some sleep." He tested the cuffs, found them securely fastened to both his wrist and hers. Irritated as much with himself as he was with her, he slid his bedroll closer to hers and lay down, all too aware of her every movement as she settled into her sleeping bag next to him.

Tense minutes ticked by. Exhaustion tugged at his body, but sleep eluded him. He listened to the wind, the ping of snow against the windows on the north side of the cabin. He tried not to think about the woman lying beside him, about all the things she'd told him, but his efforts were in vain. He wanted to look at her, wanted to see what her face looked like in the firelight as she slept, but Jake was far too smart—and far too cautious—to give in to the urge.

Sighing, feeling restless and unsettled, he laced his free hand behind his head and stared at the ceiling, resigned to a very long and very cold night.

Abby couldn't believe he'd cuffed his wrist to hers. Of all the security measures he could have taken, that was the absolute worst. How on earth was she going to get to the key and unlock the cuffs with her wrist cuffed to his?

Minutes stretched into hours, second by excruciating second. Abby tried to sleep, but she was too cold and much too wired. The storm raged outside the windows, but she paid no heed to the shrill of the wind. Every sense she possessed was honed on the man lying next to her. She knew she was crazy for entertaining thoughts of escape. The storm was worse than dangerous. Of course, the term was relative when she knew this duty-bound lawman lying beside her was going to do everything in his power to make sure she spent the rest of her life in prison.

Abby figured this was another one of those times that called for desperate measures.

She wasn't sure how much time passed. For hours Jake tossed and turned and grumbled. For a while she feared he wouldn't sleep at all. But finally exhaustion won, and he stilled. His breathing became slow and regular. Only after he began to snore quietly did Abby risk moving. Easing up onto one elbow, she looked over at him. His eyes were closed, yet even in sleep he looked dangerous. Like a predator that lured its prey closer by feigning sleep, then devouring it when it ventured too close.

The thought made her shiver.

Keenly aware that she was about to cross the point of no return, she glanced down at his belt and spotted the pouch where he stored the cuffs. Cautiously, she leaned over him and reached for the pouch. She knew the odds of her pulling this off were slim to none. But she also knew this was her only chance, and she didn't intend to waste it.

Her heart hammered wildly when her fingers came in contact with the pouch cover. Gritting her teeth against the tension twisting her muscles into knots, she tugged on the flap. The snap popped, sounding like a gunshot in the silence. Abby held her breath, certain the noise had wakened Jake. Painful seconds ticked by as she waited for his eyes to open. Terrified to move, her face inches from his, her heart pounding out a rapid tattoo, she squeezed her eyes closed and said a silent prayer.

She was so close to him, she could feel the warm brush of his breath on her cheek. Even after a full day of hard riding, she could smell him, that woodsy sent that reminded her of an alpine meadow at dawn. If she moved a fraction of an inch, she would touch him and risk wakening him. Her nerves skittered wildly at the thought. Grappling for control, she took a deep, silent breath and opened her eyes, determined to go through with this.

The fire cast shadows on the planes of his face. His dark brows knitted as if he were troubled even in sleep. Lordy, she'd never seen a man with lashes that long before. An odd sensation fluttered low in her belly. Mercy, he *was* something to look at. Too bad he had that badge clipped to his belt, and the determination to ruin her life....

Appalled that she could feel something as insane as attraction at a time like this, she refocused her attention on her search for the key. Easing two fingers into the pouch, Abby felt around. Relief swamped her when her fingers came in contact with the speck of cold steel. For a full minute she didn't move, didn't even breathe, until the hot rush of emotion subsided. Nothing had been easy for her in the past year, and she was having a hard time believing something as risky as this would go as planned.

Maybe Lady Luck wasn't so bad after all.

Careful not to touch Jake or jar his other wrist, Abby fished out the key. Stealthily, she eased away from him and onto her side. Trapping the cuff to the floor with her free hand, she used two fingers to insert the key into the lock and twisted. The cuff popped open.

Slipping it off her wrist, she looked around for something solid enough to hold an enraged man—at least for a little while—and decided on the chair. It wouldn't stop him, but it would definitely slow him down. Hopefully, long enough for her to get away.

Jake wasn't sure what woke him. The cold, maybe. It was vicious and deep and had been seeping into his bones for the past hour or so as he'd drifted in and out of sleep. Or maybe it was the silence. The wind still rattled the walls, but the silence had a different quality this morning. The only sound came from the hiss of embers in the fire. It was almost as if he were alone....

Raising his head abruptly, he glanced over to where his charge should have been, felt the sharp stab of adrenaline in his gut.

''What the—''

He jumped to his feet. The chair she'd handcuffed him to clattered against the plank floor. He stared at the empty sleeping bag.

Damn crazy woman had cuffed him to the chair!

Stiff from sleeping on the floor, he dragged the chair over to the door and yanked it open. The horse was gone. Rebel Yell looked at him with gentle brown eyes.

Well, at least she'd left him the mule.

Cursing her for being so damn determined, cursing himself for being so damn stupid, he stalked to the center of the room, the chair clattering along beside him. He couldn't believe he'd done something so incredibly dumb!

You should have left her cuffed to the chair.

But the part of Jake that was a man knew why he hadn't. Last night when she'd looked at him with those stunning violet eyes, he'd felt it all the way down to his toes. Eyes like that could make a man do foolish things. Foolish things like believe an incredible story fabricated by a disturbed young woman obviously willing to go to great lengths to regain her freedom.

He'd bought it hook, line and sinker.

Maybe he was a bigger fool than he'd thought.

A glance out the window told him the worst of the storm had passed but the snow was still coming down. If the wind let up, the chopper would be out and looking.

The thought of what he'd let happen sent a sharp jab of shame through him. If he didn't find her, he was going to have some major explaining to do. Not only to the corrections officials, but to his own department as well as the RMSAR team.

Hell, this was a mess.

Damn woman.

Reaching into the compartment of his belt, he felt around for the key. Of course, she'd taken it with her. What self-respecting convict wouldn't?

Grasping the back of the chair, Jake raised it over his head and brought it down hard on the floor. Wood splintered. The cuff sprang free. Scooping his duster off the sleeping bag, he jerked it over his shoulders and headed for the door at a dead run.

With a little luck, he might be able to find her before she got into any more trouble.

Chapter 6

"Okay, horse, these are the ground rules." Abby held on to the horn while the animal lunged through deep powder. "I tell you where to go. You obey, unless there's a bottomless crevasse I didn't see, and in that case, feel free to disobey. Got it?"

The horse took another bone-jarring lunge. Abby held on for dear life, praying she'd put the saddle on right. She'd been in such a hurry, she couldn't be sure. So far, so good.

"Easy, big girl. Take it easy. Just...don't get stuck."

She'd known this wasn't going to be easy. What she hadn't expected was for the snow to be the problem. It was hip-deep where the wind had whipped it into drifts. Travel would be difficult at best, impossible if she wanted to be truthful about it.

Abby didn't have time for impossible. This was her last chance at freedom, and she didn't intend to blow it.

If all went as planned, she'd reach the highway by dusk. Hopefully, she could hitch a ride with a trucker who didn't ask too many questions and be in New Mexico by dawn.

It was a desperate plan. But no matter how badly the odds were stacked against her, Abby knew there *was* a remote possibility she could pull it off. If she could just get out of the immediate area, she had a chance. If she could get to Grams's house, she might actually succeed.

The sound of a gunshot jolted her so badly she nearly lost her balance. Brandywine stopped her forward motion, turned her head and pricked her ears forward. Turning in the saddle, Abby looked over her shoulder, felt her heart plummet into her ankles.

Jake.

He was a quarter mile away. With the light snow falling, she couldn't see his face, but his form was unmistakable. Black Stetson. Long duster. He was on the mule and heading in her direction at a very fast pace. Oh, she bet he was mad as a hornet.

A rise of fear made her heart bang hard against her ribs. The realization that he was coming after her drove a spike of panic straight through her.

Another shot rang out. Abby ducked instinctively. A silly reaction considering she was out in the open without cover. But she knew Jake wouldn't shoot her. She wasn't sure *how* she knew that, but she did. He'd merely fired his rifle to let her know he was there. That he was coming after her.

Abby had absolutely no intention of getting caught.

Nudging the horse with her heels, she clucked and leaned forward in the saddle, the way she always did with Mr. Smith's Shetland ponies. "Come on, girl. Let's go."

The horse lunged over another snowdrift. Abby clutched the horn, urging the animal forward with her heels. Three more lunges and the snow became a bit more shallow. The horse broke into a trot. She rode another fifty yards, then stopped at the edge of a sparse forest of lodge-pole pine and aspen. Turning in the saddle, she searched the horizon, but man and mule were nowhere in sight.

Where on earth had he gone?

Feeling the hairs at her nape stand on end, she urged the horse into a faster trot and started into the trees. Every cell in her body was being jostled by whatever gait this horse was trained to take, but she was making good time. She supposed she could put up with the jarring as long as it was putting some distance between her and Jake. Her brains might be scrambled by the time she got to the interstate, but at least she'd be free.

Another twenty yards and the trees opened to a gently sloped hill with a deep gully washer that stretched like a scar to a frozen pond at the base. Steering the horse clear of the gully where the snow had drifted and was probably chest-deep, Abby guided the animal north, toward Interstate 70—and hopefully a trucker in need of some company.

She'd just passed a tall jut of ice-crusted granite when a noise behind her made her turn in the saddle. Her pulse jumped at the sight of man and mule bearing down on her. For a split second Abby stared, incredulous that he'd been able to cover so much ground so quickly and sneak up on her. Yelping once, she slapped her hand down on the horse's rump. "Go!"

The animal lunged forward, but it was too late. The mule was already alongside her. Jake yelled something but she didn't understand the words. Out of the corner of her eye Abby saw the gunmetal gray of his eyes, the firm set of his mouth. His angry expression told her he wasn't going to make this easy for her.

Gloved hands reached for her mount's reins. "Hold it right there!"

"No!" she shouted back.

But he was too fast. Her horse spun, kicking up snow. Jake's knee bumped hard against hers. She saw his gloved hands reaching for her and she screamed. Twisting in the saddle, she shoved at him with both hands. She may as well been trying to move a mountain. Strong arms went around her waist, toppling her balance. She screamed again, felt her foot slip from the stirrup. She reached out to grab hold of the horse's mane, but her fingers found only air.

An instant later the ground rushed up and knocked the breath from her. Next to her, she heard Jake grunt. The horse shied away, then stood watching them with her ears pricked forward. Reminding herself that this was her last chance at freedom, Abby tried to scramble away. Before she could move, a strong hand shot out and gripped her shoulder. Abruptly, she was flipped onto her back. Thinking fast, she tossed snow in his face. He spat, but it didn't faze him. She saw a flash of angry gray eyes, and the next thing she knew Jake was on top of her.

"What the *hell* do you think you're doing?" he snapped.

Defeat tasted bitter at the back of her throat. She fought him for all she was worth, squirming and kicking out with her feet. Animal sounds tore from her throat. Snow flew like powder, coating her face, getting into her eyes and mouth, creeping down the back of the duster she'd worn.

"I'm not going back!" she shouted. "Damn it, let me go!"

"Calm down," he snapped.

"Get off of me!"

"Stop fighting me and I will."

"I can't breathe!"

"Yes, you can. Just…calm down."

"I'm not going back. I don't care what you do to me. I'm not going. I'd rather die first." Her breath rushed raggedly from her lungs.

"Keep this up and that can be arranged."

Turning her head, she blew out a mouthful of snow. "You could've shot me, but you didn't, did you, tough guy?"

"You keep pulling stupid stunts like this and you won't

need any help from me. You'll get yourself killed all by yourself.''

"Get off me!"

"Not until you calm down."

She tried to slap him, but he easily deflected the blow. "Don't make me cuff you," he snapped.

Blinking the snow from her eyes, Abby glared up at him, breathing hard, defeated and angry. "Okay. I'm calm, damn it."

He was breathing hard, too, his nostrils flaring slightly. He'd lost his hat at some point and there was snow in his hair. His jaw was set and firm. Anger shone bright and hot in his eyes, but Abby also saw something else. Something she didn't want to deal with. Something she certainly didn't want to name.

His face was only a few inches from hers. His hands had captured hers and held them firmly above her head. His body was flush against hers. Her legs were apart, and his body was resting solidly between her knees.

Oh, my.

Awareness of their precarious position zinged through her like a bullet. The cold and the anger and the hurt melted away beneath the heat. In the span of an instant the dynamics of the situation flip-flopped. Suddenly, Abby was no longer a convict, but a woman who hadn't been held for a very, very long time. Jake was no longer an iron-hearted lawman determined to bring his fugitive to justice, but a man with hungry eyes and a mouth that could tempt even the most cautious woman.

Abby definitely fell into the cautious category. In the last year and a half, she'd been hurt and betrayed and forgotten. But she was still a woman. A woman who'd been alone for so long she couldn't even remember the last time she'd been held. Or listened to. Or even looked at like a human being.

Jake Madigan looked at her like she mattered.

She didn't plan on kissing him. It was an impulsive, stupid thing to do. But one moment she was staring at that chiseled mouth, the next she'd leaned toward him and pressed her lips against his. He jolted as if he'd been hit with a thousand volts of electricity. His entire body went rigid. She felt his grip on her wrists loosen. Then, growling low in his throat, he moved against her, pushing her more deeply into the snow. His mouth softened against hers. He kissed her back, tentatively at first, and then with an intensity that stole her breath.

Abby had been kissed by men before; she wasn't a stranger to intimacy. But the things Jake Madigan did to her mouth dazed her. She'd thought by distracting him that she would be able to take control of the situation. Somewhere in the back of her mind she vaguely remembered that she had a plan. But one taste of the silky, dark depths of his mouth and her plan was forgotten.

She didn't remember opening her mouth to him. But the next thing she knew her tongue was warring with his. A war she was destined to lose because the man made her head spin. Her body burned where he touched her. She couldn't think, couldn't remember, why she should run away from him.

He kissed her as she'd never been kissed in her life, until she was mindless except for the need streaming through her. Everything around her faded to gray. The snow beneath her turned liquid and warm. He pressed against her, his mouth working magic on hers. Vaguely, she was aware of him releasing her hands, and spearing his fingers into her hair.

Arousal coursed through her veins like liquid fire, pooling in the pit of her belly and streaking to the place where she felt the hard pulse of him against her. He growled something dark and forbidden in her ear, but Abby was beyond understanding words. She knew what he wanted; she knew what she wanted.

She knew better than to offer an open invitation to disaster. This man was going to ruin her life. He was going to use her for his own pleasure, make promises he had no intention of keeping, then discard her the same way Jonathan Reed had.

Abby knew better than to let herself be swept away. But Jake's kisses were like an avalanche, shaking her and tumbling her until she was senseless.

Jake knew what it was like to want a woman. It was part of being a man, and he accepted it without complaint. It was a sweet ache that intensified over time and needed to be taken care of on occasion. That had always been fine by him. Jake kept it under control. No problem.

Only this time he didn't quite have a handle on the control thing. Here he was, lying in the snow, kissing a convict, knowing better, but unable to stop because she tasted so damn good. He'd never wanted a woman the way he wanted Abby. She was the only woman he'd ever known who could break his control with nothing more than a look. Wreak havoc on his common sense with little more than a touch. Jeopardize the strict code of honor by which he lived because he couldn't bear to see her hurt. He'd never given up those things for anyone. Certainly not for a felon.

But her mouth was wet and soft beneath his, and he couldn't get enough. She tasted sweet and mysterious and forbidden, and the need for more pounded through him like a drum. He could smell her hair, a tantalizing mix of woman and the out-of-doors. He ran his hands through the unruly locks, felt them tangle in his fingers. Cradling her head in his hands, he angled her mouth and kissed her deeply.

When she mewled and shifted her body closer to his, Jake felt his brain rattle, his common sense scatter like dandelion seeds in a high wind. He was painfully aroused, his body rock hard and crying out for release. He knew he should stop kissing her. Logic demanded he put a stop to this before things got out of hand.

Things had already gotten out of hand.

While his intellectual side knew fully this was a mistake, his body didn't give a damn one way or another. His mouth fused with hers. He wanted his hands on her flesh. Wanted to look into those violet eyes of hers and see them wild with desire. He skimmed his hands down her sides. Her body felt fragile and small beneath his hands. The gloves hindered him, he wanted them off. Wanted to feel her bare flesh, but he was afraid if he paused to remove them the moment would be over.

He didn't want this to end.

The blood rushed through his veins like a freight train barreling down a rickety track. He was breathing hard, his body trembling like that of a love-struck teenager. He barely heard the dull thud in the snow less than a foot from his head. At first he thought Abby had kicked off her shoes, but inexplicably his nerves jumped.

An instant later a rifle retort sounded. Breaking the kiss, he hovered over her, dazed, every nerve in his body screaming. "What the hell?"

Looking bewildered and thoroughly kissed, Abby tried to rise. "That was a—"

Jake shoved her back down. "Stay down."

"But that was a gunshot!"

"I know what it was. Stay down."

"Someone's shooting at us!"

"Well, that's a hell of a deduction." Scrambling to his feet, Jake looked frantically around, cursing himself for having let down his guard. "We're sitting ducks here."

Abby got to her knees. Her hair was damp from the snow and tangling around her face. Even with his heart pumping pure adrenaline, Jake couldn't help but notice how beautiful she looked, how badly he'd wanted to finish whatever it was they'd started.

Spotting the ravine a dozen yards away, he motioned toward it. "I want you to run to that ravine, get down on your belly and don't move until I get there."

"But where are you—"

"Just do it. Don't argue. I'm going to get the horse." He looked over his shoulder to where Brandywine pawed at the snow twenty yards away. "We're in big trouble without the horse." He gazed at Abby, felt his heart do a weird little dip in his chest. He knew she would probably make a run for it. But to keep her out of the line of fire, he found himself willing to take the risk.

"Can you do that for me?" he asked.

She nodded.

Another shot echoed.

"Stay low. Go!" Jake shoved her toward the ravine, then sprinted toward Brandywine, praying the sniper's shooting wasn't as good as his timing.

What the hell had he been thinking kissing her like that?

Another shot rang out just as Jake snagged the reins. Vaulting onto the horse's back, he nudged her into a racer's sprint toward the ravine. A bullet ricocheted off a rock face less than three feet away. Staying low, he unsheathed the rifle, turned in the saddle and squeezed off two shots in quick succession in the general direction of the sniper. Resheathing the gun, he took Brandywine down the side of the ravine. The terrain was too rough for a horse, but he figured it was a lot safer than getting shot at.

Who the hell was shooting at them, anyway?

He reached the bottom of the rocky ravine a moment later. He was shaking, anger and fear and the remnants of arousal hot in his blood. He sat there, reining in his emotions for several seconds before realizing Abby was nowhere in sight. A ribbon of fear slithered through him. He found his eyes scanning the area for blood. Relief crackled through him when he spotted the tracks. Out of the sniper's line of vision, but barely. He took Brandywine down the ravine, through snow that was chest-deep.

Damn crazy woman was going to get herself killed.

Pulling up on the reins, he tracked the path to the bottom of the hill. He spotted her just as she entered a sparse copse of aspen. She was running away from him again.

Clucking to Brandywine, Jake eased the animal over the rough terrain and into deep snow. The horse lunged, but he moved with her in perfect balance. Not wanting to be left alone, Rebel Yell picked his way down the rocky side of the ravine, lagging about thirty feet behind.

At the bottom of the hill, Jake urged Brandywine into an extended trot. Because of the deep snow, Abby wasn't making very good time. But she hadn't stopped, either, hadn't so much as looked back since they'd started this crazy chase.

What could the woman possibly be thinking? It wasn't as if she was going to get away. And who had been taking pot shots at them? In the back of his mind, he'd been hoping it was a stray shot from a hunter. But Jake knew better. And for the first time, he considered the possibility that there was a sliver of truth to what she'd told him.

He was less than fifty feet behind Abby when he realized what she was going to do. The realization made his blood run cold. "Abby! No! Stop!"

The pond was a hundred yards wide, the frozen surface covered with new snow. Abby stepped onto the ice without hesitation and began trudging across, slipping, her gait broken.

Jake brought his horse to a sliding stop at the edge of the ice. "Abby! The ice is thin! Abby! Damn it!"

She didn't look back.

Working the duster from his shoulders, Jake watched, his

chest so tight he could barely breathe. Surely she knew the ice wasn't thick enough in the center of the pond to hold her weight. When he'd started his ride yesterday, the temperature had been nearly forty degrees. He wondered what kind of desperation would push someone to do something so foolhardy.

A loud *crack!* sounded.

Feeling helpless and angry and scared, Jake stepped out onto the ice. "Stop! Abby, damn it, the ice isn't going to hold!"

Thirty yards away, she came to an abrupt halt and froze, her arms out. She didn't turn to face him, didn't speak. Jake could see her breaths puffing out into the cold air in front of her.

"Okay, Abby, I want you to stay calm," he said. "I want you to take a deep breath. Then I want you to get down on your belly and slide back over here. Can you do that for me?"

Slowly, she turned. "Are you lying to me, Jake?"

Her face was almost as white as the snow. "I wouldn't lie to you about something like that."

"Is the ice going to break?"

He didn't know for sure. But he'd heard the crack. Surely she had, too. "I want you to get down on your belly. Right now."

Holding her body perfectly still, Abby knelt, then lay flat on her stomach.

"Good girl. Now, I want you to crawl over here."

"What about the jerk with the gun?"

"One disaster at a time, okay? We'll deal with him in a minute. You just move nice and slow."

"Okay."

Jake scrubbed his hand over his face. He felt the cold sweat beading on his back. Abby crawled across the ice, her hands and knees digging into the snow. He could see where the water was coming through the cracks in the ice, darkening the snow. She paused to look at it.

"Don't look at it," he said harshly. "Look at me. Don't stop. Come on."

Her gaze met his. The power of her gaze made his knees go weak. He remembered the feel of her beneath him when they'd kissed. The softness of her body. The sound of her laughter the day before. All of those things collided in his mind. Abruptly, he realized how important it was to him that nothing happen to her.

"You're doing fine," he said.

"That's what people always say right before they screw up."

"You're not going to screw up."

"That's what I thought, too." She tried to smile, but he saw fear in her eyes. "I'm really good at screwing up, Jake. I do it all the time. My entire life is one big screwup."

"No it's not." He rubbed his temple. "Keep moving."

"I'm getting wet. The water—it's coming through the cracks."

"When you get close enough, I'm going to toss you a branch. I want you to grab it and hang on to it. Then I'll come out and get you, okay?"

The ice cracked again. A sickening sound that echoed off the surrounding trees. Jake saw Abby jolt. He saw terror in her eyes, and then the pond simply swallowed her.

Chapter 7

Jake had seen someone drown once. When he was sixteen years old, he'd seen Jimmy Baine fall through the ice on a pond during a hockey game not far from his father's ranch. It had taken the rescue team more than forty minutes to retrieve Jimmy's body. That was the day Jake had decided to get into search and rescue.

He didn't intend to let this lovely young woman die such a horrible death.

Twenty yards away, he could see Abby's head above the water. She tried to grab onto the jagged edge of the ice and pull herself up, but the ice kept breaking away. Jake knew in another five minutes she wouldn't have the strength. Another ten and she would be too weak from hypothermia to keep her head above water.

"Hang on!" he shouted to her. "I'm coming in for you!"

"Jake!"

He looked desperately around for a branch. A long, strong one that wasn't rotted from lying on the ground too long.

He felt the seconds whizzing by as he sprinted over to an aspen and broke a good-size branch from the trunk. Stripping off the smaller branches, he raced to the frozen bank of the pond. He didn't pause to think about the consequences as he stepped out onto the ice. A crack sounded on the other side of the pond. A terrible, hollow sound that reminded him of a power line snapping under pressure. He got down on his hands and knees and crawled, crossing the ice at a dangerous pace.

"Abby!"

"I'm here." Her voice was already thready and weak.

Jake feared the hypothermia was already taking hold. It could set in within minutes under these conditions. He stopped three feet away from her, afraid to get any closer without risking breaking through the ice himself. "Grab onto this branch. I'm going to pull you out."

"Okay. Hurry, it's…c-cold."

"Don't think about the cold. Just do as I say." Lying as flat and still as he could, he shoved the end of the branch toward her. "Take the branch."

Her hand came up and out of the water, her fingers closing around the branch.

"Good girl," he said. "Put both hands around it."

Even from three feet away he could see that her fingers were blue as she wrapped them around the branch. "Okay."

"Hang on. I'm going to pull you out."

The ice cracked beneath him. Water turned the snow to slush as it seeped through the cracks. Jake rolled, felt the ice sag beneath him.

Damn, he didn't like the way this was shaping up.

Extending his arms over his head to more evenly distribute his weight, he inched toward the shore. He heard the ice around Abby breaking as he pulled her through it.

"I—I can't g-get out," she sputtered. "It keeps b-breaking."

He glanced at her, saw terror in her eyes. Her lips were blue, her face ghastly pale. She'd only been in the water a few minutes, but it didn't take long for hypothermia to zap the life from someone. "Don't let go of that branch," he snapped.

Pushing himself onto his knees, he tugged on the branch. Abby's shoulders came out of the water. She put her knee up on the ice. Her coat was soaked, her hair dripping and wet. Jake held his breath, prayed she kept her grip, that the ice would hold. He pulled steadily, hauling her halfway out of the water.

"Hold tight," he said, and dragged her out of the water so that she was lying on her stomach on the ice.

He knew better than to go to her. The ice couldn't possibly hold their combined weight. But for the first time in a long time, Jake broke the rules. He went to her, swept her into his arms and carried her to shore.

Abby figured if Jake didn't kill her for running away, the cold was going to finish her off for sure. It was brutal and tore into her like a voracious beast whose fangs sank all the way to her bones. It sucked the air from her lungs, the warmth from her blood. The air was so cold against her skin it seemed to scorch her until she burned all over. Her entire body quaked violently as Jake carried her to shore.

All of her clothes—including Jake's extra duster—were soaked. Considering it was just a few degrees above zero, she didn't think things could get much worse. Well, if she didn't take into consideration the guy with the rifle taking shots at them.

"Abby. Look at me. I'm going to take you back to the cabin and get those wet clothes off you."

"God, Jake, I—I'm...f-freezing."

"Just keep talking, okay?"

She focused on him, felt her world tilt when she saw the

sharp-edged concern in his eyes. There were a hundred things she wanted to say, but her teeth were rattling together uncontrollably. The shivers were so violent, she couldn't speak.

"I guess I s-screwed up again, huh?" she managed to say after a moment.

"I reckon you did."

"I—I'm s-sorry."

"I know. Just…hang on. I'm going to get you up on Brandywine and we're going back to the cabin, okay?"

She tried to nod, ended up jerking her head once. "You're g-getting w-wet."

"Not as wet as you. You feeling okay?"

"Just…r-really c-cold."

But the cold didn't seem quite so savage when she was cradled in his arms. In fact, she was beginning to feel almost comfortable. Her hands and face were numb, but there wasn't really any pain. The cold burned, but it no longer hurt. If she closed her eyes, she could almost imagine it as heat. She relaxed against him, imagining his warmth sinking into her.

"Keep your eyes open for me, okay?"

The edge in his voice tugged her back. She opened her eyes, found him staring down at her, his gaze suffused with worry. "Stay awake for me."

"I'm okay, Jake. Really. I just…"

"Abby, damn it, keep your eyes open."

She hadn't even realized they'd drifted shut again. "I'm okay. I'm not even that cold anymore."

"That's because you're hypothermic." He struggled through the snow toward the horse. "Talk to me."

"About what?"

"Anything." He looked down at her. "Except the weather."

She smiled, intending to answer, but the words drifted

from her mind. Exhaustion tugged at her. She knew everything would be okay, knew he would take care of this. He felt so strong and warm and solid against her as he carried her toward the waiting horse. She wasn't sure why, but she felt safe wrapped in his arms. He'd saved her life. With a little luck she could still make it to Grams's....

Abby tried to keep her eyes open. She tried to think of something to say to him. She wanted to ask him about the sniper, but her mind seemed to drift aimlessly. Vaguely, she was aware of him struggling through the deep snow, breathing heavily in the cold, thin air, his arms tight around her. He said something, but her mind wasn't listening....

Abruptly he set her on her feet. "Come on, honey. On your feet. I want you to walk. Let's go. One foot in front of the other. Can you do that?"

"Yeah...okay." She hadn't intended to slur her words. She felt light-headed, as if she'd had one too many glasses of wine. Must be the cold zapping her.

"Come on. Walk."

Vaguely, she was aware of her arm around his neck. Her feet were numb. Her hair was beginning to freeze. She looked down at the ground and ordered her legs to move. She could do this. She'd spent the past six months getting into top physical condition. It wasn't as though a little cold water was going to put her down.

The instant he let her go, her legs melted like butter on a hot skillet.

Cursing, Jake swept her back into his arms. "I should have known you wouldn't cooperate," he growled.

Abby rode the haze, fighting the sleepiness plaguing her and the confusion playing with her mind. She knew she should be afraid, knew she was in trouble. As a nurse, she knew hypothermia was serious business. She just couldn't muster the energy to get too worried about it.

Jake kept talking to her, pressing her, asking her questions. She tried to rally her mind to answer, but after a while the responses got all jumbled and she could no longer find the words.

Jake Madigan never panicked. The emotion just wasn't part of his persona. Panic caused smart people to act stupid. It caused even pros to make mistakes that could end up costing someone a life. Panic was the kiss of death in any emergency situation.

But even knowing all of those things about himself and about what he did for a living, Jake felt the sharp edge of fear slice him and go deep. The woman in his arms couldn't weigh much more than a hundred pounds soaking wet. She looked incredibly fragile, her face as pale as death....

"Abby. Abby! Come on. Open your eyes. Talk to me."

"I'm...okay."

Her words were slurred, her voice so low he had to crane his neck forward to hear her. Hell, she was already in the first phase of hypothermia.

"Didn't mean to...screw up," she whispered.

"You're going to be all right." She had to be all right. Jake would never forgive himself if something happened to her. She was his responsibility. *His.* And he didn't intend to let either of them down. "Just hang on, okay?"

His legs shook as he caught Brandywine's reins, then set Abby gently in the saddle. Swinging onto the horse, behind her, he nudged the animal into a reckless gait through the snow.

He knew he should have his rifle unsheathed and ready, but there was no way he could handle a semiconscious passenger and the rifle at the same time, so he did his best to approach the cabin from the opposite side—out of the shooter's line of vision—praying whomever had been using them for target practice earlier had gotten the message that Jake was armed and more than ready to retaliate.

He stopped Brandywine at the back of the cabin a few minutes later and jumped to the ground. The place looked deserted, but he wasn't taking any chances. Abby was as still as death when he eased her down off the horse. He would have felt better if she'd been shaking, but she wasn't.

Unholstering his H&K .45, he kicked open the cabin door and quickly searched the premises. No one had been there. Back outside, he tied the horse to the lean-to, then scooped Abby into his arms. It had been more than twenty minutes since she'd fallen through the ice. It was imperative that he warm her body quickly. He had to get those wet clothes off of her. If she was aware enough, he needed to get some warm fluids into her.

He didn't relish the idea of undressing her. He didn't want to know what she looked like beneath those clothes. But Jake was too much of a professional to let anything as banal as lust interfere with his job. Setting her on the floor a few feet from the fire, he quickly tossed two logs onto the embers, and put a pail of water on to boil. When he turned to Abby, she was sitting up, trying to toe her shoes off, but her movements were sluggish and weak. Her eyes focused on him, but they were glassy. Blue tinged her lips.

"I've got to get these wet clothes off of you," he said. "Can you help me out?"

Embarrassment flared briefly in her eyes. "I can...do it."

"Sure you can. I'll just...give you a hand, okay?"

"Just let me..." Her hands fluttered at the zipper of her jumpsuit, but her fingers were too stiff to function.

"This isn't the time for modesty, Abby, okay? I'm a professional. You can trust me."

"I can *do* it...." Her fingers fumbled the zipper. "Damn it."

"Let me take care of you, okay?"

Jake knew he couldn't wait any longer. Every minute counted when her body temperature was dropping. They were hours away from the nearest medical facility. The cabin was barely above freezing inside. He didn't have an IV or heated oxygen or even a warming blanket to treat her with should this turn serious.

He knelt beside her. "I put some logs in the fire. It'll be warm in here in a few minutes."

She had the zipper partway down, but he could see she wasn't going to succeed. Her hands were blue. The ends of her hair had frozen. Setting his jaw, he reached for the zipper. She tried to push his hands away, but he firmly set them aside. With impersonal efficiency, he stripped the jumpsuit from her. Lifting her slightly, he worked the wet material from her body and tossed it aside. Down to her bra and panties, her flesh was colorless and cold to the touch.

Jake handed her one of the blankets. "Here."

"Thanks."

"Sit up for me." Putting his hand beneath her shoulders, he helped her to a sitting position. He kept his eyes averted as much as possible when he unhooked the wet bra from around her. He tried not to think about that crazy kiss they'd shared, or the way his body jumped to attention every time he thought about doing it again.

Quickly he wrapped her in his sleeping bag. "Better?" he asked.

She nodded.

"Take those wet, uh…underwear off, too," he said. "I'll hang them by the fire to dry for you."

Looking embarrassed even through her weakness, she reached down and removed her panties. Without looking at them, Jake moved to the hearth and draped them over the rustic mantel. He tossed another log onto the fire. The cabin was beginning to warm up, but it wasn't well insulated. The water had started to boil, so he lifted it from the embers and took it over to the table. He removed a package of instant soup from his saddlebag and made a cup, and took it back over to her.

"I want you to sip this," he said. "Slowly."

Her eyes were clear when she looked up at him. Relief swamped him when he saw that she was shivering again. That was a good sign; her body was trying to warm itself.

"What kind of soup?" she asked.

"Hot." Kneeling beside her, he helped her to sit up again. "I hope it's better than your coffee."

"I didn't think I'd ever be glad to hear one of your smart-aleck comments."

"I've got more where that one came from." She took the cup, but her hands were shaking so violently, she could barely hold it. Jake steadied the cup, and she sipped tentatively. "You saved my life," she said after a moment.

Her gaze locked with his. The impact made him feel gut-punched. How was it that this woman could undo him without saying anything? Just hit him with those violet eyes and he was a goner? He tried to blame his reaction on the close call with death and the remnants of fear left in its wake. But he knew there was a hell of a lot more going on between them than that.

"You didn't leave me much choice," he said.

"I thought the ice would hold."

"If you'd gone under I might not have been able to get to you." The thought made him feel nauseous. He tried to be angry, but he was still too scared. "Hell, Abby, you could have drowned."

"I warned you I was really good at screwing up, so stop yelling at me."

"I'm not yelling. I'm just trying to figure you out."

"Don't bother. I don't even have myself figured out, so it's probably a losing proposition for you."

He thought about that for a moment, then let it go. "You gave me your word you wouldn't run away."

She turned those eyes on him. Even though he'd moved back to a safe distance, her gaze touched him with the intimacy of a caress. "How far would you go to stay out of prison if you were convicted of a crime you hadn't committed?" she asked.

"I'd go through the proper legal channels before I'd risk getting myself killed."

"Those proper channels failed me, Jake. They cost me a year of my life. A year of hell that I won't ever be able to get back. Am I supposed to just stand by and let the legal system destroy my life?"

"The legal system is all you've got."

"No. I've got the truth."

He hadn't expected her to say that; felt his walls go up. She was going to tell him something he didn't want to hear. She was going to ask him to trust her. Jake wasn't up to it. Not now. Not ever. It didn't matter that for an instant, when she'd told him about the death of her patient, when he'd seen the devastation in her eyes, he'd almost believed her.

Rising, he scooped his rifle off the floor and set it on the table within easy reach. He looked out the windows on the east side of the cabin, studied the ridges beyond for the sniper, but the snowscape outside remained serene. Without looking at Abby, he picked up her jumpsuit and sneakers. The jumpsuit was waterlogged and still frozen in places. The bra was nothing more than a thin scrap of cotton. Hell. Trying to ignore the silky feel of it in his hands, Jake hung both over the back of a chair and set it next to the fire. When he turned back to her, she was still watching him with those eyes. Those beautiful, haunting eyes that had kept him awake until the wee hours of morning.

"Are you warm enough?" It was a dumb question considering her teeth were rattling like dice in a roulette wheel.

"I don't think I'll ever be warm again."

"Yes, you will." He went to her and knelt, putting the

cup of soup to her lips. "Drink it. I'm not kidding around. You need fluids. It'll help warm you up."

She sipped. "Why was someone shooting at us?"

He held the cup for her and urged her to take another sip. "I was just going to ask you the same question."

What little color she had in her cheeks fled. Her eyes were troubled and dark against her pale flesh. Jake steeled himself against the sudden need to raise his hand and touch her cheek. But he wouldn't do that to himself. Wouldn't do it to her. Certainly not after what had happened between them earlier.

"Maybe it was a hunter, and he didn't even realize—"

"Hunters don't shoot at people, Abby."

"Well, maybe it was an accident. A stray bullet."

Frustration, with her and the situation, made his voice gruff. "Those shots were taken from at least a half mile away. Those bullets were close. Too close. That takes some marksmanship. The guy has a long-range rifle and knows how to use it."

Jake didn't want to ask her about who might be trying to kill her. But after what had happened with the sniper just now, he was forced to reconsider his original judgment about her guilt. "Last night, you told me you thought someone was trying to kill you."

She didn't respond, but he saw the dawning realization in her eyes, the quick stab of fear.

"Who do you think is trying to kill you?" His own words echoed inside his head like the cliff-hanger of a badly written play. Jake studied the soft lines of her face, her worried eyes, and wondered how she'd gotten herself into such terrible trouble.

"You're not going to believe me," she said after a moment.

"Try me."

She hesitated, and Jake got an odd feeling in the pit of

his stomach. A gut feeling that told him there was more going on than he'd initially realized, a hell of a lot more than she'd told him. And he knew none of it was good.

"My guess is that Dr. Jonathan Reed wants me dead," she said after a moment.

"Who's that?"

"He's the chief of surgery at Mercy General."

"Why does he want you dead?"

She pulled the sleeping bag up to her chin. Jake could see that her teeth wanted to chatter, but she kept them still by clamping them together. "Because I know something about him I'm not supposed to know."

"Like what?"

Abby didn't answer.

Jake studied her closed expression, felt that feeling in his gut augment. He wasn't sure exactly what it was that had his suspicions kicking in. Maybe the way her entire body had stiffened when he'd pressed her about Reed. Jake couldn't pinpoint what was going on, but his years of experience in law enforcement told him she wasn't lying. Still, it didn't make a damn bit of sense that she wouldn't talk to him.

"Why do you think he wants you dead, Abby?" he repeated.

A tremor went through her body. With a sudden burst of insight Jake knew her shaking wasn't from the cold. She was trembling because she was afraid.

She started to turn away, but Jake reached out and grasped her bicep, stopping her. "Why?" he pressed.

Easing her arm from his grasp, she looked directly at him then. The kind of stare that was so intense he wanted to look away but couldn't.

"Because he's a murderer," she said after a moment. "And he knows I know it."

Chapter 8

Abby had known telling the truth would be difficult. She'd been through the interrogation nightmare a hundred times with the cops. Another hundred times with her lawyers. None of them had believed her then. She didn't expect Jake to believe her now.

It was a crazy story, and she wasn't certain of any of it. She knew how it would sound to Jake. Like a desperate lie based on some bizarre Hollywood movie. She didn't want to look into his eyes and know he thought she was a liar— or crazy.

"That's a serious allegation," he said after an interminable moment.

"Murder tends to be pretty serious."

He studied her for a moment, his expression inscrutable. "Tell me what you know." When she hesitated, he added, "I can't help you unless you talk to me."

She held his gaze, felt the familiar pinging of her heart against her ribs. She wanted badly to confide in him, longed to tell him everything and get it all out in the open. Even so, she wasn't sure if she could bear it if he didn't believe her.

"It's a crazy story, Jake."

"I'm a cop, remember? Crazy's right up my alley."

"You're not going to believe me." She looked down at her hands, realizing that was the worst part of this. Knowing he wasn't going to believe her. No one else had. Over the past year she'd learned to live with that. But she knew it would be infinitely worse with Jake.

"Let me be the judge of that," he said. "Just...tell me what you know."

Closing her eyes, Abby sucked in a fortifying breath. "I'd been working at Mercy General for about two years when I met Jonathan." The normal tone of her voice surprised her, considering she felt as if she were coming apart inside. She told herself it didn't matter what Jake thought of her. Abby didn't *want* it to matter. But at some point in the past two days his opinion had become important to her. "Jonathan was a heart surgeon. He was talented. Dedicated. And brilliant. Everyone wondered why he stayed at such a small hospital. He always said it was because that was where he was needed most. He was well respected at Mercy and throughout the medical community. He was older. Influential. I was an emergency room nurse and we became... friends."

Jake's eyes sharpened on hers and she resisted the urge to squirm. She'd already resolved not to tell him just how close she and Jonathan had been. The shame and humiliation were too great. She'd resolved to keep that part of it separate—the betrayal, the lies, that the man she'd been sleeping with...a man she'd given her naive heart to...had lied to convict her to save his own neck. She knew it would only muddy the waters if she got into the personal aspects of the case. She had to keep this impersonal. She had to sound credible to Jake if she wanted him to believe her, if she wanted his help.

She desperately needed both.

"I was devastated after my patient died that night," she continued. "There was an investigation. At first it was routine. But after the autopsy report got back to the cops, they started sniffing around the hospital, asking questions, and eventually the finger was pointed at me. I couldn't believe it when charges of negligence were brought against me. I was put on administrative leave without pay. A couple of weeks later, I was arrested for murder."

Abby looked away, unable to hold his gaze. The arrest had been devastating, both professionally and personally. Two detectives had come to her apartment on a Saturday afternoon. They'd cuffed her just outside her door as her neighbors looked on in astonishment. She'd been taken downtown, booked and sent to a cell. It had been the most shocking and humiliating experience in her life.

Remembering, she turned away from Jake's discerning eyes to stare into the fire. "It took me two days to make bail." Two hellish days of not understanding why she'd been arrested, of not knowing if or when she would ever be free. Two nights of wondering why her lover hadn't come forward to help her. "I had a lot of time to think during those two days. All that time, I kept thinking the police would realize it was all a big mistake. But they didn't. My bail was set at five hundred thousand dollars the following Monday. My grandmother put up the cash. And I knew I was in very serious trouble."

"What did you do?"

"The instant I got out, I started...researching."

"Researching what?"

"Well, I'd seen some things at the hospital in the last couple of months."

"Like what?"

"Things that didn't mean much at the time," she hedged. "But when I added them all together, I started getting suspicious."

"Suspicious about what?"

The laugh that escaped her tasted bitter on her tongue. "You know, I felt incredibly guilty about that patient's death. I had nightmares for weeks. I couldn't sleep, couldn't stop thinking about him. I couldn't bear to think I was responsible for that man's death. I almost convinced myself that maybe I *had* made a mistake. Maybe I *had* screwed up and injected him with the wrong medication.

"Anyway, I was doing a lot of soul searching at that point. A lot of thinking. Recalling everything I did that night. Recalling things that had happened over the last few months at the hospital. I'd remembered hearing about another unexplained death a few months earlier. I had a good friend who worked in the records department. Her name was Kim.

"I called her and asked to see the records for that patient. Kim was afraid for her job and refused, but she liked me and wanted to help. She knew me well enough to know I would never make a mistake like that. When I kept pressing her for help, she finally agreed to leave the door and file cabinets of the records room unlocked one night.

"I sneaked into records and spent a couple of hours going through the files. And I realized Jim wasn't the only homeless person who had died at that hospital."

She took a deep breath. "I didn't have much time, but in less than two hours, I was able to find out that in the prior six months, four other destitute people—three men and one woman—had been brought in to the emergency room for relatively minor injuries or illnesses, and never left. People who were homeless, without any money and without family. No one to ask questions if they were to die unexpectedly.

But before I could make copies, one of the security officers caught me in records that night.''

"Oh, Abby.'' Shaking his head, Jake dragged a hand through his hair.

"He called the police. God, it was a nightmare. I got arrested again. I mean, this guy caught me red-handed. I tried to tell the cops what I'd found, but no one would listen. No one believed me. And any defense I may have had went downhill after that.''

Jake nodded, knowing how bad something like that would look to the police. "They thought you were trying to cover your tracks.''

She nodded. "I wasn't. I was looking for information. Anything that would prove I was innocent.''

"Did you find proof?''

"It took me a while to figure it out, but I finally did.'' Abby took a deep, shuddering breath and looked at Jake.

His eyes were the color of a thunderhead, his jaw set as if in stone. "Tell me,'' he said.

"Each time those patients died, Dr. Jonathan Reed was the doctor on duty.''

"That doesn't prove anything, does it?''

"Each of those patients were cremated after their deaths,'' she said.

"A lot of people choose to be cremated these days.''

"Each time Reed was the doctor who pronounced them dead.''

"That's still not proof.''

"There's a reason those people died, Jake. There's a reason why their bodies were cremated. There's a reason why they were chosen. And there's a reason why all of those things happened on Reed's watch.''

"Abby, are you telling me this respected surgeon killed four homeless people? What possible motivation could a man in his position have to do something like that?''

Abby swallowed. Her mouth was dry. Her heart was beating fast and unevenly. She was still cold, only now the ice seemed to be seeping from the inside out. "I think Reed murdered those people for their organs."

Jake wasn't the kind of man to react, but Abby saw him recoil, saw the flash of surprise in his eyes. She held her breath, waited for the disbelief to follow. When it didn't come, she lowered her head and put her face in her hands and fought a hot rush of tears.

"Do you have anything to back that up?" he asked after a moment. "Any kind of proof?"

Taking in a deep, calming breath, she raised her gaze to his. "No."

"Abby…you know how that sounds…"

"Of course, I do," she snapped.

"You could have fought this legally."

"He was going to kill me."

"You could have asked for protection."

"Jake, I was dying in prison," she cried. "A little bit every day. I couldn't bear it. Having my dignity and my humanity stripped away a little bit at a time. I didn't even feel human some days. It was like my mind and my body no longer connected. My God, I didn't kill that patient. I couldn't bear the thought of spending the rest of my life in prison for something I didn't do."

For the first time, his gaze faltered, and Abby knew he understood. He was in law enforcement, after all. He'd been inside prisons before. He knew what it was like.

"How do you tie this in to black market organs?" he asked.

"When I was in prison, I had access to an entire library. I was going through archived newspapers and ran across an article from the *Rocky Mountain News*. Two years ago, there was a story done on Jonathan Reed when he became chief of surgery at Mercy General. There was a photograph of him with another surgeon from Paris. They'd gone to medical school together. This other surgeon, Dr. Jean LaRue, had a four-year-old daughter who needed a liver transplant. She'd been on the recipient list for over a year, but it wasn't looking good. He didn't think she was going to get the new liver in time.

"By accident, I ran across another article from a Paris newspaper when I did a search on LaRue. It seems some miracle happened and Dr. LaRue's daughter got her new liver in time to save her life."

"How does that involve Reed?"

"The first homeless patient at Mercy died the same day Dr. LaRue's daughter received her liver."

"Connecting Reed to that patient and then to the liver transplant is a stretch, Abby. I mean, in this day and age, how could something like that work?"

"Reed has a private clinic not far from Aspen."

"Aboveboard?"

"Yes, but I think he does a lot more than treat bronchitis and set broken legs." When Jake continued to stare at her, she elaborated. "I think he has a list of recipients. Wealthy friends, more than likely.... When a possible donor checks into the hospital—a patient whose sudden death won't raise too many questions—Reed plugs the information into a computer. If he gets a match, he injects the patient and takes what he needs."

"But doesn't the patient have to be kept alive?"

"Just long enough for serology testing and testing for certain diseases such as Hepatitis C and HIV. That usually only takes about six hours. Once the testing is done, the organs can be removed from the body. The organs are then profused in a cold-storage medium high in electrolytes and nutrients. Kidneys are flushed. Then the organs are put on ice, to be jetted to wherever a recipient is already in an operating room and under anesthesia.

"A heart and lungs can only be out of the body for five or six hours, so the serology is done while the donor is alive. Kidneys and pancreas can last up to forty-eight hours. Livers up to eighteen hours." She looked at Jake. "Aspen is only an hour away by jet."

"So the timeframe is feasible."

She nodded.

"Criminy." Jake heaved a huge sigh. "It's feasible, but it's still a stretch."

"Reed is in a position to pull it off. He's an important man at the hospital. He's a trusted, respected surgeon. He's well connected. Wealthy. My God, if one of his friends were to come to him in need of an organ transplant—or even the friend of a friend or a child…Reed could have a long list of possible recipients. He could do the surgeries himself. An anesthesiologist and nursing team wouldn't be hard for him to find if he paid them enough."

She paused to take a breath. "Jake, he murdered those people. Then he kept them on life support until he could harvest the organ he needed. He put the organs on ice and flew them to his clinic in Aspen."

"How could he cover up something like that?"

"Mercy General is a small, privately held hospital. Maybe he had someone on staff helping him. As terrible as it sounds, Reed knew no one was going to ask questions about a homeless person dying. He knew his actions would never come into question. When that homeless person died on my watch, he wasn't expecting the man to have family who cared. He wasn't expecting them to ask for an autopsy. When they did, he needed a scapegoat. I was convenient."

"Damn, Abby, that's a wild theory."

"You're a cop, Jake. Tell me you believe in coincidence."

"I don't."

She stared at him, her breath clogging her throat. "You

could look into Reed's financial records. I'm betting my life he's come upon some huge sums of money in the last couple of years.''

"All we have is a *theory,* Abby. I can't act on something that's based solely on circumstantial evidence and—''

"And what? The word of a convict?''

"I wasn't going to say that.''

"You don't have to. I see it on your face.'' Wrapping the sleeping bag more tightly around her, she tried to rise.

Jake stopped her by putting his hand on her arm. "Don't walk away from me.''

"I can't stand it when you look at me like that.''

"I'm trying to take this in and make sense of it.''

Sighing, she sank back down to the floor, but the air between them snapped with tension. Jake scrubbed his hand over the stubble on his jaw. "You told me you believe someone is trying to kill you. Did Reed try to get to you inside the prison?''

"I think he hired someone to kill me. One of the other inmates came at me with a knife in the shower room.'' The memory of her narrow escape made her shiver. "She nearly got me, Jake. If I hadn't already been in good physical condition, she would have killed me.''

"Why does Reed want you dead now? I mean, you've already been convicted.''

"I don't know if you've noticed, Jake, but I've got a big mouth. I was making noise. People weren't listening, but all it would have taken was one hot-shot lawyer and Reed knew I could foil his little empire.''

"Reed didn't want to take a chance that someone might listen to you.''

"Would you?''

"You think he hired someone to track you up here?'' he asked.

"That's his style.'' Abby laughed, but there was no humor in it. "Reed never does his own dirty work. He gets other people to do it for him. He's got money. A lot of it. I'll bet he hired a hit man."

Jake contemplated her for a moment. "*Exactly* what evidence convicted you?"

"Remember when I mentioned that my prints were on the syringe in the biohazard disposal unit?" When he nodded, she continued, "That was bogus, because no medical professional injects a patient without gloves these days. Still, the syringe had traces of Valium in it. One of the other nurses saw me give an injection. But as I already told you I swear it was the tetanus injection. I swear I wouldn't make a mistake like that. I'm too careful. But no one could find the tetanus syringe. No one went to bat for me." Not even Jonathan Reed—the man she'd been sleeping with at the time.

"They left you swinging in the wind."

She nodded. "With a noose around my neck."

"Do you have any proof of any of this?"

"I've been in prison for the past year, Jake. It's not like they let me out on weekends to investigate the crime." Her voice shook with vehemence. "But I know Reed did it. Damn it, I know it."

"Why you?"

"Why me what?"

"Why did Reed choose you?"

Abby stared at him, her steadfastness faltering. "Because I was vulnerable."

"Why were you vulnerable?"

Leave it to Jake to ask the tough questions. That's what he did best. The man was a deputy, after all.

When she didn't readily answer, his cop's mask fell into place. "Abby?"

A sense of hopelessness gripped her. She didn't want him

to know why she'd been vulnerable. She knew that knowledge would obliterate what little credibility she had.

"As soon as I realized the investigation had focused on me, I went to Reed," she said, skirting the question. "I was scared and had nowhere else to turn. I asked him to support me and tell the police I wouldn't have made a mistake like that. Reed promised to do what he could." Abby closed her eyes. "Instead, he went to the police and told them I'd confessed to him."

"What?" Jake asked incredulously.

"Reed told them I was a disturbed young woman who needed help. That I was obsessed with death. That some drugs were missing from the drug locker. He told them I'd stolen drugs. My bail was revoked shortly after that."

"It was your word against his."

"Yes."

His eyes narrowed, probing hers uncomfortably. "What aren't you telling me?"

She looked away, feeling trapped. "I've told you everything that matters."

"Abby, why were you vulnerable?"

"Don't," she said.

"Damn it, if you want my help, you're going to have to trust me."

The simple request brought tears to her eyes. She longed to trust him, but knew she could never put that much of herself on the line ever again. She'd trusted Reed, and he'd cut her heart out. The betrayal had killed something inside her forever.

After several tense minutes, she turned her gaze back to him. "Reed knew about my past. He…used it against me."

"What past?"

Shame pierced her, coldly familiar and scalpel-sharp. "When I was seventeen I…had a breakdown. An emotional breakdown. I'd…confided in Reed about it. And he…used it against me. That's why I was vulnerable, Jake. That's why he chose me.''

Breakdown.

The word echoed like a scream inside Jake's head. Of all the things she could have said, that one surprised him the most. He recalled the corrections officials's warning that she was emotionally unstable. He'd put it out of his mind because he hadn't seen any evidence of instability. He considered himself a pretty good judge of a person's frame of mind, and Abby Nichols was as sane as the day was long.

Something wasn't right about this case. Something that was cunning and cruel that chafed his sense of justice like a steel rasp.

Yet at the same time an uncomfortable doubt rose up inside him. He remembered another woman he'd tried to help. A woman he'd trusted and loved. He would have laid down his life for Elaine and her sweet little boy. Instead, he'd let her twist their relationship into something ugly, then stood by dumbly when she cut him off at the knees.

Jake knew better than to get involved in Abby's plight. He'd been sharing close quarters with her and wasn't thinking clearly. He hated to admit it, but she'd gotten to him. At some point in the past twenty-four hours he'd lost his emotional distance. He couldn't think of a worse fate for a man who prided himself on walking the straight and narrow.

The kiss had changed everything, he realized. He'd stepped over a line, broken a staunch personal rule. He needed distance. Needed to get the hell out of this cabin and down the mountain before he made another mistake. A mistake that wouldn't be quite as harmless as a kiss.

But every time he looked at her, he wanted her. Wanted her in a way that was as strong as the need to take his next breath. When he closed his eyes, he could still feel the heat of her against him, the softness of her body, the sweet wetness of her mouth. And the need clawed at him, like a trapped animal desperate to get out....

Jake gave himself a hard mental shake. Sweat glistened on his brow, and he loosened the top button of his flannel shirt. Across from him, Abby stared into the fire. Even in profile, she was breathtaking. He knew better than to ask the next question; he knew it would only bring him one step closer to knowing her. He didn't want to know her. He didn't want to get inside her head or, God forbid, let her get inside his. But Jake had never been one to back away from danger.

"Abby." His voice grated like steel against steel. "Look at me."

He saw that danger clearly when her gaze met his. Tentative. Wary. So lovely he couldn't look away. The torment in her eyes was raw and hard as hell to look at. No one could fake that kind of emotion, and he knew that whatever happened here today was honest and real with no holds barred.

"How was something like that admissible in court?" he asked.

"Let's just say the prosecutor was a lot sharper than my public defender."

He thought about that for a moment, then said, "Tell me about your breakdown."

"Jake—"

"You've already told me this much. I need to know everything. Come on. Talk to me."

Her eyes skated away from his to stare into the fire. "It happened after my father died. I was almost eighteen years old. My father and I were very close. He was...a really good man." A sad smile touched her lips. "He was on his way home from work one day and a drunk driver hit his car head-on."

"I'm sorry," Jake said in a thick voice.

"He suffered multiple trauma. A terrible head injury. He was in a coma for six days. The neurosurgeon ran an EEG, and it showed there was no brain activity." Pain tightened her features, but she didn't cry. "The doctor said he wasn't going to survive. He took us into a little room at the hospital and explained the situation and told us we should discuss removing him from life support."

Cursing under his breath, Jake cut his eyes to hers. "Aw, man..."

She didn't even acknowledge him. And he knew the memory had taken her back to that little room and one of the most horrendous dilemmas a person could face.

"I couldn't believe they could suggest such a thing," she said. "I mean, I was too heartbroken to understand that he was already gone. That he couldn't come back to us. And there were other considerations. The insurance company for one. They would only pay so much and we didn't have a lot of money."

"Medical bills."

She nodded. "The doctor also told us there was a six-year-old boy in Dayton, Ohio, who needed a liver or he was going to die. He told us about a high school student in Seattle who needed a heart or she'd never see her first day of college." Her hands clenched the sleeping bag at her throat. "Mom made the decision the next day."

Jake had heard enough to know where she was going with this. He didn't want to hear it, but couldn't stop her. Not when he knew how badly she needed to tell him this. How badly she needed get it out in the open so she could purge herself of the pain she'd held inside her for so many years.

"That afternoon, they turned off the respirator," she said. "Mom and Grams and I were in the room with him. One minute he was lying there breathing as if he were asleep. Then he was just very...still. He was...gone."

Jake had seen death before. He hated it. The loss. The

unfairness. The inevitable pain it caused the survivors. That was why he'd become an EMT. Why he'd chosen law enforcement as his career. Why he volunteered for Rocky Mountain Search and Rescue.

She raised her gaze to his, anguish fresh in her eyes. "I remember telling him goodbye. I remember walking out of the room, thinking it was over. I remember wanting to cry, but realizing I couldn't. I couldn't speak. I remember people talking to me, trying to comfort me. But the grief was dark and terrible and just…crushed me. I guess I shut down. I went inside myself." She took a shuddery breath. "I stopped talking to everyone around me. After a few days, Mom got worried and took me to the doctor. He recommended a psychiatrist. The shrink admitted me to a psychiatric hospital a few days later."

"I'm sorry, honey."

"It's okay. I mean, I'm okay now."

"How long were you in the hospital?"

"About two months."

"You recovered fully."

She shot him a grateful look, but it was fraught with pain. The kind of deep, dark pain most people never had to feel. The people who did, never, ever talked about it. "The only good thing that came out of it was that I decided to go into nursing afterward."

"I'm sure your dad would have been proud."

She looked away quickly, clearly uncomfortable. "Thank you for saying that."

He wasn't sure what to do or to say next. He wanted to comfort her, but knew better than to touch her. There was something about this strong, hurting woman that made him want to protect her, made him want to take away her pain.

Jake knew he wasn't the man for the job

"Reed knew about the breakdown." She pulled the sleeping bag more tightly around her and shivered. "The prosecutor in the case got the judge to allow my records as evidence at the trial. The prosecutor put Reed on the stand. Reed testified that I was 'preoccupied with death' because of what happened to my father. He attested to this so-called preoccupation with death. He claimed that's why I killed that patient.''

The thought of dirty legal maneuverings chafed Jake's sense of justice. The thought of the pain those maneuverings had caused this woman outraged his sense of honor. ''I'm sorry.''

''The jury agreed. I was found guilty of second degree murder and sentenced to life in prison.''

The need to touch her was as powerful as any he'd known. He could picture himself going to her, pulling her to him and holding her until the tremors stopped and the words that were crowded in his throat came pouring out and chased the sadness from her eyes.

He rose abruptly. His heart hammered in his chest. He felt Abby's eyes on him, but he didn't look at her. He knew he should say something more, but he couldn't. He didn't want to see her pain or vulnerability. He didn't like the way it affected him and wasn't sure how much more he could take before he did something stupid. Like go to her and kiss her until the pain on her face was gone and she put her arms around him as she had out in the snow today.

Lifting his rifle from the table, he walked over to the window and looked outside. He tried to concentrate on the high ridge to the north, looking for the sniper, but he couldn't stop thinking about what she'd told him.

He continued to stare out the window, acutely aware that she was sitting near the fire, silent and hurting, and there wasn't a thing he could do about it. Beyond the glass, the wind shuffled a bank of dark clouds on the horizon. Snow more than likely, damn it. They needed to get down the mountain. With the weather threatening and a sniper on the loose, he knew it wasn't safe for them to stay here any longer. But Jake also knew they couldn't leave until Abby's clothes were dry and she'd recovered her strength enough to travel. Getting down the mountain on horseback in hip-deep snow was going to be tough. Jake had enough experience to know you didn't take any chances with something as serious as hypothermia in the high country.

He looked over at Abby, found her staring into the fire, the sleeping bag wrapped tightly around her shoulders. She was turned away from him, her profile delicate against the backdrop of flames. He couldn't see her eyes, but the long sweep of her lashes lay soft against her cheek. Her blond-streaked hair had dried into wild little corkscrews that fell over her shoulders in a thick mass. The firelight shot silver sparks through the blond. It looked soft. Touchable.

His gaze slipped lower and his mouth went dry at the sight of her graceful throat. He wondered what it would be like to kiss her there. To run his tongue along the delicate curve and taste the flesh. He wondered if she would taste the way she smelled. Sweet and secret and soft as wet velvet....

Raw lust struck him in the gut like a fist. Blood pooled low and hot in his groin. Muttering a curse under his breath, he turned away from her and stared blindly out at the wind-blown peaks. He thought inappropriate thoughts about the woman behind him and all the things he wanted to do with her. He thought about what all those things would cost him, and cursed under his breath.

"Is it safe for us to stay here? I mean, with that guy with the gun outside?"

Jake glanced at her over his shoulder, warning her with his eyes for her to stay away. "Why? You got someplace to go?"

She held his gaze, challenging his question. "Actually I do."

"Where?"

"I can't tell you that."

"Didn't think so."

"Jake, we could split up. You could head back down the mountain. You could tell the D.O.C. guys about the sniper. Tell them I—"

"I'm taking you back, Abby. If you've got a beef with your conviction, you'll have to fight it through whatever legal channels are left." He felt like a bastard saying that to her, knowing what he did. But the alternative was too crazy to contemplate.

She hissed an obscenity that left no doubt in his mind how she felt about those legal channels. "I could just take off."

He shot her a sour look.

"I know you won't shoot me in the back," she said.

"You know I'll come after you."

"So, we're stuck here?" she asked.

"We don't have a choice for the moment."

"You mean, because I fell through the ice and got a little disoriented?"

"You're a nurse. You figure it out."

She rolled her eyes. "Look, I'm not some Denver daisy who went out for a jog this morning. I've trained for six months for this. I'm strong and feel just fine."

"You go out in subzero weather in wet clothes and a body that was hypothermic just a few hours earlier and you're asking for trouble."

"I'm in good shape, Jake."

He didn't want to think about what kind of shape she was in. He'd seen her long, toned legs and flat belly. He'd seen the muscle definition in her arms. Yeah, she was in good shape, all right. So good, he couldn't keep his eyes off her.

Wrapping the sleeping bag more tightly around her, she approached him. "Let me go," she said.

"Abby—"

"Please."

"I can't do that."

"Why not?"

"Because I'm a cop, damn it."

"You know I'm telling the truth."

Jake didn't want to have this conversation. It wasn't his responsibility to judge her guilt or innocence or any of those gray areas in between. All he was supposed to do was take her back. And he planned to do just that come hell or high water.

He turned his back on her. "Put another log on the fire, will you?" he asked quietly. "Try to get some rest. I'm going to feed the stock and take a look around."

"Damn it, Jake—"

"Rest while you can, Abby. We leave at first light."

Chapter 9

Jake avoided going back inside until dark. He fed the stock, put some snow in a pail and melted it for the animals to drink. At noon, he tacked up Brandywine, sheathed his rifle and rode a one-mile perimeter around the cabin, hoping to spot a spent casing or some tracks or some other clue that might tell him who'd been taking shots at them. Later, he spent a couple of hours hauling dry firewood into the cabin. He even built a small bonfire on the off chance the RMSAR chopper was out looking for them. He knew it was futile; for the second day in a row, the winds were kicking in from the north and the Bell 412 was likely grounded.

But even something as futile as building a bonfire was better than going back inside. Spending time with Abby was making him crazy, filling his head with thoughts he had absolutely no right to be thinking.

But Jake knew he was going to have to go inside at some point and face her. He couldn't avoid it much longer. It was barely above zero outside. His hands and feet were numb.

His face tingled from the cold. He had to go inside. He needed to eat. He needed to rest, so he could keep watch tonight.

Hell, he was going to have to spend the *night* with her.

Jake didn't want to think about her any more. He didn't want to want her, didn't want to know anything more about her. He didn't want to know what she'd been through or how it had affected her. All he wanted was to get this job over with so he could go back to his life where things were black and white.

But for the first time in his life things weren't quite so black and white and he was scared to death that doing the right thing included helping an escaped con.

The cabin was dim when he finally pushed open the door and stepped inside. The only light came from the low, burning fire in the hearth. The tang of smoke hung in the air. It took a moment for his eyes to adjust. On the floor a few feet in front of the fire, Abby lay on her side, wrapped in her sleeping bag, asleep. She looked fragile and innocent and incredibly sexy lying there with that mane of hair spread out under her like coils of silk.

The sight of her stopped Jake dead in his tracks.

Stomping the snow from his boots, he tore his eyes from her. He went to the small table in the kitchen, picked up the kettle and filled it with snow. When he took it to the fire, she was sitting up, watching him, her face soft from sleep.

"Thirsty?" he asked.

"Yeah." She rubbed the back of her neck and looked out the window. "I can't believe I slept the day away."

"That's the hypothermia. The cold will zap you." He walked over to the window facing the ridge and pulled the frayed curtains closed.

"Do you think he's still out there?" she asked.

"I don't know." He looked at her and felt the now familiar tightening sensation in his gut. "Probably."

Scowling, Jake walked over to his saddlebag. "I've got two more meals. Do you want to eat now, or in the morning?"

"Do you have anything left to snack on tomorrow?"

"Not much. A couple of protein bars."

"Let's eat now." Rising, the sleeping bag wrapped around her, she walked over to the fireplace and lifted her jumpsuit from the back of the chair. "I mean, if you don't mind. I'm starving."

"No problem."

"I need to get dressed."

Hell. "Ah...okay."

"Would you mind turning around for a second?"

"Sure."

Because her back was already to him, Jake hesitated a moment and watched her. The lady definitely had a nice back. And he knew even after this was over, he'd be thinking about that slender back for a long, long time to come.

Turning away, he busied himself with their last two meals while Abby dressed. In short order, they were sitting cross-legged in front of the fire with their meals on their laps. They ate in silence for several minutes. Sipping water from the cup between them and savoring their last two meals. Jake had just begun to relax and believed he was going to get through this when she started in with the questions.

"So, how long have you been in law enforcement?"

"Twelve years."

"You like it?"

He frowned at her, hoping she'd get the message and cut it out. She gazed back at him, unfazed. "It's a living," he said.

She forked a piece of broccoli. "You're also with a search and rescue team?"

"Rocky Mountain Search and Rescue." He wondered if

she was merely curious or if she was going somewhere with all the questions. "Don't ask me if I like it."

"That was my next question."

"Eat your dinner."

"Hey, I'm just trying to make conversation."

Silence fell between them again when she reached over and used a small container of salt. "You ever been married?" she asked.

He shot her another dark look. "No."

"Why not?"

"Because I never met anyone I wanted to marry."

"No need to get testy."

"Yeah, well, no offense, but I'm not real big on conversation."

"Now there's a surprise." She forked a carrot, then chewed it thoughtfully. "You believe I'm innocent, don't you, Jake?"

"What makes you think that?"

She shrugged. "I can tell."

He tried to concentrate on his meal, but the chicken and vegetables had lost their taste. "This is your last meal until we get back, Blondie. I suggest you eat it while it's hot, try to enjoy it, and stop talking so damn much."

"You want to let me go, but you can't because it goes against your grain, doesn't it?"

He continued eating, avoiding her gaze. "I'm not going to have this conversation with you."

"Really?" she asked sharply.

"Really."

"You want to know what I think, Jake?"

"Not particularly." Sighing, he set down his fork and glared at her. "But I reckon you're going to tell me anyway, aren't you?"

"I think you can't trust me because someone hurt you. My guess is it was a woman. Am I close?"

Jake nearly choked on a piece of carrot. Clearing his throat with a sip of water, he set his plate down and shook his head. "Look, Abby, I really don't want to talk about this."

"Am I right?"

"No."

"Who was she?"

"Nobody."

"I think she would have had to be *someone,* Jake. I mean, you're not the kind of man who would…get involved with just anyone."

"I'm the kind of man who likes to keep my private life private."

"Since we're stuck here together for the next few hours, I thought we could use this time to get to know each other."

"I know all I want to know about you."

"That may be so, but I'm curious about you."

"I'm boring, believe me. You don't want to know."

"You're closed."

"Closed? Well, hell, maybe you could take a hint."

"You're dying to know what I mean by 'closed' aren't you?"

He scowled at her. "Not in the least."

"It means you don't invite people into your life. You don't let them get inside your head, so you don't have to care about them. It means you're not comfortable talking about yourself. You don't like people to know what you're thinking or feeling—"

"And people with hard heads like you just keep digging, don't they?"

Undeterred, she continued. "I mean, look at you. I ask you one little question and you go into a panic."

"Now that's a hoot."

"You're touchy about it, too."

Determined to ignore her, he forced a laugh and resumed

eating. "I suppose you moonlight as a shrink in your spare time."

"What did she do to you?"

"What did *who* do to me?"

"The woman who hurt you."

"Oh, for crying out loud!" Rising abruptly, he took the empty container to the trash bin in the kitchen area. Abby hadn't finished with hers, so she remained by the fire. But Jake could feel her eyes on him, like sunlight coming through a magnifying glass, burning him. Damn, the woman knew how to drive a man nuts.

He went back to the fire, and sat cross-legged on his sleeping bag. Maybe if he turned the tables, she'd stop with the questions.

He shot her a hard look. "While we're playing Twenty Questions, why don't you tell me how you broke out of Buena Vista?"

She looked up from her food and considered him. "Are you asking as a cop, or are you merely curious?"

"I'm asking because I have absolutely no intention of talking to you about my personal life. How's that?"

She took a sip of water, trying to look casual, but Jake could tell the conversation they were about to have was anything but casual for her. "After that night in the shower room, and I figured out that someone didn't want me talking to the wrong person, I realized I wasn't going to survive unless I got out. I knew someone would eventually catch me off guard. That I'd get a knife in my back or have an accident."

"The D.O.C. guys said you had a gun."

"It wasn't a gun…exactly."

"What exactly does *that* mean?"

She bit her lip. "Can I tell you this in confidence?"

"I'm a cop, Abby. I can't—"

"You can, Jake. It's just you and me here. We're stuck

together. When this is over, you're going to go back to your cop life. I'm going to go back to prison for a crime I didn't commit."

He sighed, not liking the way she'd put that. "Okay. Off the record."

"I called…a friend. I told her what was happening. I didn't want to involve her, but I was scared and desperate and we finally…came up with a plan over the phone."

"What was the plan?"

"She came to visit me."

"How did you get the gun?"

"She smuggled it into the prison in her—"

"Whoa!" Jake threw up his hands. "Stop right there."

"—panty hose."

A relieved breath slid between his lips.

"And it wasn't a gun." He must have looked at her blankly, because she explained. "It was a squirt gun."

"A squirt gun?"

She nodded. "I've never used a gun, so I probably couldn't hit the broad side of a barn. And then there's that nifty metal detector at the prison entrance."

"You mean to tell me you broke out of Buena Vista Corrections Center for Women with a *squirt* gun?"

"Turns out I didn't need it." She bit her lip. "I know it sounds crazy."

"That appears to be the theme we've been keeping."

"Evidently."

"How did you plan to clear your name?" he asked after a moment.

She slanted him a look, her eyes cool. "Are you asking as a cop, Jake?"

He stared back, realized he was—and that he would use it against her if he had to. He hoped it never came to that. Her status as an escaped con aside, he'd grown to like Abby

Nichols. Hell, he'd even developed a strange sort of respect for her. "Maybe I am."

"In that case, I'll take the fifth." Turning away from him, she walked over to the duster hanging near the mantel and pulled it down. "Nice and dry," she said to no one in particularly.

The duster made him think of that morning. She'd been wearing it when she'd left the cabin. When he'd tackled her off that horse and come down on top of her. He stared at her, willing himself not to remember the way she'd felt beneath him. The smell of her hair. The way her body had conformed to his. She'd fought surprisingly well for such a small woman. And when that hadn't worked, she'd kissed him, and Jake had lost his mind and kissed her back.

Hell.

He looked down at his hands, realizing he couldn't let what happened between them pass without comment. This situation, his relationship with this woman, was getting more complicated by the minute. If he wasn't careful, he could find himself in serious trouble—if he wasn't already. If she got back to the prison and yelled foul—or God forbid, accused him of sexual contact—Jake could very well find his career down the tubes.

"There's something we need to talk about," he said gruffly.

She didn't even bother to look at him as she folded her sleeping bag and spread it on the floor. "Oh, yeah? What's that?"

"Well, we need to discuss what happened today."

"A lot of things happened today, Jake." She sat on the sleeping bag, pulled the duster around her shoulders and shot him a challenging look. "Do you think you could be a little more specific?"

"I guess you're not going to make this easy on me, are you?"

"I guess not."

Jake scowled. "The…kiss, damn it."

"Oh. That." She busied herself smoothing the duster over her. "It was no big deal."

The offhand way she'd said the words shouldn't have ruffled him, but it did. He didn't want to admit it, but that kiss had definitely been a big deal. Considering he was an officer of the law and she was an escaped convict in his charge, Jake figured the entire fiasco was pretty damn monumental.

"Don't pull that again, Abby."

"Me?"

"Yeah, you."

"If I'm not mistaken, it takes two people to engage in a kiss."

He would have argued the point if she hadn't been right. But she was. He'd kissed her back, and he hated himself for it. True, she might have initiated it, but he should have shown a little restraint and stopped it. Why was it so hard to do the right thing when it came to this woman?

"It was…improper. I'm a cop. I shouldn't have…done that."

"Worried I might tell someone, Jake? Get you into trouble?"

That was only part of the problem. The simple part. The other part wasn't so cut-and-dried. "I'm not going to let you jerk my chain," he growled.

"Don't worry, your secret is safe with me."

This was not playing out the way he'd planned. In fact, nothing was working out the way he planned when it came to this woman.

He stared at her for a long while. She stared back, her expression challenging and, perhaps, a little hurt. He wasn't sure why, but he was having a difficult time reading her. That was unusual for Jake; knowing what people were thinking and feeling was second nature to him. That was what made him such a good cop. Why couldn't he read Abby? Why the hell was he having such a hard time doing the right thing?

"I know a lawyer," he said, after a moment. "He's top notch. Criminal law. I could ask him to look into your case."

A kaleidoscope of emotions scrolled across her features. Shock. Disbelief. Gratitude. Jake didn't want to see any of them, didn't want to know what she was feeling. He knew that kind of insight would take him one step closer to knowing her. He did not want to get any closer to Abby Nichols.

"I'm going outside to keep watch." Abruptly, he plucked his duster from the floor and started toward the door. He heard her say something to him, but he didn't stop. She was too close, and he was feeling the proximity like heat from a stove. He'd stay outside until she was asleep. At least then he wouldn't have to look into the violet depths of her eyes and think about everything she'd been through. At least then he wouldn't be tempted to make another mistake.

At least, he wouldn't be tempted to believe her.

Abby wasn't sure what woke her. One minute she was sleeping soundly in her sleeping bag a few feet from the fire. The next she was sitting bolt upright, listening...for what?

The embers in the fire hissed quietly. A few feet away Jake was huddled in his sleeping bag, his breathing regular and slow. Around her, the cabin was pitch-black and freezing cold. She shivered, not sure if it was from the cold or the uneasiness slinking through her. Rising, she moved closer to the fire and stuck out her hands to warm them.

If Jake hadn't caught up with her this morning, she could very well have been in New Mexico right now, sitting in

Grams's kitchen where she would feel safe and warm and loved.

As the rising heat warmed her fingers, she listened to the wind tearing around the cabin outside. She didn't relish the idea of venturing out in the cold, but wondered if she should just make a run for it—even in her weakened condition. She knew the hypothermia she'd suffered from earlier was the only reason Jake hadn't handcuffed her to the chair.

Biting her lip, she looked over at him, felt that odd sensation of freefalling she got every time she looked at him. Even in sleep his expression was…uncompromising. She could see his face against the firelight. The lean slant of his jaw. The thick slash of brow. Lips that were far too sensuous for a male.

Images from the kiss they'd shared earlier in the day assailed her. She closed her eyes against the heady rush of pleasure. She knew the kiss had been a mistake, but for a moment, as he'd held her in his arms and made love to her mouth with his, she'd felt cherished. As though she was beautiful and desirable and the threat of spending her life behind bars wasn't hanging over her head like a dark cloud.

Abruptly she turned away. What was she *thinking?* Just because she'd liked the way he'd kissed her didn't mean she was going to go off the deep end, did it? Abby was off men for good, thank you very much. The only reason she'd kissed him anyway was to distract him. To see if she could get to him. Men were the most predictable creatures on God's earth, and by-the-book Jake Madigan wasn't any different. If and when the time came, Abby knew she could use that weakness against him.

Even if it meant selling her soul.

She wanted to believe he'd meant what he'd said about helping her with a lawyer once they got back. She wanted to trust him. She wanted to believe him. God, how stupid did that make her? She'd once believed Jonathan Reed, too.

She'd believed his promises, trusted him. She'd covered for him and lied to the police in the process—a mistake that had ended up costing her her freedom. When it came time for him to deliver on those promises, Reed'd cut her loose.

Abby knew Jake wasn't any different. He might make promises now, while he was with her, while he was attracted to her. But after they got back, when the lust cooled and she was sitting alone in her cold cell and Jake Madigan was a hundred miles away, he wasn't going to be thinking about her. He wasn't going to go out on a limb.

If she had a lick of sense, she'd muster the strength somehow and take off right now.

She was seriously considering doing just that when a sound at the door drew her attention, freezing her in place. The wind? she wondered. Had Jake left the door open? Not likely with a mad sniper on the loose. The thought made the hairs on her nape stand on end.

The door hinge creaked. Sensing danger, Abby stepped back. Adrenaline stabbed her gut. Someone was out there. Someone was coming in.

"Jake!" she shouted.

An instant later the door burst open and swung wide. A dark shadow loomed toward her.

Abby screamed.

"Shut up, bitch!"

She heard a *whoosh!* then something hard struck her temple. Pain streaked down the side of her face. Pinpoints of light flashed, long yellow tails flaring like shooting stars. She reeled backward, realizing the son of a bitch had hit her.

"Bastard!" she heard herself say. "Nobody hits me and—"

The blast of a gun cut her words short. My God, she thought dully, he's going to kill me.

"Get down!" Jake's voice cut through her shock. Strong

arms wrapped around her and flung her to the floor. Abby screamed as she went down, but knew Jake was only protecting her. Risking his own life to keep her safe....

Another blast rocked the air. She couldn't see in the darkness, couldn't hear for the thundering of her heart. She felt Jake leave her. Heard the thud of his boots on the plank floor. She saw a shadow against the window. A dark blur moving fast. But she couldn't tell if it was Jake or the intruder.

She scrambled to her hands and knees, looked around blindly. Where was the rifle? Where had Jake put it? She heard the shuffle of footsteps across the room. Jake's curse burning through the air. Another gunshot exploded. Her ears rang with the blast. Her heart pounded like a freight train in her ears, pumping fear through every inch of her body.

Abruptly, everything went silent. Abby crouched, deaf and blind, fear slithering like a cold snake inside her.

"Hey."

Rough hands gripped her. She tried to twist away, but the hands held her firm, lifted her to her feet.

"Abby. Easy, it's me. Jake."

"Oh, Jake. He was going to—"

"Are you hurt?

"Where is he? Oh, God, where—"

"Shh. Easy. Just...take it easy."

"Is he..."

"He's gone." His hands swept down her arms, back up to her shoulders. Abby noticed he was shaking and knew she wasn't the only one who was scared half to death.

"Are you hurt?" he asked.

"I'm okay."

He hesitated as if he didn't quite believe her, then squeezed her arms reassuringly. "You sure you're okay?"

"I'm f-fine. What about you?"

"I'm ticked off."

"A little too close for comfort, huh?"

"Something like that." Still gripping her shoulders, he turned his head toward the door. It was standing wide open, snow and cold air swirling into the cabin. "Stay here. I'm going after him."

Because she couldn't speak, she nodded.

His gaze bored into hers. "We both know you're in no condition to run away, don't we, Abby?"

"Yes," she whispered, and Jake Madigan disappeared into the night like a phantom.

Chapter 10

The shakes hit her thirty seconds later. Abby was still standing where Jake had left her, staring at the door he'd closed behind him, trying to decide what to do next, when her knees turned to water. Her stomach clenched and for a terrible moment she thought she would be sick. By the time she made it to the fireplace, the tremors had grown violent, starting with her hands and traveling through her body like a shockwave.

After spending the last year in prison, she'd come to believe that she could endure almost anything, that nothing could shock her or shake her up inside.

Gunfights definitely shook her up.

She stood in the cold darkness for a long time, gripping the mantel above the hearth, listening to her labored breathing and the dull thud of her heart. She didn't know how long she stood there. Her mind kept replaying what had happened. The shock of pain when the assailant had struck her. The flash of the gun. She could feel the cold air pooling at her feet. She could hear the wind outside, feel the cabin trembling beneath its force. The stench of spent powder and violence hung heavy in the air.

She couldn't believe someone had just tried to kill her.

After a while, the shock eased its grip. Mechanically, she picked up two logs and added them to the fire. She wondered where Jake was, if he was okay. She told herself she wasn't worried about him. Jake could take care of himself. She wondered what kind of man risked his life to protect an escaped convict.

Needing something to do, she picked up the kettle, took it outside and filled it with snow. Back inside, she melted it over the fire. When the water was warm, she set about washing her face and hands. Her temple hurt where she'd been hit, but the water felt good against her skin. It was too cold for her to get really wet, but she didn't care. She felt…dirty, as if the man who'd come in out of the darkness had somehow tainted her with his violent touch.

Only then did she realize she was crying.

The realization left her incredulous. Abby Nichols didn't cry easily. But with the predawn light filtering through the grimy windows, she sloshed water over her face and neck and cried openly. She thought about Fate and all the things she'd wanted for her life. She thought about Jake and all the things she could never have. She thought about Grams, waiting in her little house in New Mexico and wished to God she could talk to her.

The water calmed her emotions, washed away the remnants of violence the man had left on her skin like a greasy smear. But it didn't help with the shaking. She couldn't tell if it was the remnants of terror or the cold that made her tremble, but she couldn't stop. For the first time since she'd left the prison, she was afraid. Someone was trying to kill her, and from the looks of things, they were pretty damn serious about it.

Abby was dressed and putting another log on the fire when the door swung open. Jake stomped in on a blast of cold air and flurry of snow. He hadn't bothered with his duster or gloves. He was shivering. She thought she'd never seen a man look as dangerous as Jake did standing there staring at her, shaking with cold and anger and something else she couldn't readily identify.

"Are you okay?" she asked.

"Fine."

"Did you find him?"

"No." He started toward her. "He was on a snowmobile."

She thought about that a moment. "Do you think it was a professional hit?"

He didn't answer right away. Abby could clearly see he was irate. His eyes were hard and dark as smoke. His jaw clamped tight. It was obvious Jake Madigan didn't like to lose.

She was still absorbing that information when he stepped close to her, his eyes narrowing. "He hurt you."

"I—I'm okay," she stammered, taken aback by the sudden intensity in his eyes.

"He hit you."

She'd nearly forgotten, though her temple throbbed dully. Oddly embarrassed, she turned her head away. But Jake lifted his hand, cupped her chin with his fingers, and forced her head around so he could see the bump on her temple.

"That son of a bitch."

"It's okay—"

"No, it's not okay. Goddamm it, he *hit* you."

She choked out a nervous laugh. "I'm just glad he didn't *shoot* me."

Jake didn't laugh. Taking her shoulders, he guided her over to the hearth, then turned her toward him to get a better look. His face darkened with fury as he inspected the bruise on her temple.

Abby had seen him angry, but never like this. She'd never seen that dangerous light in his eyes. "Jake, I'm okay," she said.

"You're bruised."

"Hey, what's a little bruise in the scope of things, you know? It's all right."

"It's not all right. Damn it, Abby, you didn't deserve that. You don't deserve any of this."

"Jake—"

"He nearly killed you." He blew out a breath. "Hell."

She wanted to tell him to calm down; told herself she could handle this man's intensity. She'd dealt with worse in the past year and a half. But Jake was quickly overwhelming her with this protective-male stuff. She wondered where it was coming from. Wondered if it had anything to do with that streak of gentleman she knew ran so deep in him.

"I'm sorry he hurt you," he said. "I wish I could have stopped it."

His gaze pierced her. Abby couldn't move. Her heart beat a rapid tattoo against her ribs. She could feel the anger coming through him into her. He was shaking, his face taut.

"I'm going to get some snow, make a compress," he said. "Stay here."

"Okay," she said, a little stunned.

He walked out the door without his coat and returned with a pail full of snow. She watched as he took a handful and wrapped a fresh rag around it. Back at the hearth, he stood in front of her and pressed it to her temple.

Abby winced.

"Sorry," he said. "Sore?"

"A little."

"This will help stop the swelling, might even help with the bruising."

"Hey, with your eye and my temple, we could be twins."

He wasn't amused. "Ha, ha."

"People are going to think we got into a fight."

"We did."

Despite the lingering fear and the cold realization of how differently things could have turned out, Abby smiled.

Across from her, Jake concentrated on keeping the ice against her temple. His left hand rested gently on her bicep. Slowly, she felt him relax one degree at a time. The hard lines of his face softened. She hadn't realized it before, but Jake Madigan made a frightening picture when he was angry.

"You're making a habit of saving my life, you know," she said.

"That's my job."

"Well, you're really good at it."

He looked her straight in the eyes. "I'm good at a lot of things."

Abby swallowed hard, felt her heart kick against her breastbone. She wanted to say something back to him, but her brain seemed to have short-circuited. She wanted to think it was because of the stress of the situation. The storm. The close quarters. The madman with a gun. But she knew her reaction had more to do with the way he was looking at her.

Images from their tussle in the snow that morning came to her unbidden. Her lying in the snow. Him on top of her, solid and warm and pressed against her as intimately as a lover. She tried not to think about the kiss—she knew better than to toss gasoline into a flame—but the memory taunted her with its forbidden sweetness. She remembered the look of utter astonishment in his eyes when she'd pressed her mouth to his. The way his body had jolted. The instant of his surrender. Then his firm mouth had taken hers captive. He'd shifted closer. The growl of frustration in his throat when he'd realized he couldn't get any closer. All the things he'd done to her mouth with his tongue....

Yes, she thought dazedly, Jake Madigan definitely knew how to kiss a woman. She wanted him to kiss her now. Wanted his firm mouth against hers. Wanted to feel him surrender to her.

Desire flickered like a hot flame in her belly. She told herself none of this was going to matter in the long run. That she could give in to the needs churning inside her and kiss this man and not suffer any consequences. It wasn't as if a kiss was going to change anything. It certainly wasn't going to mean anything. It couldn't.

She stared up at him. His flint-gray eyes had softened to the color of a twilight sky. That magical moment between day and night when the stars were born and the last vestiges of the sunset died on the horizon.

"What are you thinking?" she whispered.

"Things I shouldn't be."

"Why not?"

"Because I know better." His jaw flexed. "So do you."

Abby knew they were playing with fire, and getting much too close to the flames. She knew she would probably be the one to get burned. But for a little while she didn't want to care. She didn't want to think about repercussions or right or wrong. All she wanted was for this man to kiss her.

She knew he was going to an instant before he moved. He leaned toward her, his eyes darkening like the summer sky before a storm. Abby thought she was prepared. But the instant he touched his mouth to hers, all bets were off.

Jake didn't just kiss her. He devoured her mouth with a hunger that sucked the oxygen from her lungs and left her head spinning like a top. The floor tilted crazily beneath her. If she hadn't reached up and put her arms around his shoulders, she would have slunk to the floor into a boneless heap.

His mouth fused to hers, and Abby's senses exploded.

She tasted heat and the heady taste of aroused male. A man who knew what he wanted and wasn't afraid to take it, consequences be damned. She heard labored breathing, but she wasn't sure if it was his or hers. Bright light burst behind her eyes. All the while, his mouth danced with hers, an unyielding partner who liked to lead and didn't mind stepping on her toes.

At some point, the cold compress left her temple. She felt restless hands on her shoulders, skimming down her back, then lower. His shoulders were like steel beneath her fingers, corded and fraught with tension. It had been a long time since a man had touched her, and Abby's senses heightened to a fever pitch. Every touch, every shudder, seemed multiplied exponentially, racing through her body and exploding in her brain like a powerful drug.

His hands fell to her hips. Large hands that were calloused from manual labor, yet gentle enough to heal wounds and ease pain. He held her against him with those hands and she could feel the hard length of him at her feminine core, straining closer, burning her with the intensity of his need.

She opened her mouth, for a breath or maybe to gasp, she wasn't sure, but he took the opportunity and deepened the kiss. His teeth clicked against hers, his tongue going deep, penetrating her. Abby accepted him, rode with the dizziness stealing her equilibrium. In the back of her mind she wondered how she would survive this. If he could knock her senseless with just a kiss, how was she going to react if they took this any further?

Jake couldn't remember the last time he'd lost his head. Maybe the day he'd been fifteen and watched little Jimmy Baine get sucked under the ice.

He'd known he was going to do something stupid and screw this up sooner or later. The writing had been on the wall since the moment he'd sat in on the briefing at RMSAR headquarters and seen this woman's mug shot and those incredible violet eyes.

Kissing her like this definitely qualified as stupid.

And he'd definitely lost his cool.

But she made his blood pound like no other woman he'd ever met. One taste of her mouth and he couldn't stop. He couldn't even *see* straight. The woman made him crazy with needs he swore he'd never give in to, made him glad to relinquish the control he'd always prided himself on having. Made him wonder if maybe she was worth making a mistake for.

Need and frustration coiled and snapped inside him as he kissed her. Arousal flared hot and deep in his groin. And her mouth... Her mouth was making him nuts. She tasted sweet, like ripe, succulent fruit, and Jake wanted to devour her.

Kissing this way wasn't his usual modus operandi with women. Jake had always prided himself on being a gentleman. On being slow and thorough and sure. He respected women and treated them with dignity. He was a gentle lover and never caved in to urgency. He'd never been prone to wildly hot kisses and groping like some fuzz-face teenager struggling with his first bout of hormones.

But he couldn't stop kissing her, didn't want to stop touching her. He didn't care about consequences or regret, or pause to think about where this might lead.

Her body was soft and fragile and warm against his. Her scent was inside his head. The feel of her body against his was in his blood, setting his veins on fire. Kissing her, he ran his fingers through her hair, tangled them in the thick mass of curls. He wanted to get lost in her hair. He wanted to get inside her. Wanted to feel her wet heat wrap around him.

She was pressed snugly against him. He could feel her

breasts against his chest, her heart raging against his, and felt another layer of his control flutter away. Running his hands over her hips and sides, he slipped his hands between them and cupped her breasts. She gasped and arched. He molded her flesh with his fingers. Her breasts were small and firm and filled his palms like soft fruits. Even through the thick fabric of the jumpsuit, he could feel the hardened peaks of her nipples.

His control teetered. Growling low in his throat, he deepened the kiss. The need to touch her jumped through him like an electrical surge. Sweat broke out on the back of his neck.

Gently, he unzipped her jumpsuit, slipped his hands inside. Making a small sound in her throat, she arched against him. His knees went weak at the feel of her bare flesh against his palms. He caressed her nipples with his fingertips. She shivered in his arms. He slid his hands down her belly, over taut, quivering flesh. His fingers brushed the soft cotton of her panties. His heart went wild in his chest, the need pounding through him with every beat. She whispered something in his ear, but he couldn't hear her, didn't understand the words. Every cell in his brain focused on the pleasure coursing through him. The pressure of her mouth against his. The softness of her flesh. Her scent inside his head, driving him crazy with the need for more of her.

His fingers found the crisp curls at her vee. She stiffened against him, but he didn't stop. He separated her, then dipped two fingers into wet heat.

Abby jolted in his arms, crying out softly.

"Easy," he whispered, and began to stroke her. Once. Twice.

When she opened to him, Jake closed his eyes and he was lost. To reason. To sanity. He was as lost as any hiker had ever been in the vast wilderness of the Rocky Mountains. The ache in his groin was a physical pain. A sweet ache that echoed through his body like the flu, intoxicating him like a drug, making him believe in the impossible and want crazy things.

Sexual contact with an escaped convict was definitely crazy.

Jake had made plenty of mistakes over the years. He figured he'd learned something from most of them, and the lesson had been worth the cost. This was different. If he let this go any further, it was going to end up costing both of them far more than they were willing to pay.

What the hell was he *thinking* throwing his career away for a convict? A woman who had no compunction about manipulating him to get what she wanted? A woman who threatened his control so that he was willing to risk everything he'd ever worked for for just one taste of her mouth?

The questions dragged him back to his senses. Back to his own personal code of honor. To his career as a law enforcement officer. To his dignity. Back to a situation that was every bit as dangerous to him as the man with a rifle outside.

It took every bit of discipline he could muster to pull away from her, but he did. His body wasn't happy about it, and frustration snapped through him like a bull whip. He knew better than to risk everything for something as simple as lust.

The problem was, there hadn't been anything even remotely simple about what had just happened between them.

"This is wrong," he said in a hoarse voice.

She stepped back, her cheeks flushed, her lips kiss-bruised and wet. Grasping the edges of her jumpsuit with white-knuckled hands, she reached for the zipper and jerked it up to her chin. Her violet eyes were wide and wary and didn't quite meet his. She was breathing hard, her breasts rising and falling with each breath. He could still feel the warmth of her flesh against his palms. Her wetness on his fingers. The hard nubs of her nipples where they'd brushed against his chest. Frustration burned him. The realization of how close he'd come to making an irrevocable mistake shamed him.

"I'm...sorry," he said. "I shouldn't have let that happen."

Turning away from him, she hugged herself as if from a chill. Her shoulders were rigid. Her head down. He wanted to go to her, but he didn't. He could only imagine how she must feel. Used. Humiliated. And he refused to acknowledge the sharp edge of need stabbing him in the gut.

Jake didn't usually feel the need to talk. Silence usually suited him just fine. Even so, he found himself scrambling for something to say. "That was...my fault." The words sounded lame even to him.

"Mine, too," she said. "I mean, I don't take things like what just happened between us lightly."

"Yeah, well, here's a news flash for you, Blondie. Neither do I."

She turned to face him, her eyes seeking his. Jake stared at her mouth, aroused and wanting her no matter how wrong it was. She must have noticed because she stepped back, bit her lip. "We got...carried away. We've been...cooped up together. You know, close quarters. It could happen to anyone."

Pinching the bridge of his nose, Jake lowered his head and let out a humorless laugh. "I'm a cop, Abby. Do you have any idea what I've done by..." Hell, he wasn't sure how to finish the sentence. What *had* he just done? "Sexual misconduct with a prisoner? That's...inexcusable."

"Jake—"

"The corrections guys who take advantage of the women inmates. Hell, Abby, they're worse than scum. Damn it, it happens a lot, and I've just done the same thing."

Her eyes heated. "Is that what I am to you, Jake? An inmate?"

"I shouldn't have touched you."

"It's not like you were doing it against my will."

"I'm a cop, Abby! Do you have any idea how serious an offense it is for me to…touch you like that?"

"Afraid for your job?" she asked nastily.

It was more than his job. He didn't want to say it. But he figured they both knew it. "That was worse than irresponsible, Abby. You've got the right to file a complaint with the sheriff's department against me when we get back," he said tightly.

"I'm not going to file a complaint."

"I shouldn't have let this get out of hand."

"This isn't out of hand. We'll…take responsibility for our actions like two adults and move on, okay?"

"I can't let this matter, Abby. Damn it, I can't let *you* matter."

The flash of pain in her eyes came and went so quickly, he wasn't sure if he'd seen it at all. But he could tell by the way her eyes skated away that the statement had hurt her. She didn't cry; she wouldn't now, he knew. Abby Nichols was too tough to cry. But the pain shimmering in her eyes was unmistakable, and Jake felt like a bastard for putting it there.

He wanted to go to her, wanted to wrap his arms around her and pull her against him. He wanted to take away her hurt. Tell her that everything was going to be all right. But he knew it wasn't. Not for Abby Nichols. And, damn it, not for him.

Sleep refused to come to Jake again. He spent the pre-dawn hours walking the cabin, going from window to window, watching for the sniper, thinking about the truckload of mistakes he'd made in the last twenty-four hours. He tried not to think of the woman sleeping on the other side of the room. The way she'd felt when he'd held her. The way she bit her lip when she was nervous. The sound of her laughter. The haunted expression on her face when she spoke of the time she'd spent in prison. The way those eyes knocked him for a loop every time he looked at her.

He'd crossed a line with her. Not only with his professional code of ethics, but a personal line, too, that disturbed him even more. After Elaine, Jake had sworn he'd never be taken in again. Elaine had wormed her way into his life. Used her female charms to get under his skin, her little boy to gain access to his heart. He'd fallen for her, and she'd made a fool of him. Worse, Jake had allowed it. He'd been in so deep with her—with her child—he'd refused to read the writing on the wall. He'd compromised himself. And because he hadn't had the strength to do the right thing, he'd sold himself out and she'd stepped in and cut out his heart.

How could he even consider making the same mistake with Abby? She'd escaped from prison, tried to manipulate him with her body. She'd told him a crazy story about transplant organs and a respected doctor. Why had he let her get to him? Why on earth did he *believe* her? Why couldn't he do the right thing and turn the other cheek and let the legal system work?

Because you got it bad for her, Madigan. Just like you did for Elaine, and look where that got you.

Bracing his hand against the mantel above the hearth, Jake leaned forward and brooded into the fire. Regardless of how he felt about Abby, he was going to have to take her back. He should have felt better having made that decision. It was the right thing to do. The only sane thing to do.

For the life of him he couldn't figure out why that didn't make him feel any better.

Dawn broke with a sky full of brilliant sunshine and temperatures that hovered just below freezing. The wind had finally died and Jake fervently hoped Tony Colorosa and the rest of the RMSAR team would be out in full force.

He woke Abby when the coffee was brewed. He handed her a cup, unable to keep himself from noticing how beautiful she'd looked curled in her sleeping bag. The urge to touch her tested his resolve, but Jake steeled himself against it and put the thought out of his mind. With the same cool professionalism he used with all the prisoners he'd transported, he informed her she had fifteen minutes to wash up, eat a few nuts and raisins and meet him outside.

By eight o'clock, they were mounted up and heading east, toward the nearest ranger station. Jake was still uneasy about the sniper, so he'd decided on a secondary trail that was protected by aspen and pines and rocky ridges no man could scale on a snowmobile. It would take a little longer to get where they were going, but he figured it was worth it to avoid getting shot.

"How long until we arrive?" she asked.

Jake looked over at her, felt that familiar tightening in his chest at the sight of her. She'd found something to pull her hair back with. She looked lovely with her hair away from her face. Her cheekbones were high and tinged pink from the cold. Her brows were thin and very dark over her violet eyes. The woman made an unforgettable picture. A picture that would be with him for a long, long time.

"We should make it by dark," he said. "If the snow doesn't slow us down too much."

"This trail doesn't look like it gets used often."

"The other trail is too open. I didn't want to take any chances with the sniper."

Abby glanced over her shoulder uneasily. Her face was pale. For a second her eyes had the wild look of a scared animal, and he knew she was remembering the close call from the night before. The bump on her temple was just beginning to turn purple. Jake hated seeing it, hated knowing someone had hurt her, wanted to hurt her some more. As much as he hated to admit it, he was beginning to feel protective of her.

How you going to feel handing her over to D.O.C., hot shot?

The question made him wince. Prison was no place for a woman like Abby. It would destroy her. The notion of seeing her spirit crushed by such a harsh life tortured him. Most of the criminals he put in jail deserved to be there. Most were hardened. Violent. Remorseless. Abby was none of those things. She possessed a very real softness that made her all too human. A vulnerability she disguised with layers of toughness. But those layers were as gossamer as a butterfly's wings. He couldn't fathom her hurting anyone. Not in a million years. Yet here he was, taking her back....

A sliver of guilt pierced Jake. He wasn't sure exactly when it had happened, but at some point he'd come to the conclusion that Abby was not a killer. Even if she had injected that patient with the wrong drug, Jake knew in his gut it had been an accident. Things weren't adding up. Not the woman in his charge. Or the sniper determined to snuff out her life. And as much as he didn't want to believe it, his instincts were telling him it all had to do with one Dr. Jonathan Reed at Mercy General Hospital in Denver.

"I've been thinking about your case," he said after a moment.

She shot him a wary look.

"You've told me enough for me to know the D.A.'s case was shot full of holes." When she still didn't respond, he slowed his horse and let her pull up beside him. "I thought I'd look into your case after we get back. Check out a couple of things."

"Don't say something because you feel guilty about what happened back at the cabin."

Jake swung around to face her, quick anger snapping through him. "That doesn't have a damn thing to do with—"

"Don't say something you'll regret later. Just because we...we..."

"This has nothing to do with what happened between us at the cabin last night."

She slanted him a nasty look. "You're feeling guilty."

"You're damn right I'm feeling guilty."

"Because you acted inappropriately with a prisoner? Or maybe it's because you don't want anyone to know about it and this is your way of placating me."

Jake said nothing, his temper simmering.

"Forgive me if I don't believe you."

"Look, Abby, you've told me some things about your case that need to be checked out." When she wouldn't stop her mount, he snagged the mule's lead rope and stopped both animals. "Damn it, listen to me."

"For God's sake, Jake, don't get my hopes up." For the first time, emotion rang in her voice. It hit Jake like a tuning fork held against a broken bone. "Please," she said. "Don't make promises you can't keep. I'm really not up to the disappointment."

"Abby—"

"If you want to do the right thing, let me go."

"I can't do that."

"I'm dead if you take me back."

Jake recoiled inwardly. "I'll make sure you're put under watch."

"Oh, that's big of you. Always looking out for my best interest. A twenty-four-hour guard will be terrific—"

"The police aren't going to stop looking for you. If don't take you back, someone else will."

"I won't let them catch me."

"You're exhausted and have absolutely no way to travel."

"You could give me a head start."

Jake laughed, but it was a bitter sound in the silence of the forest trail. "And in case you've forgotten, there's a sniper on the loose who evidently doesn't want you around—"

"I'd rather take my chances with the sniper."

"Use your head, Abby. Handle this through the legal system. I'll help you—"

"Don't say it, damn you."

"This isn't personal, Abby."

"It is for me. Saving my life is very, very personal."

Jake ran his hand over his face and struggled for patience. He wasn't sure how to deal with all the bitterness and pain. "Abby...."

She wouldn't even look at him, just stared straight ahead, as if he wasn't even there. What did she expect him to say? Jeez, who knew what was going on in a woman's head at any given time? He sure as hell didn't. As far as he was concerned women really *were* from another planet.

"Do you understand?" he asked after a moment.

"Oh, yeah. I gotcha, Cop. Loud and clear."

They traveled through deep snow for another hour, tension filling the chasm between them. Jake had realized in the last few days that Abby liked to chat. He found himself missing that today. He missed her smart-aleck remarks, her dry wit, her sense of humor. He hated seeing her so discouraged, so...hopeless.

Struggling to keep his mind off of her, he focused his attention on the animal beneath him, on making good time. He kept his eyes on the surrounding ridges for signs of the sniper. He was uneasy traveling in the open, and there were several places where the trail opened up and they could easily be picked off by a sniper's bullet. The thought made the hairs on his nape prickle.

Two hours later, he pulled Brandywine up next to the mule and stopped. "You hungry?"

"No."

"You're quiet."

"I don't think there's much else to say." For the first time in a while, she looked at him. Jake almost wished she hadn't. The anguish in her eyes made his chest ache.

"But I would like to know one thing," she said.

"What's that?"

"I need to know if you believe me."

"Abby...." He sighed, not sure what to say next.

She looked away abruptly, blinking rapidly. "Okay."

"That's not a fair question," he said lamely.

She raised her hand, silencing him. "That's enough. That tells me all I need to know. Forget it, okay?"

"Damn it, it's not that simple."

"Yes, it is, Jake. It's infinitely simple. Either you do or you don't. Evidently, you don't." She stared at him, her expression level and far too calm. "I can accept that. I just...after everything that's happened, I...needed to know."

"Abby, I—"

"Don't say anything else. Please."

"Listen, whether I believe you is *not* the problem."

"Then what *is* the problem?" she cried.

"That I *do* believe you, and I don't have the slightest idea what I'm going to do about it!"

She stared at him, her expression stricken. Tears shimmered in her eyes like liquid amethysts. Then she simply broke. Lowering her face into her hands, she began to cry. It was the first display of weakness he'd seen in her and it tore at him like claws.

"If you take me back, it's over," she choked. "I can't let you do that to me."

"I'll make sure you're protected from whomever is trying to get to you."

"Forgive me if my faith in the criminal justice system is a little shaky right now."

"I've got some contacts in different police agencies. These guys are sharp. They know the ropes. Hell, I'll look into your case myself. I'll do everything in my power to—"

"Let me go, Jake."

"I can't do that."

"Damn it—"

"You can't survive up here in the high country by yourself! Look at the problems we've had since we've been up here. The storm. You falling through the ice. The sniper. I've been doing this since I was old enough to walk. You don't have that kind of experience. You don't have any gear. You don't have supplies. You don't even have a compass. Another storm comes along and you won't make it out of these mountains alive."

"I'd rather die than go back!"

Anger and guilt churned like hot tar in his gut. He pointed his finger at her, felt his lips pull back in a snarl. "Don't let me hear you say that again."

"Why not? I'm dead either way. At least if you leave me up here, I'll have a fighting chance."

The thought of her dying such a needless, senseless death sickened him. "That's a chance I'm not willing to take."

"You take me back and it's out of your hands."

A cold fist of dread twisted savagely in his gut and for a moment he couldn't take a breath. "I know the ropes, Abby. I'll talk to D.O.C. I'll—"

"Do you actually think the cops are going to believe you after...this? They're going to take one look at...us and the accusations will start flying."

He didn't want to believe it, but he knew it was true. A male officer and a female inmate trapped in a cabin for two days was fair game for anyone's imagination. "They're not going to know anything happened between us." God, he hated the way that sounded. Officers of the law who took advantage of female inmates were lower than scum in Jake's mind. Saying out loud what he'd allowed to happen between them made it sound as though he was no better, as though he'd taken advantage of a situation. That was twisted as hell, and it made him feel lousy.

"If you feel the need to tell someone about what happened, then you should," he said evenly. "I'm not going to ask you to protect me. I was clearly out of line."

"Stop being so damn honorable, will you?"

He didn't see anything honorable about anything he'd done since setting foot on this mountain with her, but he didn't say as much.

"Jake," she said quietly, "the moment you speak out on my behalf, you know what the reaction is going to be." She looked down where her hands twisted on the horn. "Tell me someone isn't going to jump to conclusions about...how we spent two days together in that cabin."

She had a point. A filthy point that stuck in his craw like a needle. Jake hated it more than anything. Taking off his hat, he raked his fingers through his hair and cursed.

What a mess.

He was about to suggest they get going and discuss this on the way, when sudden pain streaked through his left side, just below his rib cage, as if someone had slammed a red-hot branding iron into him. Jake grunted, the impact nearly knocking him from the saddle. An instant later, a rifle retort echoed in the distance.

Vaguely, he heard Abby's voice call out to him. He looked down, saw a tear in his duster. Opening it, he saw blood coming through his shirt on his left side, just above his belt. Oh hell, he thought dully. He'd been shot.

Glancing up at the ridge to the north, he thought he saw movement, and slid the rifle from its sheath. Taking aim, gritting his teeth against the pain, he squeezed off two shots.

Behind him, he heard Abby urging the mule closer. "Jake!" she cried. "My God, you're bleeding!"

"I'm okay." He motioned toward the line of trees. "Take cover!"

But she kept coming, and there was only one way to keep her out of the line of fire. Leaning forward, he grabbed the mule's lead rope and nudged his mare into a gallop.

"Hang on!" Clutching his side, Jake took them down a treacherously steep ravine toward a copse of aspen, praying the bullet wound in his side wasn't as bad as it felt.

Chapter 11

Abby should have been accustomed to medical emergencies. She'd been an ER nurse for more than four years at Mercy General, after all. She'd seen all kinds of injuries from motor vehicle trauma to heart attacks to sprained ankles and broken bones. She'd even seen a bullet wound once when a local police officer had gotten into a shootout with a robbery suspect.

She wasn't sure why she was panicking now, but she could taste it at the back of her throat like the bitter aftertaste of rank medicine. At least she'd survived the ride down the side of that blasted ravine. Jake must have been thinking she was some kind of trick rider, taking the animals down a treacherous slope like that. As she slid off of Rebel Yell, she promised herself if they ever got out of this mess, she was going to kill Jake Madigan.

He was already off his horse and lashing the reins to a low branch of a nearby pine when she reached him. His back was to her, but she could hear him cursing.

"Son of a—"

"Let me see it," she said, coming up behind him.

On an oath, he turned to her. Worry quivered through her when she saw the sweat beading on a forehead that was nearly as pale as the snow.

"I think he just winged me," he growled. "But it hurts like hell."

"I'm a nurse. Let me see it."

Clutching his side, he walked over to a fallen tree and leaned against the gnarled trunk of a piñon pine. Abby followed and brushed the snow from the trunk. "Sit down," she said.

Jake yanked off his duster and jacket, then pulled his shirttail out of his jeans. "Damn it, it burns like a son of a—"

"Yeah, well, bullets tend to do that when they rip through flesh."

He scowled at her. "I was wondering when you were going to get around to your smart remarks."

"Just trying to keep your mind off the pain." Lifting his shirt, Abby glanced down at the wound and swallowed hard. The bullet had dug a jagged path just over his lowest rib. It would require a few stitches, but it didn't look as if there was a hole so the slug probably hadn't lodged inside his body. Of course, it could have broken that rib....

"It's just a graze," she said.

"Lucky me."

"It's bleeding pretty badly, but I don't think it's life-threatening."

"Things are definitely looking up," he said through clenched teeth.

Her hands trembled when she reached up to unbutton his shirt. She tried not to look him in the eye as she worked the buttons, but she could feel his gaze on her. Like the sun warming her skin—and her knowing it would be burned later. She wasn't sure if it was the remnants of adrenaline or being this close to Jake, but her blood was pumping furiously.

"I need to stop the bleeding," she said.

"I'm leaking bad, huh?"

"Bad enough. You're going to need stitches. Where's the first-aid kit?"

"Saddlebag. Right side."

Rising, Abby jogged over to Brandywine and flung open the saddlebag. She took out the kit and walked back over to Jake and knelt in front of him. "This is probably going to hurt."

"It already hurts."

"Well, then it's going to hurt even more. I've got to apply direct pressure to stop the bleeding. Bullet bounced off your rib. I think it may be cracked or even broken."

"Just my luck."

She tore open the cover off a sterile gauze, set it against the wound and pressed it down with the palm of her hand.

Jake groaned. "You weren't kidding, were you?" he snarled.

"Sorry. The rib?"

He jerked his head. "Yup."

She hated hurting him, but they were both medical professionals and knew there was no other way to stop the bleeding. "This should only take a few minutes."

"Take your time," he said dryly.

Trying to ignore the sight of his naked abdomen—and her reaction to him—Abby maintained pressure for several minutes. His abdomen was rock hard beneath her fingers and rippled with muscle. She was aware of Jake leaning back against the tree, his arm raised so she had access to his side. She was aware that his body was damp with sweat despite the frosty air—and that every thirty seconds he looked over his shoulder toward the trail.

''I keep wondering how that sniper found us,'' he said after a moment.

Abby lifted the gauze and checked the wound. Much to her relief, the bleeding had slowed. ''I'm going to disinfect, okay?''

Jake nodded, but his eyes were still on the ridge above them and to the north. ''If RMSAR hasn't found us yet, how the hell is this bozo doing it?''

He winced when the antiseptic hit the wound. Abby tried not to notice his muscles tightening beneath her palm. Or the thin layer of fine black hair that ran down his washboard belly to disappear into the low rise of his jeans. But her every sense was honed on Jake. His closeness. His scent. That he knew how to kiss a woman senseless....

''I don't get it,'' he said. ''The only people who knew I was coming up this way to look for you were the people in the briefing room the morning I left.''

''Yeah?'' Abby secured the bandage over the wound. ''Who was that?''

''Buzz Malone. He's the team leader. A couple of medics. Tony Colorosa, our chopper pilot.'' He paused. ''And two suits from D.O.C.''

A chill climbed up Abby's spine. A chill that had absolutely nothing to do with the temperature. And everything to do with the possibility that someone in a position of power within the Department of Corrections didn't necessarily want her to make it back to the ranger station. At least not alive.

She lowered Jake's shirt. When she looked at him, his eyes were already sharp on hers. ''Any idea what's up with that?'' he asked.

''I don't know,'' she said slowly.

''Reed's a doctor, right?''

Her pulse jumped at the mention of his name. ''A surgeon.''

"He's well connected?"

She nodded. "A philanthropist. Charismatic. And very wealthy."

"Money can buy a lot of things."

"People included. What are you saying?"

"Just thinking out loud, mostly."

"You think Reed is behind all of this, don't you?"

"Don't you?"

She thought about it for a moment. "He knows I'm on to what he's been doing. I mean, I've got a big mouth. I've been telling anyone who would listen."

"Can't blame you for that." Jake contemplated her. "Let's think about black market organs for a second."

"Okay."

"Hypothetically speaking, who are his clientele?"

"Wealthy people from all over the world. People who need transplant organs or whose children need them. Most of these people are already on a recipient list. But there just aren't enough organs to go around. I mean, when it comes right down to it, money doesn't really matter when you're waiting for a heart or kidneys or a liver. All the money in the world can't make there be enough organs for everyone who needs one. Everyone is pretty much equal. I mean, at least when it comes to money. Age is sometimes taken into consideration."

"So, there's a donor list," he began, "but because there aren't enough donors, sometimes the people on the list die before a viable organ becomes available."

"Maybe Reed found a way around that little problem." The thought made Abby feel sick to her stomach. The organ donor programs across the country were vital, life-saving programs, and made possible by generous people who were kind enough to sign up so that someone who desperately needed donor organs could live. That Reed would take such a worthy program and sully it for the likes of money outraged her.

Another thought occurred to her then. One that made her blood run cold. "If we don't make it back, no one will ever know."

His eyes turned to steel. "We're going to make it back."

She wondered how he could be so sure when he was sitting there with a bullet wound in his side. "Lady Luck has a bad side, Jake. I've seen it too many times in the past year and half to discount it now."

"I've got a bad side, too," he said fiercely. "Believe me, you don't want to see it."

Abby looked over her shoulder at the ridge to the north. "Do you think your search and rescue friends are out looking for us?"

"No doubt about it. The chopper is out. Maybe the ATV in the lower elevations. The snow is hindering them. But they're looking. You can count on it."

"I'm sorry I destroyed your radio, Jake. That was really a stupid thing to do."

He looked at her soberly. "If you hadn't, you'd be in a six-by-six cell right now and no one would ever know about Reed."

The mention of a prison cell made her shiver, but she quickly shoved the feeling away. She couldn't think about going back or all the things that could happen when she did.

Then the realization of what he'd said struck her. She looked at him and blinked, realizing belatedly that he was watching her.

He must have deciphered her thoughts from the look on her face because he smiled. "You were wrong about me," he said quietly.

"What I am, Jake, is confused. I have no idea where I stand with you."

"I believe you about Reed," he said after a moment. "I

believe you about all of it. The only question that remains is how we're going to handle it.''

Abby had never been much of a crier. Even before this mess she'd never been prone to tears. But hearing those words put a fist solidly in her throat. Tears burned behind her eyes. She blinked rapidly to suppress them, but they spilled over anyway.

Gazing steadily at her, Jake took off one of his gloves and thumbed a tear away. ''That was supposed to be good news.''

''It is.''

''Don't cry. That really tears me up.''

''Don't let it get to you too much. I mean, you've been shot.''

He smiled wryly. ''I'll keep that in mind.''

Using the sleeve of her duster, she rubbed her eyes. ''I don't know where that leaves us, Jake.''

''That leaves us with a big problem.''

Her heart stuttered. Another tear slipped down her cheek and he caught it with the backs of his fingers. ''I'm in a position to help you. I'll do my best. No matter what happens, I want you to believe that, okay?''

Disappointment cut her, but Abby steeled herself against it. She didn't have room for disappointment. Jake was going to help her. He was an officer of the law. Just because for one crazy second she'd wanted more didn't mean he was going to oblige.

Abby didn't want promises. Invariably they ended up broken. Jonathan Reed had left her with enough broken promises to last her a lifetime.

Drawing a shaky breath, she looked around. ''What do we do now?''

Jake stepped back, worked his hand into his glove. ''Our number one concern is to avoid that sniper.''

''Sounds like a solid plan. How do we do that?''

"We head south. It's rougher terrain, desolate as hell, and will end up taking a little longer, but these animals are experienced trail animals. The sniper is on a snowmobile. He's got speed, but we'll hear him coming from a mile away."

"What about food?"

"We're down to our last two protein bars." He scowled. "We need to be sure to take in plenty of fluids. I'll melt some snow later. We're at nine thousand feet. Between the cold and the altitude, it's easy to get dehydrated."

"Right."

His expression turned serious. "If the weather turns, Abby, we could get into trouble."

She saw the worry in his eyes and her heart melted a little. He wasn't worried about himself, she realized. He was concerned about her. Aside from Grams, she couldn't remember the last time someone had been concerned for her, certainly not a man. "The weather's going to hold," she said.

"How do you know?"

"I think we've already used up all our bad luck."

He chuckled. "I was thinking the same thing."

"How long before we reach the ranger station?"

"Tomorrow morning."

"Can you travel?"

"Hey, no problem. Bullets bounce right off me, you know? Ribs of steel." He straightened, but Abby could see it was an effort for him to keep from grimacing. She'd seen the bullet wound. Even if it wasn't life-threatening, she knew how much pain it was causing. And she knew it wasn't going to be easy for him to travel rough terrain on horseback in hip-deep snow.

"You'll need antibiotics," she said. "Maybe a tetanus shot."

"It'll keep." He looked up at the sky. "We might get lucky and see the chopper. I've got a couple of flares."

"In the saddlebag?"

He walked over to the saddlebag and removed a cylindrical flare. "Just hold the flare dead center, like this." He demonstrated. "And strike the tip against a tree or a rock. One end will flame and start smoking like crazy."

"I'll remember that."

"Let's make some time."

Jake smelled it before he actually saw the rising steam or heard the gurgle of water.

"What on earth is that smell?" Abby asked.

He stopped his horse and peered into the gathering darkness. "Sulfur," he said.

She parked the mule next to Brandywine and stared into the trees. "Sulfur?"

He glanced over at her and his heart bumped hard a couple of times against his ribs the way it always did when she was close. They'd been traveling over rough terrain and deep snow for nearly four hours. But even exhausted and scared and cold, she was incredibly beautiful. At some point her hair had come loose and coiled like springs around her shoulders. Fatigue shadowed the fragile skin beneath her eyes. But her eyes still had that vital light that was the force of her personality. He'd found himself watching her a dozen times throughout the afternoon hours. Found himself wondering if anyone had ever loved her. If a man had loved her. If Abby had loved him back....

Banking the thought with ruthless precision, Jake clucked to the horse and moved into a small clearing surrounded by jutting rock and piñon pine. Near an outcropping of jagged granite, fog rose out of the earth like ghostly fingers.

"I feel like I'm entering the enchanted forest," Abby said from behind him. "What *is* this place?"

He grinned. He almost couldn't believe it. "A hot spring," he said.

"I've never seen anything like it." She gaped at the bubbling water and thick bank of swirling fog that hovered above. "It looks...surreal."

"There are quite a few hot springs in the area. There's one not far from Aspen. It draws a lot of tourists year-round and from all over the world."

"Can we...get in?"

"As long as the water temperature isn't too hot."

She stared at the rising steam. "I don't know about this...."

"I don't know about you, but I've never been so glad to see hot water in my life." Turning in the saddle, Jake glanced over at her and grinned. "You'll love it."

Careful not to jar the wound in his side, he used the stirrup and dismounted. He lashed Brandywine to a sturdy lodge-pole pine, loosened the girth of the saddle, then proceeded toward the bubbling pool. "A couple of young park rangers were seriously burned up in Yellowstone a few years back when they jumped into a hot spring."

"How awful."

"We'll be a little bit more cautious." He could feel the heat even from three feet away. After two days and two nights of hard riding and sponge baths, he was more than ready for a dip.

"How are you going to check the water temperature?" she asked from behind him. "We're both pretty cold. You know what long periods of exposure to cold does to a person's sense of temperature."

Remembering the first-aid kit, he walked back over to Brandywine, opened the saddlebag and removed a thermometer from the kit. "I knew I'd need this someday."

"Well, that's pretty handy."

He looked up to see Abby sliding off of Rebel Yell. He watched her slide the lead over the animal's head then tie him next to Brandywine. He couldn't help but wonder how she would look with all that wild hair tangling over her bare shoulders, her body immersed in hot mineral water....

He turned away and strode to the water's edge. The warm steam felt heavenly on his cold, chapped face. Squatting, he submerged the thermometer. "I'll keep it in there for a minute or so and see what the water temp is. If it's under a hundred degrees we should be good to go."

She came up beside him. Her leg was right next to his face. He remembered from the day he'd undressed her that she had long, slender legs with just the right amount of muscle definition. Her skin had been creamy white and soft as velvet. He wanted to lift his hand and touch her, but he didn't dare.

He pulled the thermometer from the water, felt a grin emerge. "Ninety-two degrees."

"That means we can...bathe?"

Rising to his full height, he looked down at her. "We can do a lot more than that."

The words hung between them like a faux pas at some fancy dinner party. She opened her mouth, her eyes widening slightly. Realizing that hadn't sounded at all how he'd intended, Jake cleared his throat. "What I meant to say was, aside from cleaning up and warming up, I can use the warmth to melt some snow for the horses. And refill our water bag."

"Oh. I mean, sure. I mean...I know what you meant."

"Right."

"Yeah." She nodded vigorously, but she didn't meet his gaze. "Um...is there anything I can do to help?"

"Why don't you fill the pail with snow, tie the rope off on the branch up there above, and set it in the water? I'll feed the horses the last of the grain."

"Oh, Jake, they're going to be hungry in the morning."

The realization that she was worried about the animals going hungry warmed him. No, Abby Nichols didn't fit the profile of a convict. Certainly not a murderer. The only question that remained was what he was going to do about it.

You're going to take her back anyway, aren't you, sport?

The question had been eating at him all day, like a voracious acid that continued to devour long after it had been washed away. Jake had tried to justify what he had to do; he was only carrying out the job he'd been hired to do, for God's sake. He knew it was guilt playing on his conscience. Guilt with a little bit of lust mixed in. The thought shamed him, but he refused to believe his feelings for her went any deeper. That would be just too hard to deal with.

As much as he hated the thought of taking her back, he knew there was no other way to handle this. It was crazy to think anything could be resolved by hiding out in the mountains in the middle of winter.

"You know, Abby, we're going to be pretty hungry, too, come morning." He looked at her and grimaced.

She pulled the pail from the saddlebag, then turned those eyes on him. Jake could tell by her expression that she already knew what he was going to say next.

"We've got to keep riding," he said after a moment.

"In the dark?" Desperation flickered in her eyes.

Jake knew she'd been hoping for another night of freedom—instead of a few short hours. It was killing him to do this. But he didn't have a choice. Damn it, he didn't.

"The ranger station is only a few hours from here. We'll stop for a while to clean up and rest, but we can't stop for the night. I don't want to risk running into bad weather or having to deal with the sniper again."

She looked down at the pail, but not before he caught the flash of pain in her eyes. She'd looked gut-punched. God, he hated hurting her. Hated it more than anything in the world. Why in the hell did this have to be so difficult? Why did he have to care about this woman?

The realization of just how much he cared for her sent a swirl of panic through him. He reassured himself it was just his libido talking. He was a man, after all; she was an attractive woman. They'd been keeping close quarters for two days now. He couldn't help it if there was some kind of sexual chemical reaction between them every time they got within shouting distance of each other. He was going to keep this impersonal. He was going to take her back. He was going to do the right thing if it killed him.

"Okay," she said at last. "We go back."

"We don't have a choice. I'm sorry."

She didn't say anything, but just looked at him with those incredible eyes. Only now they were filled with a profound sadness than made him feel like a bastard.

God, he hated this.

He took the pail from her. "I'll take care of the horses. Why don't you grab your protein bar if you want it and go ahead and get in the water?"

"Oh, well…sure. I mean, I'm starved." Pausing, she turned back to him and cocked her head. "Whatever happened to those peanut butter cookies?"

Jake felt a little sheepish. "I was running low on grain, so I…fed them to the animals."

"The cookies?"

"Well…Brandywine loves peanut butter."

She stared at him a moment, then a laugh broke from her throat. It was a melodious sound that rippled through the frigid air and echoed off the bare-branched trees like the sound of birdsong. Jake soaked in the sound of it, let it warm him from the inside out. When she smiled, he smiled back. It was a simple moment. An honest moment that shouldn't have meant anything to either of them. But it was exactly the kind of moment he'd come to cherish in the last two days. Exactly the kind he was going to miss when this was over.

* * *

Abby was uneasy as she stepped out of her jumpsuit and draped it over the gnarled branch of a low-growing juniper a few feet away from the spring. Not only was the air freezing cold, but her modesty made undressing a personal discomfort as well. Taking her clothes off in subfreezing temperatures was bad enough—but it was even worse knowing Jake was only a few yards away taking care of the animals. The spring was hidden from his view—and it wasn't as if she didn't trust him. She did. Well, at least when it came to his being a gentleman. What she didn't trust was the annoying little explosion of desire that went off inside her every time she looked at him. And the crazy notion that her feelings for him went deeper than the flesh.

She was totally insane to be attracted to a man like Jake. A man of honor, full of promises and an uncompromising sense of right and wrong. Jonathan Reed had taught her a hard lesson about those things, and Abby had sworn she would never subject herself to that ever again. But even the pain of his betrayal wasn't enough of a deterrent to keep her from considering jumping into the fire all over again with Jake.

He was as hardened and cold as the Rocky Mountains themselves. He didn't care about easy when it came to right and wrong. He followed the rules even when those rules were wrong, even if those rules were going to destroy her. And he was damn well going to take her back to prison no matter what the cost to either of them.

She squeezed her eyes shut against the thought. In the past twenty-four hours, things had gotten complicated. If she was going to escape and clear her name she had to forget about Jake and his promise to help her. She'd made the mistake of trusting him, of believing he could help her. Just like she had with Reed—and look where that had gotten her.

No, she couldn't give up her original plan. She couldn't let Jake talk her out of what she needed to do. She'd already given the legal system ample opportunity to get to the truth. Lady Justice had let her down.

Abby's life was on the line. The burden of proving her innocence now lay squarely on her own shoulders. She didn't intend to blow it. She would take a few minutes to warm herself and get clean. Once they were back on the trail, she would take off. Jake was injured; he wouldn't be able to ride hard enough to catch her. With a little luck, she would be sitting in the cab of a Peterbilt, heading west toward Grams's place in New Mexico by dawn.

The air was bitterly cold against her bare skin. Shivering, her body covered with gooseflesh, she stepped over to the pool. The spring was six feet across and surrounded by rock. She dipped her toe into the bubbling mineral bath. The warmth beckoned her. Knowing she didn't have time to waste without risking Jake catching her in her birthday suit, she stuck her entire foot into the water, and felt for the bottom with her toes to see how deep it was. Three feet down, the sandy bottom met her foot. Stepping into the pool, Abby sank into the water up to her chin. Her body sang with the zing of sudden and unexpected warmth. The heat shocked her with pleasure. Sighing, she leaned her head against the rock behind her and looked up at the sky.

Dusk had fallen gray and cold. The branches above the pool were shiny and black from the steam that had risen and frozen to the bark. She could hear Jake over by the horses. He was talking quietly to his mare. She smiled, thinking of the peanut butter cookies. The man definitely had a soft spot for his animals.

She wondered why that same soft spot didn't apply to her.

"How's the water?"

Abby looked over to see Jake standing a few feet away.

He looked like some kind of apparition as she stared at him through the undulating fingers of steam. She watched, mesmerized as he slipped off his duster, draped it over the low branch of a tree, then toed off his boots.

She fully intended to answer him, but the realization that he wasn't going to stop with the duster and intended to strip right down to his birthday suit and get into the small pool with her rendered her speechless.

Standing there in his worn jeans and flannel shirt, he looked rugged and as dangerous as a rogue cougar. Two days of black stubble darkened his lean jaw. His gunmetal eyes were level on her, and she realized he was always looking at her as if he were trying to work through a complex problem. She wondered if she looked at him the same way, if he had any idea just how complicated the emotions twisting through her had become.

His hands went to his belt buckle.

Abby averted her gaze. "You're not coming in *now,* are you?"

"You don't expect me to stand out here and freeze my toes off while you're soaking in all that heat, do you?"

"No, it's just that...it's just that, I'm not...dressed."

"Well, I hope not. It's not like we have a clothes dryer up here."

"Well, you're not going to..." She could barely say the words. "Take your clothes off, are you?"

"I'm not getting in there with them on."

"How can you just...strip like that?"

"Blondie, I don't know if you've noticed this about me yet, but I'm not the modest type."

Oh, yeah, she'd noticed all right. Risking a look at him out of the corner of her eye, she shivered despite the heat radiating into her body. Oh no, the man wasn't shy at all. He was bold and confident and...unsettling. She saw all of those things and then some when he stepped out of his jeans and draped them over his duster. The flannel shirt went next and his muscled chest loomed into view, tapering to a flat stomach, lean hips and thighs sprinkled with black hair. He looked incredibly sexy in those snug boxer shorts. When his fingers slid into the waistband, she turned her head.

Heat that didn't have anything to do with the water crept into her cheeks. "I just thought you could...give me a few minutes in here alone."

"Oh, well...make up your mind. It's getting a little drafty."

His voice was directly over her, but she didn't dare turn around or look up. She knew he was naked, and she had absolutely no intention of seeing Jake Madigan without his clothes. "Just...hurry up and get in, will you? And stay on the other side of the pool. I'll just...close my eyes."

The water rippled as he stepped in. After a moment, Abby opened one eye and looked over at him. Mercy. Not looking the least bit embarrassed about his state of undress, he stood in the pool, letting his body acclimate to the heat, then sank into the water up to his neck. His face screwed up, and he rose gingerly until the water only came up to his naval. "Ah, damn. I forgot about the bandage."

Concern fluttered through her when she realized the bandage had gotten wet. Forgetting about her state of undress, she moved closer to him. "I'm not sure this was a good idea. I mean, the heat could start that bleeding again," she warned.

"It's okay. It'll be worth it to get warm."

"I'll put a new bandage on it when we get out."

Leaning back against the rock he closed his eyes. "I'd forgotten what it was like to be warm."

Abby moved to the other side of the pool, keeping one eye on Jake. She knew better than to indulge herself watching him. She had enough on her plate without adding regret to the heap. But it was hard not to look at him, even harder not to like what she saw. Not to want. In the last hours, she'd come to realize there was more to Jake Madigan than she'd ever imagined. She wondered where this might have led if the circumstances had been different.

Abby crushed the thought before it fully materialized. She'd had her fill of men. Even honorable men like Jake. She'd always believed Jonathan Reed was an honorable man. The people of Mercy General still believed it. They didn't know that a predator existed beneath that perfect image. That beneath all that education, the righteous drive to heal the sick and wounded, the genteel manners of the talented surgeon and philanthropist was the heart of a killer shark.

Hapless Abby had fallen hook, line and sinker for the act. When the going was good and easy, he'd loved her as if there was no tomorrow. When things had gotten tough, he'd disposed of her like a pair of soiled examination gloves. It shamed her now that she'd loved him back. That she'd loved him even after he'd testified against her. That she'd been willing to settle for that.

God, she'd been naive.

"What are you thinking?"

She started at the sound of Jake's voice, the water stirring around her. She opened her eyes, found him staring intently at her. She felt stripped bare by that piercing gaze, felt as though he'd been reading her mind.

"Nothing," she said after a moment.

He continued to stare at her, his expression hard and slightly perplexed. "You were thinking about something. You get that little crease between your eyebrows when you think. It was working double time just now."

She stared back, feeling as if she'd been caught with her hand in the cookie jar, and glanced over at her clothes draped over a branch a few feet away. "You know, I think I've had enough of this heat...."

"I've got something on my mind, Abby," he said. "I'd like for you to hear this."

"I'm not sure now is the time to discuss it," she said quickly.

"In a few more hours, it'll be too late."

"I don't want to discuss this." Turning slightly, she started to reach for her jumpsuit, but Jake's arm rose out of the water and stopped her.

"If I'm going to help you, you've got to be honest with me," he said.

She looked down where his hand clamped around her wrist. "I have been honest."

"Really?"

"Really."

"Then why didn't you tell me you were in love with Dr. Jonathan Reed?"

Chapter 12

The words jolted her like a power surge through her body. Abby stared at him, speechless, wondering how he could know something she'd never told another soul.

"I didn't," she heard herself say. "I mean...that's crazy."

"Love is crazy sometimes," he said, but his eyes told her he wasn't buying it. "That's why you covered for him, isn't it?"

"I didn't cover for him."

"That's why you lied to the police."

"I didn't lie."

"You suspected Reed was somehow involved with the deaths, but you trusted him too much to believe it."

"He was...he was a doctor, for God's sake."

"So you covered for him, didn't you? By the time you realized he wasn't the man you thought he was, it was too late. Isn't that how it happened?"

"I didn't cover for him."

"You didn't tell the police everything."

"I suspected, but I thought I was wrong. I just couldn't believe Jonathan would...I just couldn't believe he could do something so...horrible."

"You covered for him because you loved him, didn't you, Abby?"

Horrified, she raised her hands to her face and looked at him over her fingertips. Shame uncoiled in her chest like a sharp piece of metal snapping free, cutting her from the inside out. "No."

"You lied to the police to cover for him. In doing so, you incriminated yourself, and he framed you, didn't he?"

"Stop it."

"Didn't you?"

She stared at him, shaking inside. "I don't want to discuss this."

"The police realized you were lying. Only they thought you were lying to save yourself, didn't they? They didn't know you were lying to protect that son of a bitch Reed."

Abby felt sick inside. She felt stupid and gullible and shamed for having made such a terrible mistake. For loving a man who'd reciprocated by destroying her.

Pressing her hand to her stomach, she turned away from Jake. A sob tore from her throat as the pain broke free. Pain she'd kept secret and tucked away in a place deep inside her.

"I can't talk about this," she whispered.

"We all make mistakes, Abby. We fall down. We get back up. It's not the end of the world."

"Not you, Jake. You don't make mistakes. Not like me."

He laughed then. Not cruelly, but with an honesty that caught her and wouldn't let her go. "You're kidding, right? You really believe that about me?"

She nodded. "You're not gullible."

Jake couldn't believe she had so much faith in him, and so little in herself. "I wrote the book on gullible."

"Did not."

It surprised him that he could smile about it now. At the time it had felt as if he were having his heart ripped out. "I asked a woman to marry me three years ago," he began. "There was a forest fire up on Elk Ridge. Took out half a dozen homes. The RMSAR team and I worked in conjunction with the smoke jumpers. A woman and her boy were left homeless." Jake could still see Richie's face on occasion. Still thought about him. Still loved him when it didn't hurt too much to acknowledge it.

"Her husband had deserted her a few months earlier. I couldn't see a mother and her son homeless, so I invited them to stay at my cabin with me until they could find a place to live and get on their feet again." Remembering how naive he'd been, Jake sighed. "I...ended up getting involved with this woman, Elaine. I was crazy about her. Crazy about her kid, Richie."

"What happened?"

He looked over at Abby, saw the solemn look in her face. He hadn't wanted to open up to her, hadn't wanted to reopen these old wounds, but he needed her to trust him and figured if he shared some of his own past mistakes with her, she would be more likely to do so with him.

"I asked her to marry me after knowing her only a month. By then we were sleeping together. It didn't even cross my mind that she wasn't what she appeared." Humiliation scraped at him, but he shoved it back. "The day after I asked her to marry me, I came home from work and she was gone."

"Oh, Jake...I'm sorry."

He raised his hand. "She didn't just walk away, Abby. She took everything I had that wasn't nailed down. Cleaned out my bank account." He cut Abby a hard look. "I'm a cop. You think I checked up on her?'' He shook his head. ''I had so much faith in my ability to read people, it didn't even cross my mind.''

''Did the authorities catch her? I mean, did she get away with taking your money?''

''I figured the money was my own damn stupid fault, so I didn't pursue it. My main concern at the time was for Richie. I had a hell of a time trying to decide how to handle it.'' He looked over at her, felt the kinship between them grow even as he questioned his own judgment for the second time in his life. ''I called Child Protective Services, filled them in on what happened and left it in the hands of someone who knew what the hell they were doing.''

''I'm sorry,'' she said.

''So, you see, Abby, you're not the only one who's made mistakes. Everyone makes mistakes. Even me, and I'm a cop.''

She looked down at the water swirling around her, looking as lost as anyone Jake had ever seen.

''Are you going to talk to me?'' he asked.

She didn't answer, didn't even look at him.

''Abby, did you know what Reed had done?''

''Not at first.''

''How did you find out? What did you see?''

''I saw him inject a patient once. I knew he'd been alone with the other patient, too. I knew he'd performed a late-night surgery in the old wing of the hospital. A wing that was no longer used for surgery.''

''You confronted him about that?''

''I asked him about it later, but he said he'd only given the man a B-12 shot. That the surgery was actually an autopsy observed by some interns and that I'd misunderstood what I'd seen.'' She risked a look at him. ''I believed him.''

''Did he ask you not to tell the police?''

''Yes.''

"So you didn't?"

She nodded. "I didn't say anything about it until after Reed took the stand in court and testified against me."

"Oh, Abby." Jake ran a hand over his face. "Were you sleeping with him?"

The question went through her like a bayonet. Shame and humiliation bled freely from the wound deep inside her. "Yes."

"That's why you covered for him, isn't it? That's why you lied to the police…to protect him, isn't it?"

"He asked me not to tell them."

"Weren't you worried about yourself?"

"I was innocent. I had nothing to hide." She looked across the water, at the snow and the trees through the steam. "It never crossed my mind that he'd done something improper. Or that he would frame me for it."

"He turned on you, though, didn't he?"

"Yes." She was crying openly now, her sobs echoing hollowly within the frozen branches and the rising steam. She knew she was losing it, her emotions, her dignity. But Jake had pushed her too far and she couldn't stop the long-denied emotions from pouring out.

"He came to me when I was out on bail. Came to me with roses and promises. He said it would all be over the next day. That my case would be dismissed. He had a dozen lawyers working on it around the clock. High-dollar lawyers who would see to it that I was exonerated." A bitter laugh choked out of her. "He seduced me that night. With his lies. His promises. He used me. I was stupid enough to—"

"No."

The angry tone of Jake's voice jerked her head up. "No," he repeated. "You weren't stupid, Abby. Don't ever let me hear you say that again."

"I slept with him that night, Jake. My fate had already been sealed and he used me one last time. He told me he loved me. And I loved him back. How stupid is that? How do you think that makes me feel?''

"Used. Betrayed. Hurt." His jaw worked angrily. "But not stupid. Not ever."

"I let him do that to me."

"He lied to you, Abby. You loved him. You trusted him. It wasn't your fault."

Jake couldn't stand to see her shaking, couldn't stand to see the tears on her cheeks and the ravaged look in her eyes. He knew better than to go to her, knew that would only be asking for trouble. But he wasn't a strong enough man to resist.

Before he realized he was going to move, he was touching her, pulling her to him. He saw the startled look in her eyes, but that didn't stop him. She resisted for an instant, her hands pressing against his shoulders, then she relaxed and her body came full-length against his.

Pleasure zinged through his brain like a high-speed jet. The knowledge that he was about to make a fatal mistake collided with logic, exploded. Jake crashed and burned. He fought the need rampaging through him, but the feel of her against him vanquished the last of his resistance.

And he realized his feelings for Abby Nichols weren't just physical anymore.

The knowledge sent a spark of terror to his brain. He knew caring for her was a mistake, knew fully what it could cost him, both personally and professionally. But he couldn't bear to see her hurting like this.

Jake wrapped his arms around her and held her tightly against him. He soothed her pain with his hands, stroking the back of her head, her neck and shoulders. He spoke quietly to her, telling her he would make things right. He would get to the bottom of this. He would look into her case.

He made dangerous promises he wasn't sure he could keep.

His thoughts fizzled when she shifted closer. His brain went into a stall when the hardened tips of her breasts brushed against his chest. The slick flesh of her belly was taut against his. The swift rush of blood to his groin made him groan. He knew she could feel the hard shaft of his arousal against her, but she didn't pull away and neither did he.

She sobbed quietly in his arms, her arms around his neck. Jake stroked her, telling her everything would work out, that he would make things work out. Slowly, her sobs quieted. He knew he should let her go and step back. He knew they were playing with fire. Knew they were both going to get badly burned. She was an escaped convict; he was an officer sworn to uphold the law. It was worse than unethical for him to hold her this way. To touch her like this. To want her, tomorrow be damned. As a cop, his career was on the line. As a man, his personal code of honor.

Neither of those things mattered when she pulled back and he saw his destiny reflected in the violet depths of her gaze.

"I'm sorry he hurt you," Jake said, his voice rough.

"I'm okay now. I've been okay for a long time."

"It still hurts you."

"I'm in prison because of him."

Fury rushed through him, but he stomped it down. Barely. "Not for long."

She stiffened in his arms, but Jake caressed her shoulders, her cheek, forcing her to relax against him. He wanted her against him. Wanted that more than his next breath.

"Don't promise something you can't deliver," she said.

"When I find him, before I ruin his life, I'm going to deck him."

"You're a cop, you can't—"

"I'm also a man and I damn well can."

His chest constricted when she smiled. The sight of it did something to him. Something that made his heart pound, made it hard to take a breath. He wondered if she had any idea what she did to him. That with only a look or a sigh or a smile she could turn him inside out. He hurt for her. Emotionally because of the terrible injustice that had been inflicted upon her. Physically because he wanted her so badly the need was an ache that went all the way to his bones.

"This is a dangerous game we're playing, Abby."

"I know. I've never been much good at it."

"You're better than you know."

"Yeah, well, so are you."

Bringing his hands out of the water, he skimmed the sides of her face with the backs of his fingers. "Maybe we're both a little crazy to even be considering it."

"Definitely crazy. Maybe even a little insane."

"I'm going to make things right for you," he whispered. "I promise."

"Jake, you're a cop. This…what we're doing could—"

Leaning forward, he brushed his lips against hers, quieting her. He knew she was right. But right had gone out the window along with his common sense the moment he'd felt her against him.

Jake knew he'd stepped over the line, knew if he let this go any further there was no turning back. But with the swirl of hot water on his skin, the Colorado sky full of stars around them, and the feel of Abby's soft body against his, the barriers between them melted away.

"I'm going to help you, Abby," he whispered. "Tell me you know that."

"I know."

Her eyes devastated him when she looked at him. The need to protect her, to possess her, overwhelmed him

Somewhere in the back of his head a tiny voice of reason cried out he was crazy for getting involved. But he silenced the voice with ruthless accuracy.

Jake no longer cared about the rules. Right or wrong had melded into a shade of gray and he could no longer distinguish one from the other. He didn't want to think about his career or how this would affect it. All he knew was that he wanted this woman in his arms. Wanted her more than his next breath. Wanted her so badly he was shaking.

"I know you're innocent," he said hoarsely. "I know you didn't kill anyone. If it's the last thing I do, I'll get you out of prison."

When she pulled back to look at him, the tears in her eyes devastated him. "Why are you crying?" he asked.

"Because you've given me hope."

Lowering his head, he kissed the tears from her cheeks, first the left side then the right. "I want you," he whispered to her. "I know I shouldn't. I know there are a thousand reasons why I shouldn't have you. I've been fighting it, Abby. But you're so close I'm touching you, and I've never felt so alive. Things have never felt so right for me. Not with a woman. Not ever."

He kissed her temple, the lobe of her ear, skimmed his mouth down her neck. She shivered, and he felt her nipples harden against his chest.

"I want you. I've wanted you since the first time I saw you," he said, emotion raw in his voice.

The tears in her eyes glittered like faceted stones. "Wanting like that could cause us some problems, Jake."

Holding her lovely face between his hands, he kissed her. "Stop making so much sense," he said.

The taste of her mouth heated his blood. The restraint coiled inside him sprang free, a shackle snapping, releasing the beast. He felt out of control, the threat of an irrevocable mistake taunting him, but Jake didn't care. All he cared about was the woman in his arms. The woman who'd been hurt and betrayed.

The woman he wanted to make love to.

Silently, he vowed to see her through this. He vowed to make things right for her. And if it was the last thing he did, he vowed to see justice served.

She sighed, and the last of his control fled. Urgency burned him. He deepened the kiss and she opened to him. He reveled in the velvety interior of her mouth. He fed on her like a starving man, devouring the sweetness of her lips. The feel of her body against his maddened him. He'd wanted to take this slow, give himself a chance to cool off and to think about what he was about to do. Jake wasn't used to tumbling headlong into disaster. But that's exactly what he did. Whispering her name, he skimmed his hands down her shoulders to her breasts. Utter perfection met his palms. He heard her gasp, but he didn't stop touching her. He couldn't even if he'd wanted to. The madness had him firmly in its grip, and he'd given up on trying to fight it.

He stroked the tips of her breasts, her tiny nipples beading beneath his touch. He was aware of her labored breaths in his ears. The bubbling of the water swirling around them. The warmth of the rising steam caressing exposed flesh.

"Stand up," he whispered.

She looked at him, her eyes wide and uncertain. "Jake—"

He smiled. "I love it that you're shy."

"I'm not. It's just…cold."

"I'll keep you warm."

Taking her hands in his, he eased her to her feet. The cold shocked his skin as he rose up out of the water. Her beauty shocked his senses. The moment didn't seem real. He stared at her, awed and reeling and a little overwhelmed as the moisture from their bodies evaporated into the frigid air.

"You take my breath away," he whispered.

She smiled. "That's just the cold."

He laughed. "I know the difference, Blondie. Believe me, what you do to me has nothing to do with the temperature."

Cupping his hands, he captured a handful of water, then let it cascade over her shoulders and breasts. She shivered, and he leaned forward and kissed her softly on the mouth. The taste of her intoxicated him like a powerful narcotic. He skimmed kisses down her throat, running his tongue over her flesh, tasting her, licking the water from her skin. A tremor went through her when he reached her breasts. Leaning forward, he took her nipple into his mouth.

Vaguely, he was aware of her hands going to the back of his head, pulling him closer to her. He suckled her. Crying out, she threw her head back, trusting him, and Jake swore he would never betray that trust.

Not wanting her to get chilled, he kissed her neck, then slowly made his way back to her mouth. Putting his hands on her shoulders, he lowered her into the warmth of the water. Pleasure sang through him. The warmth and swirl of the water. The taste of Abby on his tongue. The mystical beauty of the spring. The magic of the mountains. He kissed her, shutting out the rest of the world. The cold and snow faded into the background. Her being a convict, his being a cop, no longer mattered. He couldn't think of those things and make love to her.

He tore down the barriers keeping them apart. He feasted on her mouth. The sweetness of her kiss destroyed him, shaking him to his core. Need cut him and went deep, leaving a fresh wound on his heart. When her arms went around his neck and she whispered his name in his ear, Jake knew he'd passed the point of no return.

Abby knew opening herself up to Jake was a mistake. There were a hundred reasons why she shouldn't make love to him. She knew he would ultimately hurt her. There was no way any of this was going to work out for either of them. Giving him her heart was a losing proposition no matter how she cut it.

I know you're innocent.

His words played over and over in her mind like an old-fashioned record with a skip. She could never tell him how much those words meant to her. How much it meant knowing a man like Jake believed in her.

She had every intention of putting a stop to the madness. But Jake's mouth worked magic against hers, the taste of him filling her with desperate needs that refused to be ignored. It had been an eternity since anyone had touched her this way. Since a man had touched her intimately.

But it wasn't the physical sensations assaulting her senses that scared her. The emotional connection that had formed between them terrified her. Never in a thousand years would she imagine herself falling for a cop, certainly not a cop who was determined to take her back to prison.

There was no future for them. The realization broke her heart and filled her with a lover's desperation. All they would ever have, she realized, was this moment. No matter what happened, no one could ever take that away from her. Even if she went back to prison for the rest of her life, she would always have the memory of this night. This magical place. It was going to have to be enough.

Tears gathered behind her lids, but she rode with the emotion, let it guide her. The sensations carried her adrift. A tiny boat in a raging sea. Every nerve ending in her body hummed when his hands skimmed up her sides to cup her breasts. Abby had always been sensitive there, and heard herself gasp when an undulating wave of pleasure swamped her. Heat spiked low in her body and she felt her own wetness meet with the warm water surrounding her.

With gentle fingertips, he touched her face, her throat,

and shoulders and belly. All the while his mouth made love to hers. Vaguely, she was aware of the rush of his breath against her cheek. The hard length of his body just a few dangerous inches from hers. He whispered something in her ear, but she didn't understand the words. She'd moved beyond understanding, her senses overloaded with emotion and physical sensation.

Gliding his hands down her flat belly, he caressed the curve of her hips, the smooth line of her thigh. Arousal flared hot and deep inside her when his fingers whispered across her vee. She uttered his name. He answered with a kiss that devastated her with its sweetness, and she opened to him. A single, earth-shattering stroke and she saw stars. The pleasure jolted her. She couldn't breathe, couldn't speak, couldn't form a single coherent thought.

"Easy," he whispered. "Let me touch you."

"This is…too much," she said.

"Honey, I hate to lay this on you right now, but the best is yet to come."

She nearly came up out of the water when he began stroking her. Long, sure strokes that set her on fire. She clung to him, dazed by the sensations coursing through her. Abby had never considered herself a sexual person. What few past relationships she'd had, had been luke warm at best. The strike of a match that burned down quickly.

Jake Madigan set her ablaze.

Control fluttered away as his fingers worked their magic. He held her close, speaking softly to her. Words that shook her mind and fed the flames devouring her body. Abby arched in his arms, her senses exploding. Wave after wave of pleasure assaulted her, overloaded her brain. Her cries echoed off the tree branches and surrounding rock. Her body shook uncontrollably while the flames licked at her, burning her. She writhed in his arm, feeling wanton and out of control. As completion rolled over her, she cried out his name.

Emotions besieged her, shaking her, frightening her with their awesome power.

Afterward, he wrapped his arms around her and held her tightly until the tremors stopped. She lay against him with her head on his shoulder, her mind reeling, her body humming with a thousand sensations and the knowledge that she would never be the same. This had changed her. Jake had changed her. Somehow, everything had changed and Abby knew they would never be the same.

Next to her, Jake stirred. She felt him brush a kiss across her forehead. "That was incredible," he said after a moment.

"Ah...well..." Embarrassment washed over her, and she wasn't quite sure how to tell him he'd just given her the most erotic sexual experience of her life and they hadn't even made love yet.

"Don't be embarrassed," he whispered.

Feeling the blush creep into her cheeks, she turned her face up to his and gazed into his eyes. "It's never been that way for me before," she said.

"Me, too." He pulled her closer and kissed her temple. "This is going to sound corny, but it was like...magic."

Locked within his embrace, Abby had never felt so safe, so secure, so...cherished. She knew this moment was fleeting, knew once it was gone she could never get it back, so she nestled deeper into his arms and let him hold her. She put the moment to memory. Every detail. The sensation of being in his arms. The way he looked at her. The feel of his mouth against hers. The taste of him....

The next thing she knew she was being swept into his arms and lifted out of the water. Frigid air nipped at her wet flesh, but Jake's body was warm against hers. Snagging their clothes from the juniper branch, he carried her to where he'd set up camp.

"What are you doing?" she asked.

"I'm going to make love to you," he said.

"In the snow?"

He chuckled. "I thought we might try the tent."

Setting her down, he set to work unzipping the tent he'd set up. Abby watched him, anticipation and a new nervousness rising inside her. The cold stung her wet flesh, but at the same time it invigorated her. A new warmth seemed to emanate from somewhere deep inside her.

"I wish I could give you more." Lifting the flap, he ushered her inside. "You deserve more."

"Roses and champagne?" she said.

"A pretty room at a bed-and-breakfast."

She grinned at him. "An electric blanket?"

He grinned back. "Let's see about getting you warmed up."

Shivers claimed her as she slipped into the tent. She was seriously cold now. She watched, shivering, as Jake quickly zipped their bags together, then motioned for her to get inside.

Abby slid between the soft layers of cotton. Jake got in beside her and they lay on their sides, looking out at the rising steam just beyond the flap.

"I think we have everything we need right here," she said after a moment. "Look around us. The spring. The ice on the branches. The steam. This is one of the most beautiful places I've ever been."

It was true. As many problems as the snow and rough terrain had caused them in the last days, the hot spring they'd stumbled upon was one of the most magnificent places she'd ever seen.

"Are you warm enough?" he asked.

She gazed at him, felt the coil of need low in her belly. "Plenty," she said.

His jaw tightened, and she knew he was thinking of their situation. That in a few short hours he would be handing her over to corrections officials. She knew that would tear him up inside. But she also knew he would do whatever was in his power to help her.

"Don't think about it," she whispered.

"I don't want to hurt you," he growled.

"I know. I don't want that to get between us right now."

"Abby, if there was any other way—"

Unable to bear the words, she leaned forward and kissed him hard on the mouth. "Don't say it," she whispered, her lips against his cheek. "Please, just…don't say it."

His eyes were tortured when he turned to her. "Come here," he said, but reached for her before she could move. His arms enveloped her. Abby closed her eyes against the rush of emotion, the hot flash of desire. She sensed something different about him now. When he kissed her, she tasted urgency and the bitter tang of desperation. She saw that same desperation in his eyes, felt it echo through her heart. Whereas earlier he'd been gentle, solely focused on her pleasure, she now sensed he wanted to possess her, mark her, make her his.

Before it was too late.

He kissed her intimately, exploring the deepest reaches of her mouth. She opened to him, felt the sharp pang of desire in her belly.

"I swear I won't let anything happen to you," he said.

"I know."

"I'm going to nail Reed to the wall."

Abby closed her eyes against the rush of pain. He was making her hope. Making her believe it could really happen. That he would clear her name and she would be free to live her life as she pleased. She wondered if she were free, if her life would include Jake….

"Don't bring him into this," she whispered. "I don't want him here." Only then did she realize she was crying.

"Abby…aw, honey. I'm sorry…."

"Make love to me, Jake."

"You're crying. I did that—"

"No." She closed her eyes against the need pounding through her, the grief clenching her chest, the arousal coursing through her body like hot mercury. "Please…"

Kissing the tears from her cheeks, he moved over her. Abby opened her body to him, and kissed him back, pouring her heart into the kiss.

"Look at me," he said.

She opened her eyes. He put his hands on either side of her face, brushed the hair back from her temples. Passion shone bright in the depths of his gaze. She could feel his heart raging against hers. The intensity of the moment made her dizzy, as if the earth were swirling crazily beneath her.

"Everything's going to be all right," he said. "I promise."

"I believe you."

She cried out when he entered her. The slow penetration destroyed the last of her control. Her body commandeered her mind. She heard his name on her lips. Her own echoing among the bare-branched trees and ice-slicked rock. She rose up to meet him, taking him deep within her. It was too much. It wasn't enough. Her breath rushed from her lungs in a sigh. Her lids fluttered, a kaleidoscope of light exploding in the darkness.

When she opened her eyes and looked up at him, the raw emotion in his eyes devastated her, made her want to laugh, to cry, to take him in all the way to her heart and make them one. She tried to think as he loved her, tried to put the sensations and emotions into perspective. But the overload of pleasure was too much. Her body, her heart, her mind couldn't take it all in. But he didn't stop, and she accepted him until she thought she would die of ecstasy.

The first wave of her climax rocked her violently. Closing

her eyes against the power of it, she bucked beneath him, absorbing him, loving him as she'd never loved another.

Abby hadn't expected to be swept away. Not like this. She'd never expected to have her control stripped away, her soul laid bare for this man to see. She never expected him to take her to heaven.

Another wave crashed over her, and she slipped beneath the surface. The force of it tumbled her. Shook her. Her senses overloaded, an electrical circuit hit by a devastating surge. Vaguely, she was aware of her ragged breathing. The sweet ache of her body accepting his. Of Jake filling her, kissing her, whispering her name. She tried to speak to him, but the pleasure stole her ability, and she could do nothing but feel.

He didn't stop, didn't wait for her, and the sensations pounded her like a relentless sea. Abby wasn't sure how long she could hang on. The waves kept coming in quick succession, each more devastating than the first. She felt like a wave-battered beach in the throes of a storm. The pleasure seemed to be drowning her.

Her only thought as another wave rolled over her was that she'd lost her mind and fallen in love with a man who couldn't ever love her back.

Chapter 13

Jake wasn't the kind of man who lost his head. He'd been in some tough situations in his life and not once had he ever lost control or done something he knew he was going to be sorry for later.

Well, at least until now.

He'd definitely lost his head. Maybe even his mind. The only problem was, he didn't much give a damn about either of those things. Not when her body was wet and hot around his and no matter how close he got to her he knew he would never get enough.

All along he'd told himself this was just lust. But when he looked into her eyes and saw her feelings for him reflected there, something vital and profound broke free in his chest. Emotions tangled with physical sensation, the combination punching him in the gut like a set of brass knuckles.

He cared for her, he realized. Cared for her a hell of a lot more than he'd ever imagined. Cared for her so much the thought of letting her go put a knot in his chest—right about where his heart was. The rise of panic swirling in the back of his mind told him that wasn't true. He didn't love her. God, no, he didn't love her.

But Jake knew it was too late for denial. This wasn't just lust. He felt it in his heart. Heard it in every cry that wrenched from her throat. He hadn't wanted to admit it, but she'd gotten to him. Gotten under his skin and into his mind. God in heaven, she'd gotten into his heart.

The thought thoroughly terrified him.

Logic told him to put a stop to this before it went any further, before either of them said or did something irrevocable. But Jake knew they'd long since moved beyond logic.

He broke a sweat as his completion neared. He kissed her, devouring the sweetness of her mouth. He drank in the sounds of her sighs. He'd never imagined lovemaking could be like this. That it could spin him out of control like a car on black ice. That it could make him lose his head and risk everything he'd ever believed in for a woman he shouldn't trust.

A woman he trusted with his life.

The realization shattered him. He tried to block the thought; he didn't want to deal with the consequences. But it was too late.

Saying her name over and over again, he spilled his seed into the deepest reaches of her body, and tried not to think about how much this was going to end up costing both of them.

Jake woke abruptly, his heart pounding, an icy sweat slicking the back of his neck. He'd been dreaming about Abby. Dreaming about taking her back and turning her over to D.O.C. at the ranger station. His heart had broken when they'd cuffed her. Then one of the officers had removed his gun from his holster. Jake had watched in horror as the other man put his gun to her head. Jake had tried to get to her, but everything had been moving in slow motion. A gunshot rang out. She'd dropped to the ground. He hadn't been able to save her....

Shaken and disoriented by the dream, needing to feel her alive and warm against him, he reached for her. A needle of alarm pierced him when he found himself alone. Sitting up, he looked around, found the tent was empty.

Dread trickled into his mind one terrible drop at a time. Fear sat like a block of ice in his stomach, cold and hard enough to make him nauseous. The dream clung to him like a nasty, lingering illness. He told himself it was just a dream, not a premonition. Jake didn't believe in premonitions. He told himself the dream was nothing more than a manifestation of the physical and emotional stress of the past three days, brought on by exhaustion and guilt.

Stepping into his jeans, he opened the tent flap and looked out. His heart banged hard against his chest when he saw Abby in the hot spring. She'd piled her hair on top of her head to keep it dry. Her back was to him, but Jake could see clearly the graceful curve of her neck. She was humming. An old song he hadn't thought of in years about a sentimental lady. The lyrical sound of her voice warmed him. He watched her, dumbstruck by her beauty, shaken by the emotions crawling inside him.

She dipped into the water up to her chin, then splashed water on her face. Raising up slightly, she slid her hands down her arms and washed. Despite the disturbing remnants of the dream, arousal coursed through him. Her back was lovely, her bone structure angular and small. He remembered all the things they had done earlier and felt the familiar rush of blood to his groin. He knew he was getting in deep. That he was in miles over his head. Still, he wanted her. Wanted her more than his next breath.

He stepped out of the tent. Dawn had broken gray and

cold with the threat of snow to the west. The cold wasn't
bitter, and Jake figured it would be raining in the lower
elevations.

It had been raining in his dream.

Shaking off the unsettling thoughts, he stepped over to
the pool. "Morning," he said.

Abby looked up and smiled at him beneath her lashes.
"Hi."

"Sleep well?"

"Yeah. But I woke up cold."

"How's the water?"

"Lonely."

His heart gave a single hard kick, then melted. Images of
the night before spun through his brain. Remembering, he
grinned. "You're a sight for sore eyes in the morning."

She frowned, rolling her eyes upward toward her hair.
"More like I'll *give* you sore eyes in the morning."

"You're the most beautiful woman I've ever seen."

"And you're getting cold standing there without a shirt."

"Mind if I join you?"

She smiled again, that secret woman's smile that always
made him feel a little dizzy. "Only if you bring the coffee."

"Oh, right." Stepping into his boots, Jake dragged a
small butane stove from his saddlebag and set the pan of
water on the flame. He removed two cups and the tin of
instant coffee.

"I hope you're not hungry," he said.

"I'm okay."

He'd been about to say they were only a few hours from
a warm room and hot food, but he didn't want to bring that
up. Not now. Looking away from her, he waited for the
coffee.

How the hell was he going to handle this?

Minutes later, he carried two steaming cups over to the
water and set them on a flat rock. He was aware of Abby

watching him as he unzipped his jeans and stepped out of them. He couldn't hide that he was aroused, but she didn't say anything, merely watched him with those incredible violet eyes.

He stepped into the water, picked up her coffee and took it over to her. With their faces less than a foot apart, they sipped.

"You make really bad coffee," she said.

Jake tried to smile, but he couldn't. He couldn't stop thinking about the dream, about what the next hours would bring for him. For her. How had he gotten into this situation? How could he have let himself get so involved?

He'd never felt so lousy in his life. Guilt and conscience and the cold, hard knowledge that he'd put everything he'd ever believed on the line tangled in his chest. The ensuing emotions strangled him. He wasn't sure what was worse, wanting her and knowing he could never be with her. Or wanting her and knowing he was going to destroy her when he took her back.

"Jake?" she asked after a moment.

"Abby...." He didn't know what to say. Didn't know how to begin. How could he tell her how he felt without sounding like a hypocrite? *I care about you, but I care about my career more and I'm going to take you back to jail so I can get on with my life.*

Hell.

"Jake, what is it?"

Only then did he realize he was shaking. His hands were shaking so badly, he'd spilled some of his coffee into the pool. Concern glimmered in her eyes when she reached for him. Jake took a step back, but he wasn't fast enough and her hand brushed the side of his face.

He wasn't sure exactly what happened next. Just that one minute she was touching his face, the next his arms were around her and he had her up against the rocks, kissing her as though his life depended on it. She stiffened in surprise for an instant, then melted against him.

Her body was warm and supple against his. Urgent need coiled and snapped inside him. He knew she didn't deserve to be taken this way, but his desire for her was too powerful and he wasn't a strong enough man to resist. Reaching around her, he gripped her hips and brought her to him. He groaned when she opened and her legs went around his hips. He entered her with a single thrust and went deep.

Abby cried out once. Jake heard his own voice, but he wasn't sure what he'd said. His mind blanked when she began to move with him. They moved together, slowly at first, testing their limits. Jake closed his eyes against the burst of emotions. He tried to concentrate on the pleasure exploding in his body, about to reach a fever pitch. He didn't let himself think about what would happen when they reached the ranger station. He didn't let himself think of the dream or the guilt eating away at his conscience. That he was taking an innocent woman to jail for a crime she hadn't committed. He told himself he hadn't fallen for her. That the only thing between them was lust and a sort of mutual respect bred from three days of hard travel, high emotion and close proximity.

Completion bore down on him. He felt her muscles contract. Once. Twice. Jake let go of his control, and the climax crashed down on him with the force of an avalanche. Closing his eyes, he rode the waves, let the pleasure consume him.

For a few minutes the only sounds came from their heavy breathing and the wind through the trees. Jake was halfway out of the water. His back was getting cold. Abby shivered in his arms.

Gently, he lowered her into the steaming water. "You're cold," he said.

"Just my shoulders."

"I didn't…uh, mean for that to get out of hand like that."

She dipped her head, catching his gaze. "What's got you so worried?"

Jake couldn't meet her gaze, couldn't look at her after making love to her and knowing how terribly he was about to hurt her. He felt like such a bastard. "Abby…"

"Jake, it's okay."

"No, damn it, it's not. I've been beating my brains out, trying to think of a way to handle this without taking you back to D.O.C., but I can't. At least not right away."

She stared back at him, her expression stricken, and it practically killed him.

"I meant everything I said to you. I'm not going to let this go." He was still intimately connected to her. As much as he needed to touch her, as much as he loved being inside her, he couldn't have this conversation that way. Moving slightly away, he rubbed his hand over his face. "But that doesn't change what I have to do."

"Go back without me. Tell them I got away. Tell them about the sniper—"

"Abby, I hate this, but I can't do that."

"You can, Jake. Between the two of us, we ought to be able to prove what I suspect about Reed. I mean, you believe me. You know I didn't—"

"No, Abby."

She drifted back in the water, her eyes wide and accusing. "Oh, I get it, I'm good enough to sleep with, but I'm not good enough to stand up for, is that it?"

"No," he snapped. "Damn it, don't ever let me hear you say that again."

"I don't need to say it, Jake. Your actions speak louder than words."

"I can't leave you up here with no food or water or transportation and a sniper on the loose! We've had this conversation before, and I haven't changed my mind."

"What about what happened between us last night?" Panic fringed her voice. "Doesn't that mean anything to you?"

"Hell yes it does! It means a lot to me. But that doesn't mean I'm going to leave you up here to die!"

"I'd rather take my chances with the sniper."

"You have to go back. At least until I can get some proof. A few days. A couple of weeks, max. I won't let anything happen to you. Do you hear me?" One step and he was upon her. His fingers wrapped around her arms, and he shook her gently. "I'm not going to let anything happen to you. I care, damn it! I care about you more than you know, Abby. So don't go laying guilt on me. I'm doing the only thing I can. I'm doing what I think is right."

She choked out a sob. "You didn't care about right or wrong a moment ago!"

Guilt pierced him. Jake let her go and stepped back. He knew how this looked to her. That he'd used her in the worst way a man could use a woman and was about to discard her back into the same system that had let her down so horribly.

"You're going to have to trust me," he said after a moment.

"The last man who asked me to trust him sent me to prison."

"I'm nothing like Reed," he growled.

"You're just a little bit more up front about it."

"I'm not going to let you do something stupid, Abby. I'm not going to let anyone hurt you. And I'm not going to let you rot in prison for something you didn't do."

He could tell by the look in her eyes that she didn't believe him. It shouldn't have hurt, but it did. And Jake felt the pain all the way to his soul.

By the time Jake and Abby hit the dirt road leading to the ranger station, the snow had changed to drizzle. A cold, bone-chilling drizzle that invariably found its way to the skin. Abby couldn't bring herself to care about the physical discomfort. She didn't even have the energy left to shiver. Her hair was soaked, but she hadn't even bothered with the hood of the duster. In the scope of things hypothermia seemed like nothing compared to the humiliations she faced in the coming hours—and the prospect of spending the rest of her life behind bars.

Jake rode a few feet ahead of her, his expression stony. Pain sliced her every time she looked at him. He'd been watchful throughout the morning hours. He'd spoken to her several times, but Abby hadn't responded. She knew it was wrong of her, but she was angry with him. She couldn't let go of the hurt. Or the sense of betrayal that clamped down on her heart like a vise every time she thought about what he had done to her. She couldn't believe that after everything they'd shared he was going to go through with this. That he was going to turn her in. She felt the betrayal like a knife in her back.

A mile from the ranger station a chopper flew by low to the ground. Jake reached quickly for the flare, struck it against the leather sole of his boot. The flare hissed, then began spewing orange smoke. Jake tossed it to the ground.

"They spotted us," he said.

The finality of the statement sent a shiver through her. She wanted to say something, but her chest was tight with fear and dread. What was left to say, anyway?

"They'll be expecting us." Pulling up on the reins, he stopped the horse and turned in the saddle to look at her. "I meant what I said, Abby. Don't think I'm not going to keep my word."

She ignored him, focusing instead on the horizon to the west, the jagged snow-capped peaks, the hawk wheeling high above the trees by the stream that ran parallel with the trail.

Only when he dismounted and started toward her did she look at him. "Come here," he snapped.

"What are you going to do, cuff me?"

"I have a few things I want to say to you, and you're not listening."

"Look, Jake, don't make this any more difficult than it already is."

"Get down off of that mule, or I'm going to pull you off."

Cursing under her breath, she dismounted, then faced him. "Happy?"

"No. This is killing me."

"Yeah? You should try it from my perspective. It's not exactly a walk in the park."

He stepped toward her. "Come here."

She stepped back. "Why?"

"I want to hold you for a moment."

"Or maybe you want something quick and dirty before we get back to the—"

"That's enough!" he snapped. "That's not how any of this happened and you know it. Don't cheapen what happened between us because you don't like the way I'm handling this."

"I don't have to cheapen it. You've already—"

"Don't say it, Abby. Damn it, don't even think it."

The pain cut her like a knife twisting under her ribs. Unable to endure it, she reached desperately for her anger. Anything was better than the hurt. "All I know is I slept with you and now you're taking me back to prison. You claim to believe me, and yet you don't see fit to keep me out of prison."

"I'm doing what I have to do to protect both of us. I was hoping you'd have a little bit more faith in me."

"Forgive me if I don't, but it seems to me like you're mostly interested in protecting your own interests."

"I can't help you if I lose my credibility."

"We wouldn't want that to happen, would we?"

Pinching the bridge of his nose, Jake closed his eyes and cursed. "The right thing isn't always the easiest, Abby. You of all people should know that."

For the first time the parallels between Jonathan Reed and Jake Madigan were painfully clear to her. Abby didn't want to believe it, but experience told her Jake was going to feed her to the wolves to save his career. The knowledge devastated her. Jake was an honorable man, after all. A lawman who would abide by not only his personal code of honor, but by society's strict moral code. There was no place in his life for a convict.

The knowledge cut her clean through.

"Abby—" He started toward her.

Raising her hands, she stepped back. "Please, don't do this to me." She desperately needed to feel his arms around her, but pride wouldn't let her say it, wouldn't let her reach for him. She couldn't bring herself to go to him.

Jake took the decision from her. Crossing the distance between them in one resolute stride, he reached for her. She tried to back away, but he caught her hand and pulled her to him. The solid warmth of his body against hers was like coming home. Abby heard a sob; realized with some surprise it had come from her. Closing her eyes against the pain of holding him close, yet knowing they could never have a future, she clung to him for a moment.

"I know a lawyer over in Boulder," he said. "He owes me a favor. Buzz Malone and I are good friends. He's an ex-cop, Abby. He'll give me a hand. I'll find proof. I swear, I won't let you down."

"Don't make promises you can't keep."

"I always keep my word." Pulling back slightly, he

smiled at her, but the smile was fringed with strain. "You'll be all right. I'll get you put in special lockup as soon as I can. Even if it's over in another county for now, I'll work on that first, so you'll be safe. Everything will be fine. I promise."

Because she couldn't speak, she nodded. But she didn't believe him. She'd believed once too many times and the results had shattered her life.

He kissed her then. A hard kiss that shouldn't have been sexual, but aroused her nonetheless. He was the only man in the world who could do that to her. The irony that he was the same man who was about to destroy her life didn't elude her.

Chapter 14

Half an hour later Jake and Abby rode into the parking lot of the ranger station. Normally, the place was deserted this time of year; most people in Colorado preferred the ski slopes over hiking and camping in the rain. But this afternoon the place was crawling with law enforcement. Two Chaffee County sheriff's vehicles were parked outside the small, neat building. A white D.O.C. van with a prisoner cage in the rear was parked next to it. At the gate twenty yards away, a Channel Seven news van replete with a satellite dish and a smartly dressed reporter, sat with its engine rumbling like a hungry predator waiting for prey.

Jake stopped his horse a few feet from the nearest Chaffee County cruiser. He heard the door of the ranger's office slam and looked up. Two burly sheriff's deputies in matching county-issue slickers approached.

His gaze swept to Abby. Her face blanched when she spotted the two men. Her hands shook visibly as she tangled her fingers in the mule's stubby mane. She was breathing rapidly, her breaths spewing vapor as if she'd just run a mile.

"Easy, honey," Jake said quietly. "Just…stay calm. Everything's going to be all right."

He could tell she wanted to say something back, but the two men reached them and the opportunity vanished. One of the men took the mule's lead while the other walked over to Jake.

"Deputy Madigan? You okay?"

"Fine." Letting the reins fall to the ground, he dismounted. "We're both cold and hungry and tired as hell."

The door of the ranger station slammed again. Jake looked up to see Buzz Malone and John Maitland approach. Behind them, two D.O.C. officials followed. Jake recognized one of them as the suit from the morning of the briefing. It seemed like a lifetime ago. The other was a tall, big-boned woman wearing an ill-fitting uniform and a don't-mess-with-me expression.

Jake couldn't ever remember feeling so off kilter. He'd always been able to keep a handle on his emotions, on what he was thinking and feeling and doing. But he had the disturbing impression that these people were going to take one look at him and know he and Abby had become lovers. Aside from getting shot, he couldn't think of a faster way to end a cop's career.

He risked a look at Abby. Her face was still sheet-white, but her expression was composed. Even from four feet away he could see that she was shaking. Her hair was wet, and it was damn cold, but he didn't think the trembling had anything to do with the temperature.

God, he hated this.

"Ma'am, get down off the mule," instructed one of the deputies, stepping over to the animal's left side. "Right now."

"You okay, Jake?"

He dragged his gaze from Abby, caught Buzz Malone's concerned look.

"Peachy," he muttered.

"That's one hell of a shiner you got there."

"Yeah, well, it's been one hell of a couple of days."

Jake knew he should walk away now while the walking was still good. While he still could. But the very thought of leaving her tore at his insides like a vicious little animal.

He knew better than to look at her. Not when his control was tattered and he could feel the rise of her fear as surely as he could taste the bile at the back of his throat. He'd known this was going to be hard, but he hadn't imagined it would tear him up inside.

The sight of her devastated him. Even cold and wet and disheartened she was beautiful. Fear permeated her expression. She wouldn't look at him, and Jake instinctively knew why. He knew it would be too hard for her to maintain the guise of lawman and convict.

"Ma'am, I said get down off the mule." The burly deputy pulled a set of cuffs from his pocket.

More than anything Jake wanted to talk to her, to reassure her, to make her believe that he was going to come through for her.

Without speaking to the deputies or Buzz, he walked over to the mule and reached up to help her down. He was aware of the other men hanging back. He could feel their questioning gazes on his back. For the first time in his professional career he didn't give a damn.

"Come on down," he said. "It's okay."

Abby looked down at him. Jake nearly flinched at the pain in her eyes. "Easy," he said. "Slide down. I've got you."

She slid off the mule. Jake caught her at her shoulders and eased her to the ground. He felt the pull of her softness, the soft scent of her hair, the pain in her eyes, tugging at him like a powerful tide.

"You'll be all right," he whispered.

"Deputy Madigan, Officer Walters will take the prisoner from here."

Feeling shaken and off balance, he turned away. In the back of his mind he could still see the look of betrayal on her face. He could still feel the warmth of her flesh against his skin. Smell her sweet scent with every breath he took.

Buzz Malone and John Maitland were watching him oddly. Jake took a tentative step toward Buzz. The older man's gaze sharpened, but he didn't say anything. Jake could tell by the look in his eyes that he knew something wasn't right. That by-the-book Jake Madigan had stepped over the line.

Behind him, he heard the female D.O.C. officer speak to Abby. "Nichols, turn around and give me your wrists."

Jake's heart pummeled his ribs when the sound of the cuffs snapping into place reached him. He'd known they were going to cuff her, search her, interrogate her. He knew it could be hours before she got into dry clothes and got something to eat. They hadn't eaten since the day before, and he couldn't stand the thought of her going hungry.

The sound of shoes against gravel turned him around. He looked up in time to see the male officer put his hands between Abby's shoulder blades and shove her toward the cruiser. She stumbled, lost her balance and went down on her knees.

Jake saw red. He didn't remember moving. Didn't remember lunging forward and grabbing the other man's collar and jerking him around. He saw surprise on the deputy's face. Pulling back, he punched him hard. Pain streaked up his knuckles, but Jake reveled in the diversion. Anything was better than the hurt ripping through his chest.

Out of the corner of his eye he heard the female officer gasp. Then her partner hit the ground like a sack of potatoes.

"Madigan, what the holy hell are you doing?"

Vaguely, he heard Buzz Malone's angry voice. Out of the corner of his eye, he saw Abby on her knees on the wet asphalt, trembling, her head down. Jake felt as if he were having an out-of-body experience. He started toward her, but Buzz's hand on his arm stopped him.

"Cool your jets, Jake."

Temper pumping, Jake tried to shake him off, but Buzz swung him around. "Cool down, damn it! I mean it."

He let go of Jake's arm.

"What the hell's the matter with you?" The deputy he'd slugged jumped to his feet, his hand on his jaw. "You crazy son of a bitch! You hit me!"

Jake swung around to face him. "I'd better not see you so much as lay a hand on her again, hot shot. You got that?"

"She stumbled, man. Who the hell do you think you are punching me like that? I'll have your badge for that!"

"She'd better arrive in her cell in good condition," Jake snarled. "If she so much as breaks a fingernail I'll find you and make you wish you'd taken up waitressing instead of police work."

"She's a killer!" The deputy's face reddened with anger. He jerked a finger at Abby. "She shot a clerk at a sporting goods store three days ago and took some weapons. I suggest you readjust your loyalties, partner."

Jake stared at the man, temper and disbelief pummeling him like a boxer's fists. "What are you talking about?"

The deputy wiped blood from his mouth with the back of his hand. "A few hours after she escaped Buena Vista, an elderly clerk was shot and killed in a sporting goods store a few miles from the prison. A couple of guns and some cash were missing. The sheriff's office found the guns and cash in a truck parked under a bridge four miles from the prison. A truck owned by Nichols's grandmother.''

Jake hadn't expected the debriefing with Sheriff Noble to go well. That he'd punched one of his counterparts didn't help much. If it hadn't been for Jake's report of the sniper—and the bullet wound on his abdomen—he figured Zane Noble would have fired him on the spot.

Thank God for small favors.

Buzz had agreed to drive him over to RMSAR headquarters for a shower and change of clothes, but Jake knew there was more to the man's offer than simple kindness. If anyone understood Jake, Buzz did. There was no one Jake trusted more, and he figured if he was going to get to the bottom of what had happened to Abby, Buzz was the man to ask for help.

The two men rode in silence on the short drive to RMSAR headquarters, but Jake knew Buzz wasn't going to let this go without explanation. Buzz proved him right the moment they walked in the door. ''You owe me an explanation,'' he said.

''I don't have time right now.''

''Make time.''

''I need a shower, then I've got to go.'' Jake brushed past the dispatch station, toward the rear. He was shaking inside. Hell, he was shaking on the outside. He'd thought he was going to be able to handle this. Turning Abby over to D.O.C. Walking away like this. The fact of the matter, he wasn't handling it well at all.

God in heaven, he couldn't believe the accusations he'd heard about Abby.

''Go where?'' came Buzz's voice from behind him.

Jake wanted to hit something. Rage and pain tangled inside him until he felt he might burst. Both men looked up when Pete Scully came down the hall toward them. The junior medic took one look at Jake and passed by him without saying a word. Tony Colorosa wasn't so lucky.

"Hey, Madigan, looks like that hot-lookin' lady convict punched your lights out. I hope it was worth it, buddy."

Jake knew it was an innocent comment—at least as innocent as a comment such as that could be coming from Tony. But his temper was at the boiling point. He spun on Tony, grasped his shoulders and slammed him into the wall. "Shut up about her!" he snarled.

Barking out a profanity, Tony tried to break Jake's hold on his shoulders. "Get your hands off me, Madigan."

Jake held him against the wall. "Not another word about her. You got that, good buddy?"

"Madigan!" Buzz shouted. "In my office. Now!" He shot a hard look at Colorosa. "Get lost, Tony."

Jake shook the other man hard once more, then shoved him away. He didn't look back when Tony cursed him.

He was still breathing hard when he walked into Buzz's office. He knew Malone was going to grill his ass; Jake figured he deserved it. His behavior wasn't becoming to a search and rescue volunteer, let alone a sheriff's deputy. By this time tomorrow, he figured he wouldn't have to worry about either.

Hell, what a mess.

He'd never felt so impotent in his life. He would never forget the way Abby had looked at him as the female D.O.C. officer led her away. She didn't cry, but the look of betrayal in her eyes slashed him like a switchblade.

"Sit down."

Jake dropped into the sled chair across from Buzz's desk.

"What the holy hell is going on with you?"

Leaning forward, Jake set his elbows on his knees and put his face in his hands. What the hell *was* going on with him? Why was this making him so…crazy? It wasn't like him to lose control this way.

"Tell me what happened up there."

Jake didn't know where to start. He wasn't sure he even wanted to tell Buzz what happened. He'd acted worse than inappropriately, and knew it could end up costing him his position on the team. Hell, he wasn't even sure he *knew* what had happened between him and Abby.

All he knew at the moment was that he'd never hurt so badly in his entire life.

"Holy hell, Madigan, your hands are shaking."

Jake looked down at his hands and laughed, but the sound was raw and bitter.

"How bad are you hurt?"

"Not bad."

"Let me see it. If I didn't know better, I'd think you were delirious."

Scowling, curious himself about the injury, Jake raised his shirt and exposed the wound. The bandage Abby had put on it was still there. He raised one end of the tape. It was a deep gash and the bruise beneath was just starting to discolor.

"You need stitches."

"I hate to tell you this, Buzz, but stitches are the least of my problems right now."

"I'll run you over to Lake County later."

"How about Mercy General?"

The older man's eyes sharpened. "Any particular reason you want me to drive an hour out of the way?"

"Yeah." Jake looked down at his muddy boots and brooded.

"I'm listening." Rising, Buzz went over to the coffee station. Reaching far into the back of the cabinet mounted on the wall, he removed a small flask and two cups. Back at his desk, he set one of the cups in front of Jake and filled it with two fingers of amber liquid. "I keep this stuff for emergencies," he said.

"I reckon this would qualify as an emergency."

"Yeah, decking a sheriff's deputy isn't real subtle."

Jake reached for the cup and drank. The whiskey burned his throat, but he emptied the cup. "I screwed up, Buzz."

"You're not going to get an argument from me."

"No. That's not what I mean." He cut Buzz a hard look. "I screwed up big time."

Buzz sighed. "That female convict got to you, didn't she?"

"I slept with her," Jake admitted.

In the twelve years he'd known Buzz Malone, Jake had never seen the other man flinch. *"What?"*

"I said I—"

"I know what you said. What I'm wondering is why the hell you're telling me and what the holy hell you're going to do about it."

"She's innocent."

Buzz groaned. "Jake—"

"Damn it, Buzz, she's innocent."

"She murdered a store clerk, for God's sake! Why do you think that deputy was so hard on her? She stole money and guns and—"

"She didn't do it."

"How can you possibly know that?"

"Look, I know this sounds crazy—"

"It sounds a lot worse than crazy. It sounds like you did something that's going to cost you your career and you still don't have her out of your system."

It hit Jake then that he wasn't ever going to get her out of his system. The realization sent panic skittering up his spine, hitting his brain like a high-voltage spark. Fear churned in his gut. Fear of what he'd just realized, of what he'd known was true since the moment he'd first set eyes on her. Fear for the woman whose life he now held in his hands.

"I love her." His own words stunned him, rocked him to his very foundation. "God, Buzz, I love her."

Across from him Buzz got creative with his cursing. "Jake, you're tired. You've got a bullet wound in your side. You just came out of a high stress situation. Give yourself a couple of days to clear your head and cool off."

"A couple of days isn't going to cut it." Jake slid his cup across the desk. Buzz obliged by filling it.

"I need your help," Jake said.

"What you need is for Sheriff Noble to look the other way and let this go."

"Someone framed her."

"Jake—"

"If you won't help me, Buzz, I'll do it without you."

"Do what?"

"I've got a couple of leads to follow up on. I can't do it alone. I need your help."

"I'm not a cop anymore."

"Tomorrow at this time, I probably won't be, either. But I've got to work this. I've got to work it smart—"

"What you need to be working on is damage control. Hell, I can't believe you slugged that deputy. If he files a complaint, you're in big trouble."

Remembering the way Abby had looked on her knees on the wet asphalt, Jake grimaced. "He had it coming."

"If this woman—Nichols—starts spewing claims of improper police conduct, you can kiss your career goodbye."

"She won't."

Sighing, Buzz leaned forward and filled his own cup, looking as if he needed the drink as badly as Jake. "I don't have to remind you about your track record with women, do I?"

Jake knew he was referring to Elaine. Buzz was the only person who knew about her. The only person he'd confided in. He thought about Abby, tried to align the parallels, realized he couldn't. Abby Nichols was nothing like Elaine. Jake was willing to bet his career on it. Lord, he was willing to bet his life on it.

"Are you sure you want to throw your career away on a convicted murderer?"

Tossing the empty cup into the trash container beneath Buzz's desk, Jake rose. "I'm going to take a shower, then head over to Mercy General." He gave Buzz a hard look. "Are you coming with me?"

"You going to clue me in or keep me fumbling around in the dark?"

A frisson of relief went through Jake. "I'll explain on the way."

For the first time that day the cold got to Abby. As the female deputy led her to her temporary cell, it seemed to rear up inside her, and burst forth from her very bones. She began to shiver. Her teeth chattered. Her hands were shaking so badly, she could barely hold the state-issue blanket and pillow they'd given her down in processing.

Oh, God in heaven, what had she done?

The question was moot because Abby knew damn good and well what she'd done. Not once, but twice. She'd trusted a man she'd known would betray her. She'd given him her body and let him use her. Worse, she'd given him her heart and now it was breaking.

Oh, Jake, how could you do this to me?

The interview with the D.O.C. officials was a blur. Mostly, they'd wanted to know how she'd gotten out, if anyone within the prison system had helped her, and what she'd done once she was free. The cops weren't quite as nice and concentrated most of their questions about a sporting goods store clerk who'd ended up dead. From what Abby had gathered, the cops had found Grams's truck and somehow the guns and money taken from the sporting goods store had ended up in the truck. They'd been relentless in their questioning, asking the same questions over and over again. Cold and wet and hungry, by the time they were finished with her some four hours later, she was almost ready to confess just so she could get into some dry clothes.

Processing was a nightmare, but Abby had simply let her mind leave her body as she was checked into the Chaffee County jail. She was allowed a shower, given a prison-issue jumpsuit and taken to her small cell in the basement where a female deputy passed a lukewarm dinner through the bars. After arraignment the next morning, she would be transferred back to Buena Vista.

Where was Jake?

The question had come to her a thousand times since she'd walked away from him in the parking lot of the ranger station. She wondered if, after everything that had happened between them, after everything they'd shared, he believed the lies about her.

He hadn't come to see her. He hadn't kept his word and gotten her transferred to a place where she would be safe.

Oh, God, what had she done by trusting him?

Abby stared at the untouched tray of food. She knew she should eat. It had been almost twenty-four hours since she'd taken in any nourishment. But her stomach was in knots and her appetite had long since fled. Standing in the center of her cell, she felt physically ill and cold to the depths of her soul.

Jake wasn't going to come for her. He wasn't going to keep his word and try to clear her name. He'd used her; she'd allowed it. Her body. Her heart. He'd given her hope and then snatched it away. The cruelty of the act hurt more than any physical blow.

Wrapping her arms around herself, Abby sank down to the cold, concrete floor. She knew better than to cry; crying never helped anything, but the tears came in a flood. Her sobs echoed off the walls of the hollow room. She cried openly, her heart bleeding as if it had been slashed. The pain doubled her over, and that was when she knew she'd made the ultimate mistake. Not only had she let Jake use her. But she'd fallen in love with him.

Chapter 15

Jake sat on the gurney in the emergency room of Mercy General Hospital in Denver and watched the nurse inject numbing medication into the bullet wound on his side. He'd filled Buzz in on the story Abby had told him about Jonathan Reed and her suspicions with regard to the deaths of at least two homeless patients.

Buzz hadn't said much, certainly hadn't admitted to believing such a far-fetched tale, particularly with consideration to Jake's source—Abby Nichols. But Jake knew Buzz well enough to recognize the cop's suspicion in the other man's eyes. Buzz would help. And he knew if Buzz came upon one ounce of proof, he'd jump on it like a wolf on a rabbit. He'd left Jake at the nurse's station and begun the uncertain and tedious process of questioning the staff with regard to Abby Nichols, Jonathan Reed and the death of a homeless man named Jim.

"Numb enough for you, Officer Madigan?"

The nurse's voice jerked him back to the present. Jake looked over at her and forced a smile. "I don't feel a thing."

"Good, because you're going to need about eight stitches."

Nurse Holly Forbes was in her forties, with pretty brown hair and a reassuring smile. Jake watched her work the curved suture needle for a few minutes before asking, "How long have you worked at Mercy General?"

"Oh, gosh, it'll be fourteen years next month. Just doesn't seem possible, you know? Didn't even have the new wing when I started."

"Did you know Abby Nichols?"

Her hands faltered for a fraction of a second and she cast him a sidelong look. Jake stared back, trying to read her, and went with his gut. "Off the record," he said.

She resumed stitching. "I knew her. She was a very nice young woman."

"Did you know her well?"

"We were friends. Used to take our dinner break together when we worked graveyard shift. Terrible about what happened." She pulled another stitch, then snipped the end with scissors and began tying it off. "She's in prison from what I hear."

"She is."

"She didn't seem like the type, you know? Made quite a stir here in the hospital when what she did came out in the trial."

"Do you think she did it?"

Their gazes met. Jake narrowed his eyes, desperate now to read her. "Are you working on her case?" she asked carefully.

"No. I'm her friend."

"I suspect she could use a friend."

He paused, wondering how much to tell her, knowing there wasn't much time. "I don't think all the information came out during the trial, do you?"

Her previously steady hands began to tremble. "I wouldn't know."

"If you care about what happens to that young woman, you'll follow your instincts and tell me what you know," he said.

She finished tying off the last stitch and set the needle and scissors in the stainless-steel tray. "I don't know what—"

"I'm pretty good at reading people, ma'am, and you have 'I know more than I'm telling you' written all over your face."

"Deputy Madigan—"

"Her life depends on the truth," he said.

She smiled, uncomfortable. "I don't know anything for certain. And I told the police everything. But I have my suspicions, but that's all they are. Suspicions."

"Suspicions about what?"

"Look, I've got three little kids to support and no husband to help me do it. This job is important. I can't risk—"

"I promise you, this will go no further than this room." There he went again, making promises he might not be able to keep.

Another nurse came into the room. Holly smiled uncomfortably at the other woman, then looked down at the tray in front of her and unwrapped a sterile gauze bandage. "I can't discuss this here."

"Someone's trying to hurt Abby," he said. "She doesn't have much time."

The nurse closed her eyes and sighed. "The person you need to talk to quit about a year and a half ago."

"Who?" he pressed.

"Donna Sullivan. She was a nurse here."

"Why do I need to talk to her?"

"Because she knows more than I do."

"Where can I find her?"

"She used to live in Littleton. A little efficiency apartment off of Bowles. I don't know if she's still there. She never kept in touch."

Fifteen minutes later, Buzz and Jake were back on the road, heading toward the suburb of Littleton.

"What do you think?" Jake asked, after telling him everything the nurse had told him.

"I think it's worth talking to her."

"Yeah."

"Could be a wild-goose chase."

"Or maybe someone at Mercy General has a dirty little secret."

Buzz reached for his cell phone, and dialed a number, and barked to someone at the other end, "I need a background search on Donna Sullivan." He frowned. "No date of birth. Yeah, I know I'm not a cop anymore." The frown deepened. "I'm calling in that favor you owe me. Yeah, that one. Tell it to someone who cares. Call me." After disconnecting, he looked over at Jake and grinned. "Damn, I miss being a cop."

It was nearly midnight when the clang of steel doors reverberated down the long, narrow hall of the Chaffee County Jail. Abby was lying on the threadbare cot with the single blanket over her, staring at the wall. Her nerves jangled at the sound of voices. She told herself it wasn't Jake, that he hadn't come to see her. That she was a fool for thinking he would show up. But she couldn't keep the swift rush of hope from jumping through her.

The thought of seeing him again made her heart sing. God, she must look a mess. Her hair was sticking out all over the place. Her eyes felt swollen from crying. Her face was probably ghastly pale. Quickly, she ran her fingers through her hair and pinched her cheeks to give herself some color. Jumping to her feet, she ran over to the bars and strained to see down the hall.

Her heart dropped into her stomach when she saw a female deputy flanked by two men in suits. Abby didn't recognize the men. They might have been D.O.C., but she couldn't be sure.

"Nichols, stand back from the door," the deputy said.

The drill was so ingrained, Abby stepped back. The deputy proceeded to unlock the door while the men in suits regarded her emotionlessly.

"W-what's happening?" she asked.

The female deputy walked in. "Turn around and give me your wrists."

Abby's heart began to race, a cold block of dread forming in her gut. Telling herself not to overreact, that this could very well be legitimate, she took a deep breath. "Please, tell me what this is all about."

"You're being transferred back to Buena Vista."

"But I thought I was scheduled for an arraignment tomorrow morning in Chaffee County."

"Give me your wrists," the deputy said.

Ignoring the order, Abby looked at the men. "Can I see some ID?"

One of the men laughed.

"Your hands," the deputy said. "Now."

Abby started to step away, but the other woman grasped her arm and turned her around. "Don't test my patience this morning, Nichols. I'm not in the mood."

Suddenly, Abby got a very bad feeling in the pit of her stomach. She tried to stay calm, but panic was already scraping up her spine. "Please, just…show me some ID—"

Cursing, the deputy came at her. "Don't make me use the pepper spray."

Spinning away from the woman, Abby made a break for the door. One of the men stepped in front of her. She tried to push past him, but he was large and strong and stopped her cold by putting his hands on her shoulders and squeezing hard. "Calm down. We're just transporting you back to Buena Vista."

Abby winced. When she turned, she saw that the deputy had pulled the pepper spray from her belt. "Turn around and show me your hands!" she snapped.

"These men aren't with D.O.C.," Abby cried. "Please, call the judge. Call Deputy Madigan. Please, they're going to kill me."

One of the men looked over at the deputy and shrugged. "Turn around now!" the deputy warned.

Knowing there was no way to avoid the restraints, Abby turned. Roughly, her hands were pulled behind her and the nylon cuffs secured tightly around her wrists.

"Looks like we're all set." One of the men took her arm. "Is there something we need to sign?"

The deputy passed a form to the other man and he scribbled quickly. "Thanks."

Abby stared at the deputy. "Please," she said. "Call Deputy Madigan. He'll explain everything. Please!"

"Let's go, Nichols." The hand around her arm tightened and shoved her forward. Abby looked back at the deputy, saw her shaking her head.

Fear and a terrible sense of helplessness moved over her. Oh, God, she thought, no one believes me. She looked at the men on either side of her and the dread in her stomach coiled, growing into something cold and ugly and overwhelming.

"Where are you really taking me?" she demanded as another deputy unlocked a secure door that led to the outer offices.

The man on her left glanced over at the deputy and rolled his eyes. The deputy smiled.

Abby glared at the deputy. "Call Buena Vista," she

shouted. "They're not expecting me. Please! Call Jake Madigan."

The deputy shook her head. "Drive careful," she said to the two men and locked the door behind them.

Jake knew Donna Sullivan was lying the instant she opened her mouth. Fear for Abby was making him increasingly edgy. His patience had long since gone by the wayside. He listened intently as Sullivan denied knowing anything about Jonathan Reed or the deaths of the two homeless patients when she'd worked the Mercy General ER. When she ran out of things to say, he let the silence build, hoping she was one of those people who couldn't bear long, uncomfortable silences.

Shoving his hands into his pockets, he walked the small living room, aware that she was watching him, aware that he was making her very nervous. The apartment was small, but comfortably furnished. Framed photographs of two little girls in several stages of childhood adorned the walls. Pretty little girls in pigtails and pink dresses. Another photo of the same two wearing muddy sneakers and ornery grins.

Jake wondered what kind of a woman could love her children so much, yet remain silent about a such heinous crime.

"That's all I know," she said after a moment.

"I think you know more than what you're telling us, Miz Sullivan," Jake said.

"Excuse me?" She tried to look indignant, but didn't quite manage. "Look, I've told the police everything several times. I don't see why you need to hear it again. I mean, it happened a year and a half ago. The trial is over and the person responsible is being punished."

"Are you aware that lying to the police is a crime?"

"Are you accusing me of lying?"

"I'm stating a fact you may or may not be aware of."

"Look, I've told you everything I know," she repeated. "I saw Abby Nichols in the ER pharmacy that night. An hour later her patient was dead from an overdose of Valium. I testified to that. It's all I know."

"That's not the story we heard," Jake said.

"Heard from whom?" She narrowed her eyes speculatively. "Look, I know who you are. You're that search and rescue cop who was on the news earlier. Maybe you're thinking with a part of your anatomy that isn't related to your head."

He stared at her, his temper spiking. If she'd been a man, Jake would have been facing another possible assault charge.

"Let's go," said Buzz from across the room.

Jake wasn't ready to go. "This is a matter of life and death, Ms. Sullivan. Abby Nichols didn't inject that man with Valium. You know that, and so do I."

"I know no such thing."

"If I find out you're lying to me I'm going to come down on you like a ton of bricks."

Her face reddened. "Don't threaten me. I already told the police everything I know. I didn't do anything wrong. Now get out of my home. Get out before I call the police."

Buzz tried to take Jake's arm, but Jake shook him off. He pointed a not-so-steady finger at the woman. "I'll be back."

"It's over," Buzz said. "Let it go."

Jake stalked to the door, swung it open, banging it against the wall. He was breathing hard. Desperation stabbed him like a steely knife in his chest. He couldn't stop thinking about Abby, what she must be going through at this very minute.

Oh, God, he couldn't believe he'd fallen in love with a woman who could very well be facing a capital murder charge. The thought made him feel sick.

In the parking lot, Jake strode over to Buzz's Bronco, put his hands against the hood and leaned forward. He felt nauseous and out of control. He felt as if he'd reached the end of his rope.

"Cool down, Jake. Just…take it easy, man."

"I need your phone."

Sighing, Buzz reached into his pocket and passed him the phone.

Jake dialed the Chaffee County jail from memory. "This is Madigan. I want to talk to Abby Nichols." He waited, impatient and snarling while he was transferred down to the jail. Once on the line with the jailer, he repeated his request.

"I'm sorry, Deputy Madigan, but you can't speak to Nichols."

Jake closed his eyes. He'd known this would happen. He'd expected it, even. But that didn't make it any easier. As much as he didn't want to admit it, he needed to hear her voice. Needed to make sure she was all right.

"Put her on the damn phone," he growled. "Now."

"That's not possible."

"Why not?"

"Because two officers from D.O.C. picked her up for transport fifteen minutes ago."

Jake didn't remember shoving the phone at Buzz. The words echoed inside his head like a death knell. Turning away, he strode over to the SUV and slammed his fist into the fender. "Damn!"

"Whoa. Cool it." Buzz's voice broke through the veil of terror and frustration. "What happened?"

"They took her," Jake choked.

"Who?"

He turned toward the older man, his mind racing. "The jailer said they were D.O.C., but I don't think so."

"Then, who—" Buzz cut the words short.

Jake saw realization on the other man's face, felt the tourniquet of fear tighten around his throat. "They're going to kill her."

Buzz punched numbers into the phone. "We're on it."

"We're out of time." Desperation slithered inside Jake. He couldn't bear to think of someone hurting Abby. It was his fault. He'd done this to her. If anything happened to her, he would never be able to forgive himself.

The pain broke him. Guilt wrapped around him, squeezing the breath from him like a chain weighing him down. Vaguely, he heard Buzz speaking into the phone. Heart hammering, Jake stared into the night and tried to decide what to do next.

"Let's go to Chaffee County," Buzz said, handing him the phone. "We'll start there."

Numb, Jake took the phone and slid behind the wheel of Buzz's SUV. The other man didn't argue. Jake started the engine, flipped on the headlights. He couldn't shake the feeling that he was missing something. That he was about to make a mistake. But what?

Slowly, he pulled on to the street. A few yards out, he glanced out the window, found himself looking over at the apartment they'd just left. The curtain moved. Donna Sullivan had been watching them. She was the key, he realized. His best hope. His only hope.

Jake slammed his foot down on the brake, sending the SUV into a skid.

"What the hell?"

He ignored the other man's voice, jammed the gearshift into park, flung open the door.

"What are you going to do?" Buzz demanded.

"You don't want to know." Jake hit the ground running. At the apartment door, he didn't bother with a knock, kicking in the door on the first try.

Donna Sullivan was standing in the center of the living

room, a phone in her hand, her eyes as huge as an owl's. "W-what are you doing?" she squeaked.

Jake reached her in two strides, snatched the phone from her hand. "If I press redial, who am I going to get?"

Her eyes widened even more, her face paling to the color of sour milk. "I-I…"

"Who!" he roared.

"Please, don't…"

"Who are you afraid of?"

"Get out of my house. Just…get out."

Jake pressed the redial button.

Tears filled the woman's eyes. "He threatened to kill my little girls. Please don't make me talk to you."

Jake felt the words like a punch to the stomach. He remembered seeing the photos hanging on the wall in her living room. Two pretty little girls. In the back of his mind he wondered what kind of a monster could make such a horrific threat. "I won't let him hurt you or your daughters," he said quietly. "But I need a name. I need it right *now.*"

"He'll…hurt my kids. He'll do it. I know him. He's crazy."

"I'm going to take him down. Once I do, you'll never have to worry about him again. But I need your help. I don't have much time. *Please.*"

Pressing her hand to her stomach, tears streaming down her cheeks, Donna Sullivan began to talk.

Abby knew what a trapped animal must feel like. For twenty minutes she struggled against the nylon restraints, trying to wear them thin by twisting and rubbing them against the edge of the bench seat. She worked on the nylon until her arm muscles trembled and her wrists were scraped raw. But her struggles were in vain.

Oh, Jake, where are you?

She'd thought of him a hundred times in the last twenty minutes. She wondered if he was thinking about her. If he'd called the jail and knew she'd been taken. She wondered if he knew she was in danger, if he would come looking for her. The question broke her heart because she didn't know the answer.

Half an hour into the drive, the van slowed. Sliding across the unpadded bench seat in the rear, she leaned her shoulder against the woven wire of the cage and spoke to the driver. "Where are you taking me?"

"You'll find out soon enough."

She'd watched for landmarks as best she could from the rear of the van. There were no windows, but she caught glimpses of the road and landscape through the front windows. They'd entered the mountains, but they weren't on the road leading to the prison at Buena Vista. Judging from the lack of communication equipment, she wasn't even in a Department of Corrections van.

Where were they taking her?

Her question was answered a few minutes later when the van pulled onto an unpaved road. Bumping over ruts and stones the size of softballs, the van began to climb, its headlights slashing through thick pine forest. A few inches of snow covered the ground here, so she knew they'd gained some elevation. A few minutes later the road opened to a large clearing. The driver shut down the engine and both men got out.

Abby was intimately acquainted with fear. In the past year and a half she'd experienced it too many times not to recognize its jagged facets. She'd been cut by each of those facets, had the scars to prove it. Yet when the rear doors of the van swung open and the two men stood looking in at her, the terror was terrible and fresh and consumed her in a single bite. It snaked up her spine and exploded in her brain. Horrible possibilities played through her mind.

They were going to kill her. They hadn't said the words, but she knew by the way they were looking at her—as if she were a piece of litter they'd found on the street—that they were going to do away with her.

"Get out," the taller of the two men said.

Abby wasn't going to make it easy for them. She wasn't going to give up her life without a fight. When the stocky man reached for her, she leaned back and lashed out with both feet. Her right foot connected solidly with his chin. He cursed. The other man rushed forward, his lips peeled back in a snarl. She fought madly, but before she could scoot back and aim another kick, the second man had her around her ankles and pulled her from the truck.

Abby landed hard on her back in the gravel. The impact knocked the air from her, but she didn't let that stop her. She twisted away from him, and tried to get to her feet. She'd only made it to her knees when strong hands bit into her shoulders and pulled her to her feet.

Suddenly headlights blinded her. Breathing hard, she squinted, a small part of her brain praying that Jake had somehow found out where they had taken her and come for her. She drew a mental picture of him rushing to her, weapon drawn, flanked by an army of deputies. And while the deputies arrested the men who'd kidnapped her, Jake would take her into his arms, kiss her gently and lovingly and tell her how wrong he'd been, how much he loved her....

The car stopped ten feet away, jerking her from her reverie. She watched, her heart hammering like a piston as a man climbed out. She squinted against the headlights, only able to make out his silhouette. A silhouette that was disturbingly familiar....

"Hello, Abby."

Her blood ran cold at the sound of Jonathan Reed's voice.

"Jonathan...my God...."

He stepped into view. Abby gaped at him, stunned. He halted less than a foot away from her, his expression vaguely amused. It had been more than a year since she'd last seen him, but he hadn't changed. He still had the look of a wealthy doctor, an air of impatience about him. He wore perfectly creased navy slacks. An expensive leather jacket and kid-skin gloves. Cool, intelligent eyes traveled the length of her.

Without speaking he removed one of his gloves. "Ah, prison hasn't diminished your beauty. It's good to see you again."

She cringed when he reached out and gently brushed the hair from her eyes. "What do you want with me?" she asked.

"Abby, Abby, Abby." He shook his head as if she'd disappointed him. "Why couldn't you just do your time like a good little girl?"

"The police know you're behind this." Her voice shook with each word, but she didn't care.

"The police?" He arched a brow as if he found the thought amusing. "Oh, you mean that strapping young stud deputy of yours?" He clucked his mouth. "Please, Abby, you really should be more careful about who you…associate with and why."

She launched a kick at him, but Reed managed to twist aside. The man holding her arms jerked her back. "I see prison life hasn't done much to rectify that temper of yours. I'll bet you hate having people telling you what to do twenty-four hours a day."

"Why the two goons, Reed? Afraid you can't handle me yourself?"

"You still know how to push those buttons, don't you?"

"An insecure worm like you has a lot of buttons to choose from."

Anger flashed in his eyes, but he covered it with a smile.

"Still have that smart mouth, too. I always liked that about you." He removed his other glove one finger at a time. "A man in my position has to have some...shall we say...muscle."

"You mean someone to do your dirty work."

"The last transplant operation I performed earned me over two million dollars. That calls for a certain amount of...protection."

"The police know about your twisted operation. It won't take them long to come up with some proof. You might be smart, but you're not that smart. I mean, I figured it out."

For the first time he looked at her, equal to equal. "You're going to make killing you very easy."

"I think they're all easy for you."

"Tell me, dear Abby, what is so terribly wrong with what I do? What kind of an impact is an uneducated wino derelict going to have on the world in comparison to a genetic scientist with the IQ of a genius who is a few years from curing heart disease or cancer?"

Abby contemplated him, aghast at what she knew he was going to say next, appalled because she knew he truly believed it.

"Why shouldn't the derelict sacrifice his miserable life for the good of mankind?" Moving closer to her, he took her chin in his hand. "I don't use those organs for just anyone. I use them for people who can pay for them. We're talking millions of dollars, Abby. People who lead productive lives. People who have families and careers. People who will contribute greatly to our society."

"Nothing gives you the right to play God with people's lives."

"I've bestowed that right upon myself."

"I told the cops everything I know. They're on to your sick scam. Once they get proof, you're going down."

A cruel smile twisted his mouth. "By the time the media

gets finished with your…cop, everyone in the state of Colorado will know he acted inappropriately with a female convict. Everyone will know he engaged in hot sex with a prisoner while they were snowbound in that cozy cabin." A cruel laugh rumbled from his chest. "The photographs should help. Well, as long as they edit out the more… graphic details for their more sensitive readership."

Outrage flashed through her.

"Imagine the headlines. 'Deputy Beds Convict in Mountain Love Nest.'" He chuckled. "No, I don't believe your deputy will be a problem."

"He knows about the black market organs," she choked. "He knows everything. I told him all of it. And he believed me, Reed." Emotion wrenched at her with each word. Abby closed her eyes against a hot rush of tears. She didn't know for sure that Jake had believed any of what she'd told him. But she couldn't let Reed know that. "He's going to blow your little scam wide open."

Serious now, anger flaring in his eyes, he stepped close to her and grasped her chin roughly. "Ah, Abby, you overestimate your charms. I suspect your young stud wasn't quite as…shall we say…emotionally attached about what happened in that cabin as you are. Some men can be rather calculating when it comes to sex."

"That's not the way it was."

"You're a convicted felon. You're nothing more than a smear on the bottom of someone's shoe. Maybe your stud thought he was doing you a favor. Give the poor little lifer one last thrill since she's going to be spending the rest of her days in prison."

Abby tried not to let the words hurt her, but they cut her as surely and deeply as any knife. She knew that wasn't the way it had been, but the doubt was there. The sharp edge of a blade slashing her with each word.

"He's going to destroy you," she said. "He's going to

make sure you spend the rest of your miserable life behind bars.''

"Enough. I've grown bored with your dramatics." Stepping back, he nodded at the men holding her. "Get rid of her."

Terror burst like a bomb in her chest. For the first time she contemplated her life ending here and now. On this terrible night at the hands of a man she'd once trusted. Oh, God, why couldn't she keep her mouth shut? Why had she taunted him when she should have been trying to buy some time for herself?

"Why are you doing this?" she asked. "I was in prison. I wasn't a threat."

His eyes glinted cruelly as he contemplated her. Stepping forward, he pressed his mouth against hers in a sick imitation of a kiss. Abby endured the contact, closing her eyes against the revulsion rising inside her. When he pulled away, she spat.

Reed smiled. "I've experienced your charms firsthand. Let's just say any man who's had a taste of you might just fall hard enough to believe you. I didn't want to take that chance. Even with that country bumpkin cop of yours." Stepping away from her, he spoke to the two men. "Take her out into deep water, cut through the ice, weight her body and dump her."

Jake drove like a madman through the darkness, pushing the SUV to speeds that were dangerous on any highway, let alone a dirt road in the dead of night. All the while Donna Sullivan's voice rang in his ears.

Reed told me he was going to take care of her. I don't know what he meant by that, but I can only assume that meant he was going to kill her. The last thing he mentioned was the Antero reservoir....

Jake had dropped Buzz at the Chaffee County jail to work

that angle and taken off to find Abby. The Antero reservoir was located off of Route 285, not far from Fairplay. Jake broke every speed limit in the book on the drive west, pushing Buzz's SUV over one hundred miles an hour on the straight stretches of highway. Now, less than a mile away from the reservoir, he was terrified at what he might find. That he was too late. That Reed hadn't taken her there to begin with.

That he was wrong about everything and Abby was going to wind up dead because of him.

Fear crawled up and down his spine like a sharply honed spur. If Reed had, indeed, taken her to the reservoir, there was only one reason Jake could think of. Antero reservoir was deep and stayed frozen most of the winter. If someone were to chop a hole in the ice and drop a weighted body into the water, it wouldn't ever surface....

Abby tried not to imagine what it would be like to drown in the frigid water of the reservoir, to have her body weighted, the black water closing around her. Panic threatened to overwhelm her, but she fought it back. She couldn't afford to panic. She needed time to think. She needed a plan. A clear head. There had to be something she could do to save herself.

Reed walked away without looking back. She watched him go, aware of the two men standing on either side of her, the nylon cuffs cutting into her wrists. Her heart beat out a wild staccato, fear pumping through her veins with every hard beat.

"Let's go."

Vaguely, she was aware of one of the men taking her arm and guiding her toward the frozen shore of the lake. Twenty feet ahead, the other man stepped out onto the ice, an ax in one hand, a coil of rope in the other.

Abby's mind rebelled against the horror of what would

happen next. Things were moving too fast. Her life couldn't
end like this. She had too much to live for. She thought of
Jake, of all the things she wanted to say to him, all the things
they'd left unfinished. It struck her then that she'd never
heard him say he loved her. The need to hear him say the
words was an ache in her heart.

Closing her eyes, Abby stifled a sob. She knew he loved
her. No man could make love to her the way Jake had and
not love her. She'd seen it in his eyes, heard it in his voice,
felt it in the gentleness of his touch.

Oh, Jake, where are you?

"How far out we gonna take her?" the stocky man asked.

"About halfway. Ice isn't too thick yet. Hole ought to be
easy to chop out."

The man yanked on her arm. "Come on. We ain't got all
day."

Sick with terror, Abby took another step toward the ice.
Abruptly, the man holding her arm slipped. His feet went
out from under him and he went down hard on his rump.

Hope burst through her. She lunged backward, breaking
his grip on her arm. The other man turned, dropped the rope
and ax. By the time the ghastly tools hit the ground, she
was running all-out and halfway to shore.

She heard a shout. Unable to keep herself from it, she
looked over her shoulder. The second man had fallen. Another burst of hope sent her up the steep bank. She looked
wildly around, spotted the van thirty feet away and dashed
toward it.

"Stop!"

A gunshot snapped through the air. Abby didn't slow
down, didn't look back. She picked up speed and ran a
zigzag pattern, praying she didn't get shot in the back.

A moment later she reached the van. Hampered by the
cuffs, she turned, fumbled with the door handle, jerked open
the door. Fueled by terror and anger and the raw will to

live, she threw herself onto the seat. She spotted the keys in the ignition, twisted her body and started the engine.

The windshield shattered. Abby screamed, turned her head and saw one of the men running toward her, his gun leveled at her back. ''Stop!'' he shouted.

Leaning forward, she somehow got her hands on the gearshift and rammed the van into gear. Another gunshot rang out. Dropping sideways onto the seat, Abby stomped down hard on the gas pedal. The truck shot backward, the momentum nearly throwing her to the floor. She hit the gas again. Gravel spewed. She couldn't see from where she was on the seat, but the driver's side door was open. The ground blurred past as she put distance between her and the man. If she got lucky, she could get out and run into the woods and get away.

A tree slammed against the open door, ripping it off with the screech of metal against metal. Abby kept her foot on the gas, struggled to a sitting position. An instant later the truck crashed into something solid, stopping it cold. The engine sputtered and died. She looked through the windshield and tried to get her bearings. She'd backed into the dense forest adjacent to the gravel lot.

Suddenly, headlights flashed over her, blinding her. A vehicle moving fast approached. Reed, she thought, and another wave of fear sliced her. Through the open door, she saw a man running toward her. It was difficult to maneuver with her arms cuffed behind her, but she managed to get her fingers on the keys. She turned the ignition. The engine groaned.

''Start!'' she cried.

In her peripheral vision she saw a man slide to a stop at the door. He leaned in and reached for her. Screaming, Abby lashed out with her feet. ''Get away from me!''

''Easy, honey, it's me!''

The voice registered slowly. She stopped fighting, turned to look at him, felt her heart turn over in her chest. "Jake?"

He uttered her name. Once. Twice. Then he was reaching for her. Pulling her out of the truck and into his arms. A sob bubbled out of her as his strong arms went around her. His words cut through the terror and despair and filled her with hope. "Easy, honey, I've got you."

Relief made her legs buckle. He caught her just in time to keep her from slinking to the ground. "Sweetheart, are you hurt?"

"Oh, God, Jake, you came. I thought—"

"I couldn't stay away. I couldn't stop thinking about you." He looked over the hood of the van, toward the reservoir. "Are you okay?"

"I'm fine."

"Where's Reed?"

The hairs at her nape stood on end. "I don't know. He was here...."

"How many of them are there?"

"Three."

"Okay." He tugged the radio from his belt. "RMSAR Homer Two, this is Coyote One, do you read me? Over."

The radio crackled, then a voice answered. "This is Homer. What's up, Jake?"

"I'm up at the Antero reservoir. Three suspects. Armed and very dangerous. I was wondering if you guys can get Colorosa's ass out of bed and get him up here. I'll contact Buzz."

"Chopper is already en route. Buzz called ten minutes ago. ETA—now."

"I hope he has the night vis."

"He's got it."

"Over and out.

Looking quickly from side to side, Jake unholstered his

sidearm. "Are you sure you're okay? They didn't hurt you?"

"I'm fine. I'm just...really glad you got here when you did."

As if he wasn't quite sure he believed her, he ran his hands over her shoulders, down her arms. Abby could feel his hands trembling against her.

"I'm okay. Do you think you could get these cuffs off me?"

The whine of a police siren filled the air as a sheriff's vehicle sped into the clearing and ground to a sliding halt a few yards away. Jake watched two deputies disembark, then turned back to Abby. Vaguely, she was aware of him reaching into his pocket, of using a knife to cut through the nylon bands around her wrists.

"I'm sorry you had to go through this," he said.

"They were going to kill me."

"I know, honey." He took her hands in his and rubbed the feeling back into her wrists. "You're cut."

She looked down at where the nylon had cut into the flesh of her wrists. "It's okay."

"It's not. I'm so damn sorry."

She glanced through the broken windshield at the flashing strobes beyond. In the distance, the rat-tat-tat of a chopper's rotors sliced through the night air.

Jake's radio crackled as two deputies located Reed and his two goons hiding in an outhouse by the pumping station. He smiled at Abby. "Talk about appropriate setting."

"What's going to happen to him?" she asked.

"He's going to prison for a long, long time." Jake listened to the deputies' voices crackle over the radio for a moment, then glanced at Abby. "I got a full confession from Donna Sullivan."

The meaning behind the words jolted her. "Donna knew?"

"Reed had threatened her children. She's held this inside her for more than a year because she was afraid he'd murder her two little girls."

"What a terrible thing to live with."

"I offered her police protection and promised her immunity if she testifies against him." He looked beyond the truck where several deputies were tussling on the ground with one of Reed's thugs. "That will exonerate you."

The meaning was almost too overwhelming to contemplate. She would have her freedom back. Her career. Her life. The emotion that followed made it difficult to speak. "Oh, Jake…"

"Abby, I'm sorry I wasn't here for you. I shouldn't have turned you over to D.O.C."

"You're here now. That's what matters."

Leaning close, he kissed her once, hard on the mouth. It was a powerful kiss, full of tangled emotions and urgency and the jagged remnants of fear. "I've been wanting to do that since I left you," he said.

"I didn't know if you'd come. I didn't even know if you—"

His arms tightened around her, silencing her. Abby looked at him, surprised to see the glimmer of tears in his eyes. She thought he would look away, shamed by the display of emotion, but he met her gaze head-on and let the tears fall unnoticed. "I'm sorry I didn't believe in you, that I wasn't there for you. I'm sorry I let you down."

"I know this isn't what you want to hear," she said. "But I need to say it—"

He silenced her with another kiss. It wasn't a sexual kiss, but one filled with high emotion and unspoken promises. A kiss flavored by the salt of their mingled tears and the burden of all the things they'd left unsaid. "I almost lost you."

"You didn't. I'm here. Jake, we're together."

"I love you," he said roughly. "I do. I love you more than the air I breathe, more than my next breath."

"Oh, well…"

He didn't pause and the words kept tumbling out of him. "I'm sorry I didn't have the guts to admit it sooner."

"You were in a tough position."

"You were the one in a tough position. I knew you were innocent. I *knew* it. I just…couldn't put my past aside. That thing with Elaine and Richie. God, Abby, I almost got you killed."

"With all due respect, Deputy Madigan, you just saved my life."

Using the back of his hand to wipe at the tears on his cheeks, he pulled back and scowled at her. "Hasn't anyone ever told you not to argue with a cop?"

Abby choked out a laugh. "You love it when I argue with you."

He smiled at her, but quickly sobered. "Did I mention that I love you?"

"You mentioned it."

"You didn't say anything back." His gaze faltered. "Look, Abby, I screwed this up. I mean, I don't blame you if—"

"Jake, you were talking a mile a minute and didn't give me the chance to.…"

He looked at her, waiting.

"I love you, too," she said after a moment.

Closing his eyes briefly, he reached for her hand, brought it to his lips and kissed her knuckles. "You renewed my faith in love, Abby. You taught me how to trust when I was so cynical I didn't think I could ever trust anyone ever again." His jaw flexed as he fought back emotion.

"I think I've loved you since that first day up on the mountain," she said.

Tightening his arms around her, he grinned. "I fell for you right about the time you gave me that black eye."

"Oh." She choked out a laugh. "Jeez, that really was an accident."

"Sure it was."

He laughed outright. She joined him and their laughter mingled. A musical sound that spoke of life in the face of death, and hope for a future that was as brilliant as a mountain sunrise.

"How do you feel about marrying a cop?" he asked after a moment.

"I'm pretty mouthy. I hear cops hate that. Do you think you can handle it?"

"Honey, I love your mouth." He kissed her to prove it. "I plan to keep that mouth of yours too busy to do much arguing for the next couple of decades."

"Same goes, Cowboy Cop."

"I'm counting on it." He kissed the tip of her nose. "Does that mean you're going to marry me?"

"That's an unequivocal yes. Take it or leave it."

"I'll take it." He kissed her again, deeply, his mouth trembling against hers. "I'm going to spend the rest of my life loving you."

Abby leaned close to him, her heart so filled with love she thought it would burst. Their noses touched, and they grinned at each other. "You make me incredibly happy," she said.

"Honey, you ain't seen nothing yet," he said and swept her into his arms.

* * * * *

INTIMATE MOMENTS™

presents:

Romancing the Crown

*With the help of their powerful allies,
the royal family of Montebello is
determined to find their missing heir.
But the search for the beloved prince
is not without danger—or passion!*

Available in May 2002:
VIRGIN SEDUCTION
by Kathleen Creighton (IM #1148)
Cade Gallagher went to the royal palace of
Tamir for a wedding—and came home with
a bride of his own. The rugged oilman thought he'd married to
gain a business merger, but his innocent bride made him long
to claim his wife in every way....

*This exciting series continues throughout
the year with these fabulous titles:*

*Available only from Silhouette Intimate Moments
at your favorite retail outlet.*

 Silhouette®

Where love comes alive™

Visit Silhouette at www.eHarlequin.com

SIMRC5

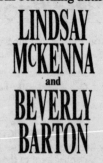

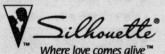

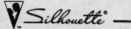

Old sins die hard...

DINAH McCALL

Why do the fingerprints of a recent murder victim in New York City belong to a man who has been dead for over thirty years? To find out, FBI agent Jack Dolan heads to the victim's last known address: a boardinghouse in Braden, Montana.

Most of the guests at Abbott House are couples seeking help from a fertility clinic, yet Jack suspects someone ruthless is lurking in the shadows. But the more he learns, the more he understands why the secrets of White Mountain must be kept hidden. *At all costs.*

WHITE MOUNTAIN

Available the first week of April 2002, wherever paperbacks are sold!

MIRA®

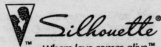

If you enjoyed what you just read,
then we've got an offer you can't resist!

Take 2 bestselling
love stories FREE!
Plus get a FREE surprise gift!